TOM GF

Borstal Slags

HARPER

HarperCollins*Publishers*
77–85 Fulham Palace Road,
Hammersmith, London W6 8JB

www.harpercollins.co.uk

Published by HarperCollins*Publishers* 2013

Borstal Slags

Copyright © Kudos Film and Television Limited 2013

Cover image produced with the kind permission of John Simm
and Philip Glenister.

Tom Graham asserts the moral right to
be identified as the author of this work

A catalogue record for this book
is available from the British Library

ISBN: 978-0-00-753647-4

Set in Sabon by FMG using Atomik ePublisher from Easypress

Find out more about HarperCollins and the environment at
www.harpercollins.co.uk/green

CHAPTER ONE

ROLLIN', ROLLIN', ROLLIN'

'Guv?'

'What is it, Tyler?'

'You're going to kill us, Guv.'

DCI Gene Hunt was driving as if the devil himself were after them. He floored the pedal, sending the Cortina shrieking through the Manchester evening like a rocket. DI Sam Tyler gripped the dashboard, as Hunt flung the car so recklessly round a bend that its offside wheels lifted off the tarmac. It dropped back heavily onto its suspension, the under-chassis scraping the road and sending out a sudden flare of sparks.

'I might kill me motor's springs, Sammy boy, but you and me is safe as houses,' Gene growled. 'It's time you stopped worrying, Tyler, and learnt to trust the Gene Genie.'

1

The Guv'nor jammed a fag into his gob, taking both hands off the wheel to light it up. He emitted a long, thick, stinking plume of smoke into Sam's face.

'Don't you go worrying your pretty little head, Tyler, I'll get us there in one piece.'

'But you're driving like a maniac, Guv. I don't know what you're rushing for.'

'There's nowt the matter with rushing. I *like* rushing. Now shut your cake-hole and look out the window like a good little soldier. Watch the world go by.'

The world was indeed going by, and at a terrifying lick. Sam watched the shopfronts whipping past outside, the names rich with memories of his own childhood: Woolworth's, Our Price records, Wavy Line. Bathed in the low, golden glow of the setting sun, the last of the evening's shoppers headed up and down the high street. Sam glimpsed a young mother, no older than twenty, in a bright-red plastic raincoat pushing twins in a buggy. A stooped old woman waited patiently at a zebra crossing, her lined, toothless face peering out from beneath a fake fur hat that looked like a giant powder puff. Hurrying past her went a mustachioed man with collar-length hair and thick sideburns, his beige trousers hugging his crotch so tightly that nothing was left to the imagination.

This is my world now, Sam thought to himself, watching a kid in a Donny Osmond T-shirt slurping on a rainbow-coloured lolly shaped like a rocket ship. *This is my world, and these are my people – for better or for worse.*

These streets, these shoppers, even the orange glare of the setting sun, all seemed much realer to him than the world he had left behind. Two thousand and six was beginning to recede in his mind – or perhaps he was just less and less inclined to think about it. With effort, he could still recall his workstation at CID with its Posturepedic office chair, its PC terminal, its energy efficient desk lamp, its neatly coiled charging cables for his mobile and BlackBerry. But such memories seemed cold and dead to him. He felt no nostalgia for the world of touch screens and instant messaging – though maybe, from time to time, his thumbs hankered for the feel of a gaming console, his taste buds for the savour of sushi, his lungs for the comfort of a smoke-free pub.

The Cortina roared ahead, its headlights blazing through the thickening gloom of evening. With a squeal of rubber, Gene narrowly avoided rear-ending a dawdling middle-aged woman in a VW. The Cortina mounted the pavement, ripped past the VW, and bounced recklessly back onto the road.

'Dopey mare in a shitty Kraut shoe box!' Hunt bellowed. 'Why the hell do they let birds behind the wheel, Tyler? It ain't natural. You might as well dish out licenses to chimpanzees.'

Sam tried to keep his mind off of his guv'nor's heart-stopping driving and turned inward instead. He thought back to how he had come to be in here in 1973 in the first place. His expulsion from 2006 had not been voluntary, nor had it been without pain. And it had all happened so fast! He could recall himself – twenty-first century DCI Tyler – pulling up by the side of the road as David Bowie played on the dashboard MP3. He could remember opening the car door and stepping out, in need of air and a moment to collect his thoughts. And then, out of the blue, came the sudden, agonizing impact of a vehicle slamming into him, the rush of air as he was hurled across the road, the bone-shattering crunch as his body smashed back down. Lying there, broken, his mind numb, he had lost all sense of space and time.

Gradually, thought had crept back into his scrambled mind. Sensation had returned to his fingers, his hand, his arm; breath returned to his lungs – and then, with a gasp, he had suddenly got to his feet and found that he was most definitely not in Kansas any more, but somewhere far, far away, well and truly over the rainbow. He was in a strange and alien world called 1973.

And, having worked so hard to escape from that world, Sam had discovered that in reality it was the one place he felt he most belonged. Unlike in 2006, here he felt *alive.*

But I'm not *alive,* he thought to himself. *In 2006, I'm* dead. *I jumped from a roof. I died. Which makes me*

– what? A ghost? A lost soul? Is this heaven? Or hell? Or something in between? Or ...?

He shook his head to clear it, refusing to submit to these overwhelming speculations. He wasn't a philosopher: he was just a copper. He couldn't answer these huge questions of ultimate reality; all he knew was that he was here, in 1973, and that it felt good. He had a job, a purpose – and he had Annie. WDC Annie Cartwright was the bright beacon at the heart of his world, the one thing more than any other that had drawn him back to this time when he'd had his chance to escape for ever. Being with her, he felt more alive than he had ever done – and that was good enough for Sam.

'Here we are, Sammo. And you say I never take you anywhere classy.'

The Cortina was nosing its way through the front gates of Kersey's Scrap Yard. On all sides stood mountains of mangled metal, cast in the raking, golden light of the sunset.

'This place is an Aladdin's cave!' said Gene, glancing about at the heaps of wreckage. 'Alfa Romeos. A couple of Audis stacked up over there. A tasty little Datsun just rustin' away.'

'Not just motors, Guv.'

Sam indicated at a mound of bulky washing machines piled carelessly amid the dead motors.

'Who the hell chucks away deluxe twin-tubs?' Gene tutted, shaking his head in disbelief. 'They've got to be worth the best part of a hundred nicker apiece.'

Passing through this mountainous landscape of scrap, Sam spied a pair of mint-coloured Austin 1300s parked up ahead.

'Patrol cars,' he said. 'Looks like uniform's beaten us to it.'

Gene slewed the Cortina to a needlessly dramatic halt alongside the two Austins, showering them with dust. He flung open the door and strode manfully out, Sam following close behind. Together, they passed a parked lorry with a big open back for transporting junk. Lodged on the dashboard of the cab was a custom-made licence plate bearing the lorry's name: *Matilda*.

Just across from the truck stood the crusher itself, a looming contraption of battered metal and massive pistons, standing still and silent with its half-digested load of ovens just visible, crunched within it. Several uniformed officers had climbed up and were trying to peer inside.

'Don't tamper with anything!' Sam called to them, flourishing his ID. 'If there really is a body inside that thing then this is a *crime scene*, gentlemen.'

'Crime scene? It's a ruddy mess, is what it is,' one of the PCs called back, clambering down from the crusher. 'You can see tufts of hair and what looks like a bit of a hand.'

'Sounds like the missus,' said Gene. He glanced across at a man in filthy overalls standing anxiously nearby. 'Are you Kersey? DCI Hunt. Tell me what happened.'

'Shook me right up,' Kersey stammered. His hands were still shaking. 'Never seen the like, not in nigh on twenty year.'

'Take your time, Mr Kersey,' said Sam.

Kersey took a breath. 'We got all this junk delivered in. Old ovens from Friar's Brook. They're knocking down the kitchens and boiler rooms over there and shipping 'em to us as scrap. The lads had just finished unloading the ovens from *Matilda*, and I was starting to munch 'em up before *Gertrude* arrives with a stack of pipes and fridges—'

'*Gertrude*'s the name of your other lorry, I take it?' enquired Sam.

'No, it's his mother, she's built like an ox,' Gene put in, sourly. Then, to Kersey: 'Keep talking. You were just starting to munch up the junk …'

'I'd just started, when I see all this red stuff running out.'

Sam nodded thoughtfully: 'So, Mr Kersey, you saw what you thought was blood coming out and you switched off the crusher straightaway?'

'Course.'

'Did you touch anything? Move anything? Poke around inside?'

'Did I 'eck as like! I don't wanna see what's in there! I just shut her down and called the law, sharpish.'

'Good man, you did the right thing. All of your co-workers are accounted for?' Kersey nodded. 'And you don't have a pet dog or anything roaming about the place?'

'There's cats and foxes and God knows what all hanging about the yard, sure,' Kersey said. 'But I never had 'em go in the crusher before. They got more sense, specially them foxes. It's a fella in there, you mark my words.'

'And you have no idea who it might be?'

'Nope. Or how he got in there. Or why.'

'Right, then!' Gene declared suddenly. 'Let's get that crusher opened up so we can have a look. You boys, stop monkeying about up there and get your arses off that thing.' The constables began scrambling back down to the ground. 'Kersey, throw the lever and open her up.'

'I – I'm not sure I want to,' stammered Kersey. His face was ashen.

'It wasn't a request, Kersey, it was a polite but firm instruction.'

Kersey froze. He'd seen more than enough blood for one day.

'Think of it like opening a present on Christmas morning,' said Gene, not very helpfully. 'A great big lovely present full of mushed up body parts. That's what I'm getting *you*, Tyler.'

Kersey looked to Sam for help.

'Show me what to do,' Sam told him. 'You don't have to watch.'

'Turn it on with the key,' Kersey said. 'Then release that handle, slowly.'

Even as he spoke, Kersey was backing away, his face turning from white to green.

'Everybody stand clear,' Sam announced. 'You all ready? On the count of three.'

'It's not Apollo 12, Tyler,' grumbled Gene. 'Just get on with it, you big fanny.'

Sam turned the starter key. The crusher's mighty pistons rattled and roared into life. Black smoke belched from the motors. He glanced around, just to ensure no one was getting too close – and at that moment a sudden flash of reflected light caught his eye. *Matilda*'s sister truck was pulling up, just beyond the parked Cortina and the patrol cars; like its counterpart, it too had a custom-made licence plate propped up against the windscreen, which bore the name *Gertrude*.

But it wasn't the sun reflecting on the lorry that caught Sam's attention: it was the sudden flash of light on the crowbar wielded by a masked man who was rushing out from behind a heap of smashed cars. The man jumped onto the lorry's running board, threw open the door and began battering at the driver inside the cab.

'Guv!' Sam shouted. His voice was drowned out by the bellowing of the crusher. 'Guv! Look!'

But nobody could hear him.

Gertrude swerved left and right, then the driver's door flew open and the driver himself tumbled out, battered and bleeding.

Leaving the crusher running, Sam bolted towards the hijacked lorry. Gene and the coppers gawped at him in incomprehension as he ran off.

'Tyler – what the f—'

'Felony in progress!' Sam shouted as he ran. 'Felony in bleedin' progress!'

The lorry turned clumsily, crashing through a mountain of metal junk. This, at last, got everyone's attention. The uniformed coppers stood and gawped. Gene reached instinctively under his coat for the Magnum.

Gertrude executed its blundering U-turn and went thundering out of the yard, smashing through a couple of parked cars in the street beyond before roaring recklessly away.

Sam reached the driver where he lay. He was splattered with blood, terrified and confused, but conscious enough to growl at Sam, 'That bastard nicked *Gerty*!'

'What the hell's on your truck that's so valuable?'

'Old fridges! Just a load of old pipes and fridges! And for that he bashed my bonce and nicked my bloody *Gerty*!'

'We'll have him!' Sam vowed. 'We will *have* him!' He turned to the uniformed officer. 'Don't just stand there, get after that truck! Get on your radios, organize a road block!' As the coppers scrambled into their little Austins and set their lights flashing, Sam called to Gene, 'I think we should stay here, Guv. We can monitor the pursuit over the radio, and make sure nobody tinkers with that crusher.'

"Monitor the pursuit'?' sneered Gene, jangling his car keys as he strode swiftly towards the Cortina. 'I *am* the pursuit, Tyler. I was *born* the bloody pursuit!'

He disappeared into the car and gunned the engine. Sam dived in beside him.

'Guv, wait, I really think we should—'

But Gene wasn't having any of it. They were off, rocketing past the marked patrol cars and ripping helter-skelter into the street. Sam flinched as the Cortina's bonnet skimmed an oncoming car with barely an inch to spare.

'Want to cast yet more aspersions on my driving, Tyler?' Gene grunted at him.

'I just want to get home alive, Guv.'

They were hurtling along, diesel smoke from *Gertrude* snorting into the air fifty yards ahead of them. Just behind the Cortina, the two patrol cars were rattling along, their lights flashing, burning out their feeble engines to keep up with the chase. The radio under the dashboard was alive with wild chatter as the word went round: truck on the rampage – heading for the heart of the city – block it, stop it, do what the hell you have to do but damn well *get it off the road*!

'*I'll* flamin' get him off the road,' Gene growled, the Magnum now in his hand, cocked and deadly.

'Guv, for God's sake, put that thing away!'

'It's *my* toy, and *I* wanna play with it!'

'You can't start blazing away in the streets, Gene!' Sam bellowed at him. 'You will *kill* people!'

'Only bad 'uns.'

Gertrude was only a few yards ahead of them now, crashing madly forward in a black cloud like some sort of runaway demon.

'It's a sitting bleedin' duck for a pot shot!' Gene declared. 'I can't resist it, I'm having a crack.'

He leant out of the window, driving one-handed, and lined up the mighty barrel of the Magnum with *Gertrude*'s rear tyres – but before he could squeeze off a shot, the truck swung suddenly to the left, smashing through a pelican crossing and sending people running in all directions. Oncoming cars blared their horns and swerved madly out of the way.

'*He's* gonna splat more civvies than *me*!' Gene spat. 'Shoot him, Tyler!'

The Cortina's engine howled as Gene floored the gas. Gertude roared right across in front of them. Gene flung the wheel as they mounted the pavement, missed a phone box by a gnat's gonad, then roared back onto the road.

'I said shoot him, Tyler!'

'Shut it! I can't hear the radio.'

'This is no time for Diddy David Hamilton!'

'The *police* radio, you cretin!' Sam leant closer to the crackling speaker. 'Sounds like somebody's got a plan.'

'Plan? What sort of plan?'

'I'm *trying* to hear!'

Between Gene's shouting and the screaming of tyres on tarmac, Sam could just make out one of the patrol cars announcing that it had cut down a back street to head off the truck. Sam glanced up and saw the little Austin pulling up bravely on the road ahead, blocking the way. The two coppers jumped out and indicated firmly for *Gertrude* to stop – stop – *stop*!

But *Gertrude* didn't. The two coppers flung themselves clear as the thundering lorry ploughed straight into their titchy patrol car and just kept going. The Austin shattered, its body crumpling beneath the mighty truck. A single wheel rolled sadly away from the mangled remains, slowed, and fell over.

'*That* was the plan?' muttered Gene, stamping on the gas and swerving around the wreckage of the Austin. He powered the Cortina alongside the truck. 'It's time for a Genie plan.'

'Not so close!' Sam yelled. 'He'll veer across and roll right over us!'

'*Roll over the Cortina?* He wouldn't ruddy *dare*!'

'Pull back, Gene!'

This time, Sam grabbed the wheel.

'*Off* the motor!' bellowed Gene, shoving him roughly away.

'You've lost it, Gene!' Sam shouted back. 'You're acting like a lunatic! People are going to get killed! *We* are going to get killed!'

'Stop being such a pissy-pants.'

The Cortina drew right up to *Gertrude*, almost nudging her filthy rear bumper with its radiator grille.

'You're bleedin' Tonto, Guv,' Sam said, shaking his head. 'You are medically a mentalist.'

'Nah, I've just got balls.'

'Look out!'

The monstrous truck cut directly in front of the Cortina, its brake lights blazing and its juddering exhaust pipe farting a great blast of filthy black fumes across the windscreen. Gene threw the wheel and the Cortina ducked away as *Gertrude* cut across a corner, burst through a line of parked cars and then flattened a street lamp.

'He must *really* want them fridges,' said Gene. 'Keep your shell-likes stuck to them police reports, Tyler. I want to know exactly where that truck's headed.'

Gene floored the pedal and jerked the wheel wildly to the left. The Cortina zoomed down one narrow street after another.

'What are you going, Guv?' asked Sam, bracing himself in his seat. 'Overtaking it so you can face it head on? That's insane! You saw what it did to that Austin!'

'This ain't a chuffin' Austin, you tart. Now keep listening!'

Sam strained to hear the radio: 'Lansdowne Road – Ellsmore Road – now he's cutting across that bit of grass outside the Fox and Hounds – wrong way up Farley Street – Left into Rokeby Crescent …'

'Has he reached the top of Keyes Street yet?'

'Nearly.'

Without warning, Gene slammed on the brakes, throwing Sam hard against the dashboard.

'You could've warned me you were gonna do that, Guv!'

'Why didn't you clunk-click like Jimmy tells you? Folks die.'

Gene threw open the door and swept out into the street. He strode, straight-backed and narrow-eyed, to the middle of the road, and there he made his stand, his off-white leather loafers planted squarely on the oil-stained tarmac. The smooth barrel of the Magnum glittered dully in the golden-red rays of the setting sun.

Sam stumbled from the car, watching Gene feed fresh rounds into the gun to make up a full barrel.

'Guv? What are you doing?'

Gene gave the Magnum a flick of the wrist. *Ka-chunk!* The barrel snapped back into the housing, ready for action.

From the twilight shadows at the far end of the road there came a clamour and a roar, as if a rampaging, diesel-powered dragon were approaching.

Gene rested his finger on the trigger of the Magnum. He stilled his breath. He focused. He flexed and limbered his shooting arm; tilted his head; made the vertebrae in his neck go crack.

And then *Gertrude* appeared, rattling out of the shadows at speed, making straight down the road directly for Hunt. Its bank of headlights flared, turning Gene into a motionless silhouette.

'Guv, that thing's going to slam straight into you and just keep on rolling.'

'It will not pass,' Gene murmured, almost to himself.

'It's going to flatten you, Guv, *and* the Cortina!'

'It – will – not – pass!'

Gene raised the Magnum.

The truck blasted its horn, sending a ragged spear of steam stabbing up into the darkening sky. Gene replied with the Magnum. Fire spat from the muzzle. *Gertrude*'s windscreen exploded. A second shot cracked the radiator grille and thudded into the engine block. A third, fourth, and then a fifth ripped one after the other through the front axle.

But it was the sixth that delivered the sucker punch. It smacked through the bonnet and struck something – something vulnerable, something vital – deep inside *Gertrude*'s rusty bodywork. The truck screamed like a transfixed vampire. The cabin lurched forward as the axle beneath it gave way and flew apart, busting the chassis and driving the front bumper into the tarmac like a plough. Sheer weight and momentum carried the broken-backed monster forward a dozen or more yards, gouging a furrow in the road and throwing up showers of stones and debris, until, with a shuddering crack, the truck jolted to a stop. The man in the mask came catapulting through the jagged remains of the windscreen and fetched up in a ruinous heap at Gene Hunt's feet. The cargo of old fridges and metal piping crashed and smashed like a steel wave that broke over the cab and cascaded deafeningly all over the road. *Gertrude*'s mortally wounded engine spewed a noisy jet of steam and then died. The headlights went dark. The scattered metallic debris came to rest. A last shard of glass fell from the windscreen and tinkled onto the road. Silence settled over the twilit street.

Gene glanced about at his handiwork, nodded to himself, and blew the smoke from the muzzle of the Magnum. Another job well done.

17

'You *are* mad,' said Sam, shaking his head slowly as he looked from the gun to the shattered remains of the lorry, from the bloodstained man crumpled at the Guv'nor's feet to the Guv'nor himself, standing there in his camel-hair coat and black-leather string-backs, wreathed in a slowly arcing aura of gun smoke. 'This isn't law enforcement – this is some sort of crazy macho playground you're romping around in, you and your bloody Magnum. This isn't what I signed up for. This isn't the job I know. What the hell am I doing saddled with you, Gene?'

From the corner of his mouth, Gene replied, 'Go on home to your kids, Herb.' He leant over the groaning man sprawled at his feet, kicked away the now-dented licence plate bearing the name *Gertrude*, and said, 'And as for you, sunshine, you're nicked – what's left of you.'

CHAPTER TWO

SLEEPING BEAUTY

The truck thief lay motionless in the intensive care ward, a cluster of clumsy plastic tubes tied with bandages to his nose and mouth. Beside him, a ramshackle tower of boxlike machines wheezed, chugged and beeped, keeping the lad in the bed on the very cusp of life. A nurse checked a paper read-out covered with wiggly lines, twiddled a fat dial or two, and fidgeted with the hem of the starched white sheets.

'You're not relatives,' she said to the two men standing at the foot of the bed. 'What are you? Police?'

'DI Tyler,' said Sam. 'This is DCI Hunt. We've just, um, arrested this man.'

'How? By dropping an anvil on him?'

'He pranged his stolen motor,' put in Gene. 'I think he might have bumped his noodle.'

'Sorry to have to bother you with this, Nurse,' said Sam, 'but does anyone here have a clue as to this young man's identity?'

'No.'

'When he was undressed, was there no ID found on him? No wallet, nothing like that?'

'His personal things are over there,' said the nurse, indicating a small wooden locker. 'But there's nothing of interest, just shredded rags. We had to cut his clothes off when he came in here – what little clothing hadn't been cut off him already.'

She stared fiercely at Gene.

'He tripped on a kerb stone,' said Gene, innocent as a cherub. 'Anyway's up, we need to have a chat with him.'

'You'll find that rather difficult, officer. He's still unconscious.'

'My uncle's unwashed pantaloons he's unconscious! He's faking it. I can sense it. Sleeping Beauty here can hear every word we're saying – can't you, old son?'

'He's certainly not faking anything,' said the nurse, aghast.

'Is he not? Let's put it to the test, why don't we?' He strode over to the bed, took hold of the truck thief's ventilator tubes, and gave them a rattle. 'Wakey, wakey, pretty baby, or I wrench these gizmos out your epiglottis and shove 'em right up your—'

'For God's sake!' the nurse spat, shoving Hunt back.

20

'You two are leaving right now. *Right* now! Or else I'm calling the police.'

'Calling the police?' said Gene, fishing out a packet of Embassy No. 6s. 'There's a flaw in your logic there. See if you can spot it.'

'This boy is unconscious, and likely to remain so for some time – assuming he ever recovers at all,' the nurse said fiercely.

'I've been telling my DCI the same thing,' said Sam, deeply uncomfortable to be associated with Gene when he was behaving like this. 'Come on, Guv. This lad's not going anywhere, we can always see him another time. They'll let us know when he comes round.'

Truculently, Gene jabbed a cigarette between his lips. The nurse gave him a look: *Don't you dare …!* Fixing her with a fierce look of his own, Gene raised his lighter, toyed at the flint with his thumb – then eased off.

'Don't take it personal, luv, I've had a day,' he said. 'Tyler – let's roll.'

Sam apologized to the nurse for his DCI's atrocious behaviour, and turned at once to go. He reached the plastic swing doors that led out of ICU into the busy corridor beyond, but found he was alone. Glancing back, he saw Gene rummaging through the small wooden cupboard which contained the tattered, blooded remains of the truck thief's clothes. As the nurse furiously declared that she was going to get the porters to throw him out, Gene suddenly raised aloft a folded sheet of paper.

'Nothing but rags?' he said. 'This could be vital.' And to Sam: 'See what happens if you take these medical birds too serious?'

He shoved the piece of paper into his pocket and – to Sam's infinite relief – strode briskly through the swing doors and away along the corridor.

'What a filthy, arrogant, reckless brute,' the nurse said, shaking her head. 'He should have been a consultant.'

They emerged into the cold night air outside the hospital. Ambulances clanged by. Gene sparked up his cigarette and drew deeply on the nicotine as if it were the very elixir of life.

'You need to clean your act up, Hunt,' Sam challenged him.

'And you need to unclench those lily-white arse cheeks of yours, Tyler. We're none of us in this job to make nurses happy – well, not like that, anyway.'

'She's got grounds to lodge a serious formal complaint against you. You assaulted a man on life support!'

'I wobbled his pipes, that's hardly an assault,' Gene said dismissively. 'And you're forgetting – Uncle Genie had a ferret about and came up *this*.'

He held up the folded piece of paper. It was dotted with the truck thief's blood.

'It better be worth it,' said Sam, watching Gene unfold it. 'What is it? Looks like a letter.'

'A spot of bedtime reading. Let's see how it compares to Dick Francis, eh?' Angling it towards the light coming from a sodium lamp, Gene perused it for a moment. 'Nice handwriting. Very neat.' And then he started to read it out. "Dear Derek ...' That our lad in there, you reckon? 'Dear Derek, so brilliant you could make time for a visit. Really good to get time with you again. Tell Auntie Rose not to fret so much.' Gene shot Sam a serious look. 'I hope he *did* tell her. I won't have Auntie Rose worryin'.'

'Get on with it, Guv.'

Gene peered closer at the letter, falling silent, his eyes narrowing, his expression darkening.

'Guv?' Sam asked.

'My God, Tyler!'

'Guv, what is it?'

Gene gave Sam an intense look. Gravely, he announced: 'It's Fluffy, Sam. She's back on the tablets.'

Sam looked blankly at him. 'What?'

Gene read out, ' 'Don't forget to give Fluffy her special tablets – take her to the vet in Lidden Street if she gets sick again.'' Gene looked up sharply from the letter. 'Sam, this stuff is dynamite.' He balled the letter in his fist and bounced it off Sam's chest. 'Too exciting for *me*. I'll never get to sleep after that.'

Sam retrieved the screwed-up letter, flattened it out, and glanced over the rest: "… if she gets sick again. It's very important I can trust you to look after her. See you again soon I hope. Love – Andy.' Andy,' he said. 'Derek and Andy.'

'Those names don't mean anything to me,' said Gene.

'Me neither. But look here – there's a rubber stamp at the top of the letter approving it for posting. It says 'HMP Friar's Brook'.'

'HMP!' scoffed Gene. 'It's just a bloody borstal, Tyler. A kiddies' lock-up for scallies whose balls ain't dropped. That's where his mate Andy is, is it? Doing a spot of bird in the nippers' clinky? And what high-profile criminal caper did he mastermind, d'you think? Clocked some old granny for her pension book and Green Shields to pay for Fluffy's suppositories? Or is he the Mr Big behind the Manchester used-fridge mafia?'

'Something weird's going on here,' said Sam. 'It's not those fridges that lad was after, it was something else. But what? And is there a connection between him and the body in the crusher?'

Silently, Sam and Gene stood beneath the black, starless sky, waiting for inspiration to strike.

With an exaggerated sigh, Gene chucked away his dog end and declared, 'I've 'ad enough of this bollocks. Hozzies give me the bleedin' 'abdabs. I'm closing shop for the day. The Genie wants his beer. C'mon, Tyler, let's leave chatterbox in there to suck on his pipes and dream of fridges, and get ourselves down the Arms for a few swifties.'

'I think I'll give it a miss this time,' said Sam. 'I'm going to swing by the station then head on home. I really do need some kip.'

'DI Tyler needs kip more than beer,' sighed Gene, rolling his eyes. 'Kids today. Lightweights. A bunch of ruddy lightweights.'

When Sam got to the station, he found Annie Cartwright's desk empty, and the sight of her chair and neatly piled paperwork made his heart ache for her.

Carefully, he sealed the letter from 'Andy' in an envelope and wrote on the front, 'See what you make of this – are there any hidden clues???' He left if tucked into Annie's typewriter. It pleased him to have any opportunity to show that he took her seriously, that he valued her mind and police skills, that he saw her as an absolutely integral part of the team. Looking at the envelope left in the typewriter, it occurred to Sam that it was almost a love letter, from him to her.

It's the first time I've left a bloodstained love letter! he thought.

A bloodstained love letter. All at once, the humour of the phrase curdled within him. He felt an icy coldness in the pit of his stomach, as if he was suddenly aware of being watched by malevolent eyes.

Sam glanced anxiously about, but the CID office was empty. And yet the fear remained. He knew that somewhere out there, hiding in the shadows but drawing steadily closer, was something evil. He had sensed it first as a vague apparition on the very margins of perception, and tried to dismiss it as a figment of his subconscious. But then, later, he had somehow recognized that same spectral presence reflected in the monstrous tattoos of bare-knuckle boxer Patsy O'Riordan. At the fairground, pursuing Patsy into the ghost train in an attempt to arrest him for murder, Sam had encountered an even stronger manifestation of that same horror – a rotting corpse, standing upright and seemingly alive, dressed in a sixties Nehru suit. The vision had vanished almost at once, but it had struck Sam with more immediacy and reality than just a trick of the mind. Whatever it was, it had been real – and it had been aware of both him and of Annie.

'The Devil in the Dark …' Sam murmured to himself. It was the name he had given this abominable thing. And briefly, after Patsy O'Riordan's death, he had heard its voice, issuing momentarily from the mouth of a young scally Sam was passing in the street:

'I'll keep coming at you, you cheating bastard. I'll keep coming at you until I've got my wife back – my wife – mine.'

'You won't mess with my mind,' Sam said out loud,

as if the Devil in the Dark could hear him. 'I'm strong. Annie's strong. And all your lies and mind games will get you nowhere. Our future is our own – and there's nothing you can do.'

He found himself holding his breath, waiting for an answer. But there was nothing, just the sound the of the night cleaners starting up their hoovers in nearby offices.

Sam looked back down at the letter resting on the typewriter, silently wished the absent Annie a good night, and then headed out. He'd go home, alone, knock back a couple of bottles of brown ale and fall asleep. A dull, lonesome end to yet another chaotic day on the force with Gene Hunt.

In a corridor leading to the main doors, Sam came across Chris and Ray. They looked red-faced and out of breath. Ray was reviving himself by drawing heavily on a cigarette, wiping the sweat from his blonde moustache with a rough, fag-stained finger. Chris was finger-combing his hair and readjusting his knitted tank top, which had been pulled askew.

'I hope you two haven't been fighting,' Sam said, striding towards them.

'Not with each other, Boss, no,' Chris said. There was a zip-up sports bag at his feet, which he picked up gingerly.

'We just been banging up a poofter,' announced Ray with contempt. 'A right little pervert, Boss, delivering filth to some other pervert. We caught 'em at the hand-over. Show him the bag, Chris.'

Chris thrust the sports bag at Sam.

'Take a gander inside that, Boss – *if you dare*,' Chris said, backing up as if the bag might go off at any moment.

Sam looked into the bad and was confronted by a messy stash of photos. It was all boys together – in bed, in the shower, on a grubby sofa, on a bare floor – with masses of pallid, spotty male flesh on display. The harsh flash used to take the pictures did the models' skin tone no favours at all.

'It's baffling!' put in Chris. 'Why would a fella want to look at other fellas' meat-'n'-two? I mean – a bird wanting a look, yeah, I can get me head round it sort of – but a *bloke*?'

'It's a sickness, is what it is,' opined Ray.

'Oh, grow up,' said Sam, zipping the bag shut. 'It's just a bit of gay porn – get over it. And from what I've seen, it's not exactly top quality.'

'I wouldn't know,' muttered Ray, uncomfortable with the whole situation.

'Why'd you even bother nicking somebody for carrying this stuff?' asked Sam. 'It's hardly the great train robbery.'

'We saw this lad carrying that bag, Boss, acting shifty,' Ray explained. 'So we followed him to the park. It was obvious there was going to be a handover, so we waited to see who turned up. We concealed ourselves cunningly in a shrub. But then the lad sort of … spotted us.'

'What do you mean, 'sort of' spotted you?'

'It weren't me, Boss, it were 'im!' Ray jabbed a thumb towards Chris.

'I've got a problem that needs tablets!' Chris protested. 'I can't help meself. The gas builds up and it hurts me tummy. I got no choice but to …' He mimed a vile pumping action with his fist. 'If I don't let it out I could do meself an injury. Blokes die. It's medical, Boss. I tried changing me diet, but it sent me the other way, all bunged up and solid, you know what I mean? Like trying to drop a lump of coal.'

'I get the picture, Chris, thank you,' said Sam.

'I'm on charcoal tablets,' Chris went on. 'They turn your tongue black, but it's a price worth paying.'

'I said I get the picture, thank you. Okay, so Chris quite literally blew your cover and the suspect spotted you. What happened next? Run off, did he?'

'Like a shot,' said Ray. 'I shouted at him to hold up but he kept legging it. So I brought him down with a rugby tackle and there was a bit of argy-bargy.'

'And that set me off again,' Chris grimaced. 'Like flippin' Hiroshima.'

'We had to nick him, Boss, he was acting so suspicious,' Ray went on. 'And besides, we didn't know what was in that bag. Could've been drugs. Could've been guns.'

'Them photos could lead us to an international porn ring,' said Chris, pointing at the bag. 'This could be *big*, Boss!'

'I doubt it,' said Sam. 'These pictures were probably snapped off locally. Look at them, they've been taken in somebody's crappy little flat. It's small beer. Amateur night. Let the lad go and get back to nicking *real* villains.'

'He *is* a villain, boss!' Chris insisted. 'A jail bird. He's done time before. He told us on the way in here. He did a stretch at Friar's Brook and he begged us not to send him back there. Practically crying he was.'

'Like a nancy,' growled Ray.

Sam's ears pricked up: 'Friar's Brook? He's done time at Friar's Brook borstal?'

'That's what he said, Boss.'

Friar's Brook borstal was where the junk metal was being brought in from at Kersey's yard, and it was also the source of the letter found on the lad who'd stolen the truck.

'This young man you arrested, what's his name?' Sam asked.

'Barton. We stuck him in Cell 2.'

'Barton …' Sam mused. Then he said, 'You two knock off for the night. The Guv's already down the boozer, he'll be missing your company.'

'You not coming, Boss?' Ray asked.

'No. I want to speak to this lad Barton. I'm interested

30

in Friar's Brook and he might have something useful to tell me about it.'

'And what about – *that*?' Chris indicated nervously at the sports bag full of shoddy gay porn.

'I'll hang onto it,' said Sam flatly. 'For my private use.'

Chris's mouth fell open. Ray scowled, uncertain, disturbed.

'What's the matter, boys?' Sam added camply, arching an eyebrow. 'Afraid of your own feelings?'

'You shouldn't joke, Boss, not about stuff like that,' said Ray darkly. 'You'll get yourself a reputation. C'mon, Chris, let's get down the Railway Arms. The Guv hates to drink alone. And besides, his sense of humour's more – more *normal* than some.'

As the two of them headed off together, Sam called out to them, 'Oh – and Chris?'

'Boss?'

'Those charcoal tablets you're taking. Don't overdo 'em, they're carcinogenic.' And when Chris stared blankly at him, Sam added, 'They give you cancer.'

'Give over, Boss!' scoffed Chris, waving him away. 'They ain't no worse for you than fags.'

Sam headed back down to the cells. He reached the heavy door of Cell 2 and opened up the spyhole. Inside he saw Barton pacing anxiously about, sweating and chewing his nails. He was older than Sam had imagined, with rough skin around his neck and face, and collar-length hair that was well overdue for a wash. If he'd been an inmate at Friar's Brook borstal, it must have been some years ago.

'Barton?' Sam called through the spyhole. 'My name's DI Tyler. I want a word.'

Barton turned with a start and at once dashed over.

'Officer!' he cried. 'Sir! You gotta get me out of here! Please! *Please*, sir! I'm begging you! I'm no nonce. I'm just the courier. It's *them* what takes the pictures, sir, not me.'

'I'm not really fussed about all that.'

'They take 'em in one of the flats on the Hayfield estate. Dirty pictures, sir. I just deliver 'em. They pay me a couple of bob, I need the cash, but I don't get involved or nuffing 'coz I'm not like that, honest I'm not, sir! Please, sir, please, you gotta let me out of here!'

'Barton, take it easy. There's nothing they can charge you with except some trumped-up nonsense about resisting arrest. And if you cooperate with me I can see that charge is completely dropped.'

'Really? Really, sir?' Barton pressed his face hard against the spyhole. 'You'll let me go? You mean it?'

'Of course I mean it. But in return, I want to ask you a few questions.'

'Oh thank you, thank you!' grovelled Barton, thrusting his fingers through the spyhole and waggling them. 'I knew you'd help me! I could see you were different, you're not like the others. You've got kind eyes.'

'I have?' said Sam, suppressing a grin.

'Yes, yes, sir, you have, very kind eyes! And a kind face, sir! A very, very kind face.'

Sam laughed.

'I mean it!' Barton cried. 'I know, I know, you think I'm a nonce talking like that. They *all* thought I was nonce, back in Friar's. That's why I don't ever want to go back there. They gave me a hard time. A *hard* time, sir!'

'Friar's Brook is what I wanted to ask you about. What's it like?'

'Terrible, sir! They nearly killed me! It was awful. They said I was a nancy, they said I'd got my dick out in the showers and tried to – they said I wanted to – that I … It weren't true, I swear it, sir! I never did nothing! I'm no poofter I like big tits and that!'

'When were you at Friar's Brook?' asked Sam.

'Last year.'

'Rubbish. It's a borstal. You're way too old.'

'Too old? I'm seventeen.'

Sam was taken aback. The heavy features, the skin roughed by cold shaves and alcohol aftershave and a diet of instant mash and fish fingers – could that really be the face of a teenager?

No moisturizers for men in the seventies. No skincare regimes, no fruit juice, no five-a-day. It's all harsh winds

33

and fag smoke and chips cooked in dripping for lads like this.

'I can't never go back to Friar's,' Barton hissed. 'It's hell on earth.'

'The other inmates pretty rough, are they?'

'Not the inmates, sir.'

'What, then?'

'If I tell you what's so terrible about that place, sir, will you promise to get me out of here?' Barton pleaded.

'Sure. I promise.'

'Okay. Since you're kind.'

'I'm all ears,' said Sam. '*And* kind eyes. Go ahead, tell me what's so terrible about Friar's Brook.'

Barton dropped his voice to a hoarse whisper. He pressed his mouth against the spyhole and breathed a single word, '*McClintock*.'

And with that, he fell silent.

Sam waited for something more, but he got nothing.

'Is that it? 'McClintock'?'

Barton nodded. He glanced about in terror, as if by uttering the name he was at risk of summoning the devil.

'And who is this 'McClintock'?' asked Sam. 'An inmate? One of the warders?'

'Go and find out for yourself, sir,' Barton whispered. 'Then you'll see. *Then* you'll see.'

'Barton, I promised to help you, and I will. But in return you promised to give me information.'

'And that's what I did, sir!'

'A single name and some veiled hints isn't much for me to go on.'

Barton crept forward again and peered out through the spyhole. 'Just remember that name, sir. *McClintock*. Go to Friar's Brook, sir. See what you will see.'

Sam shrugged. 'Well, what can I say? Thanks for your cooperation. Now – you get yourself some rest. I'll make sure you're out of here as soon as I can.'

'You mean that, sir? You won't be sending me back there?'

'We've got bigger fish to fry, Barton. Now go to sleep. And don't have nightmares.'

Still anxious, but less so than before, Barton crept back to the mean little seat that ran along the cell's back wall and settled himself on it. He folded his legs primly, and gave Sam a coquettish smile.

'Thank you, sir,' he said. 'You're different. I can see that.' And, just as Sam closed up the spyhole once more, he caught Barton's voice, 'Be dreaming of you, PC Brown Eyes.'

CHAPTER THREE

MRS SLOCOMBE'S PUSSY

Alone in his flat, Sam dumped a set of dirty plates into the sink and left the washing-up for tomorrow. It would take half the night to get enough hot water to fill the basin, and he was in no mood to sit up, not after the day he'd had. All he wanted was beer and a doze in front of the telly.

He carried a bottle of brown ale over to the TV. The screen glowed. Cash registers clinked and clanged. A funky bass guitar started up. A woman's voice intoned flatly:

Ground floor: perfumery,
Stationery and leather goods.
Wigs and haberdashery.
Kitchenware and food. Going up!

'A bottle, a chair, and a few old gags about Mrs Slocombe's pussy,' Sam said to himself, cracking open the beer. 'That'll do me. That'll do me just grand.'

He swilled back a warm mouthful of brown ale and let his mind drift. But at once he was disturbed by the memory of a voice – a man's voice, very harsh and brutal, issuing incongruously from the mouth of an immature young scally.

'I'll keep coming at you, you cheating bastard. I'll keep coming at you until I've got my wife back – my wife – mine.'

'Just ignore it,' he muttered to himself, trying hard to relax. 'It's just mind games. Annie's never been married.'
Annie. Married.

The image floated into his mind of Annie dressed all in white, with a lace veil, appearing in the aisle of a crowded church. The organ struck up the Wedding March. Sam pictured himself, all togged up in his morning suit, getting to his feet and turning to watch her walk slowly towards him.

This beautiful fantasy made his heart turn over. But then, unexpectedly, his dream was invaded by interlopers. Horribly familiar faces appeared amid the assembled guests. First he caught sight of Chris Skelton, uncomfortable in his cheap suit, a wilting flower hanging limply from his button hole as he pulled a leering, Sid James-ish face at Annie: *ooh 'eck, cop a load of that!*

Beside him, with his collar un-ironed and fag burns on his shirt, stood Ray Carling. He nudged Chris with his elbow – *when the boss gets tired of her, he can always chuck her over my way* – and swigged flagrantly from a pewter hip flask.

Just across from them was Phyllis, all made up and kitted out in her finest glad rags, but looking as scowly faced and unimpressed as ever. She shot Sam a sour look that said *a girl like that – settling for a no-good little 'Erbert like you.*

'Give me a break guys,' Sam whispered to himself, emerging from his fantasy and taking another swig of beer. Then he settled back again, let sleep tug at his eyelids and the emanations from the TV wash over him like a lullaby.

INT: GRACE BROTHER'S DEPARTMENT STORE – DAY

With her bright orange hair and thick multi-coloured make-up, Mrs Slocombe folds her arms and looks disapproving.

MRS SLOCOMBE: That new girl who's started – Miss Belfridge, she calls herself. Nothing but a floozy! She's in line for a promotion already, and all because she wiggles her hips and flutters her eyelashes!

Captain Peacock looks at her across the top of his glasses.

CAPTAIN PEACOCK: Do *you* feel ready for a promotion, Mrs Slocombe?

MRS SLOCOMBE: I do! I'm totally up for it, Mr Peacock! If only someone would give me one!

CAPTAIN PEACOCK: If I had the power, Mrs Slocombe, I'd happily give you one right now.

Mrs Slocombe simpers and pats her orange hair.

Nearby, Mr Spooner and Mr Humphreys overhear their conversation.

MR SPOONER: Promotion? Personally, I'm not much interested in climbing the corporate ladder. What about you, Mr Humphreys? Would you rather be on top?

MR HUMPHREYS: Ooh, I'm quite happy near the bottom.

The TV burbled on.

Slipping back into his wedding fantasy, Sam tried to

ignore the faces of his colleagues amid the pews. Damn it all, this was *his* dream! Those bastards had no right to gatecrash it!

He tried to fill his imagination with the image of Annie in her bridal gown. She looked – and how could she not? – wonderful. He allowed a pale aura of light to shimmer around her, a soft-focus haze that gave her an almost ethereal radiance. Subtly – perhaps a little tackily – he made her eyes glint alluringly beneath her veil as she turned to smile at him.

The priest stepped forward to read the wedding service. But Sam's imagination decided on a cruel casting decision.

'Oh no, not you!'

There was a panatela smouldering unashamedly in the priest's gob. He tugged at his dog collar to loosen it, sniffed, glanced about, and reached under his cassock to flagrantly shepherd a wayward bollock.

'Shall we crack on with and adjourn to the bar?' grunted Father Hunt. 'The padre is parched.'

'You're just bloody spoiling it, Guv. You're always bloody spoiling it.'

INT: GRACE BROTHER'S DEPARTMENT STORE – EVENING

Later that evening, everyone's working late.

Bald, jug-eared Mr Rumbold appears dressed in an overcoat and carrying an umbrella. With him is an extremely attractive young new employee, Miss Belfridge. Mr Rumbold is clearly excited by her company.

MR RUMBOLD: Since we're finishing late tonight, I promised to accompany the lovely Miss Belfridge safely to her front door.

CAPTAIN PEACOCK: Isn't that rather out of your way, Mr Rumbold? You don't live anywhere near Miss Belfridge.

MR HUMPHREYS: *I* can give you a lift home, Miss Belfridge. I've got my mother's motorbike and sidecar.

MISS BELFRIDGE: But Mr Humphreys, I thought you were completely the other way.

MR HUMPHREYS: *(Purses his lips)* That's a wicked rumour.

Drifting on the outskirts of sleep, Sam tried to rearrange his fantasy. He blotted out Gene and Ray and the others and tried to replace them. But who with? He wanted to imagine Annie's father proudly escorting his beautiful daughter up the aisle, but Sam had no image of the man.

I don't really know anything about Annie's father, he thought, sleepily sipping more beer, and sliding further into the warm bath of sleep. *In fact, I don't know much about her past life at all. Bits and pieces. She may have mentioned something about brothers. Are they in the Force too? Does she come from a police family? And what about her childhood, all those years before I met her?*

He began to imagine old boyfriends she might have had over the years. There would have been no shortage of willing candidates. Spotty, callow-faced youths, trying to impress her at the disco, or deep-voice uniformed coppers with little intelligence and even less imagination, offering her a future of child-rearing and domestic servitude.

Sam felt waves of jealousy lap at the edge of his dozing mind. To think that he could so easily have missed his chance with Annie, that he might have lost her to some schoolyard boyfriend or dull-as-ditchwater lug in uniform. Just to *imagine* her with somebody else made his muscles tighten and his stomach clench.

But she's not *with somebody else – she's with* me. *More or less. Pretty much. In a manner of speaking.*

There *was* no husband, emerging from the shadows to reclaim his runaway bride. Whatever the Devil in the Dark may be, it was not Annie's husband. It was impossible. It was unthinkable!

MR HUMPHREYS: Wait there, Miss Belfridge, while I get my motorcycle things. I stuck my helmet round the back.

CAPTAIN PEACOCK: Stuck it round the back, Mr Humphreys? I hope you haven't put it anywhere that might cause a blockage.

MR HUMPHREYS: It's only a small one, Captain Peacock. I could probably stick it anywhere and nobody would notice.

MRS SLOCOMBE: Well I hope you don't try sticking it under my ladies' counter, Mr Humphreys! *I'd* certainly notice! There's no room down there to accommodate your helmet.

MR HUMPHREYS: Are you giving me backchat, you orange-haired bitch? Jesus Christ, you need to learn some bloody manners!

Since when did Quentin Tarantino start directing Are You Being Served?, Sam thought. He forced his eyes open and looked at the TV screen, and was disturbed to see Mr Humphreys stride furiously across to Mrs Slocombe's counter and lay into her with both fists. As Mrs Slocombe went down, curling into a foetal position, Mr Humphreys slammed his foot into her, over and over again, aiming kicks at her back, her legs, her head.

MR HUMPHREYS: Still feel like showing me up in front of people, do you? I can't hear you, you cheap little bitch! *Do you still feel like showing me up!* Answer me, you filthy whore!

I don't remember this episode, Sam thought dopily. *I must be dreaming. This can't be real – this must all be some sort of—*

'No, Sam – it's very real,' said a horribly familiar voice. The Test Card Girl was standing right beside his chair, clutching her blank-eyed dolly. 'Can't you see who the lady is – the one lying on the ground, being hurt?'

His voice thick and slow with sleep, Sam muttered, 'It's Mrs Slocombe.'

'Is it, Sam? Or is it really somebody else ...?'

Forcing his eyelids apart, Sam peered at the screen. Mr Humphreys – not that it looked at all like Mr Humphreys any more – was still kicking the hell out of a woman on the ground. But, where there had been orange hair and a frilly blouse and frumpy shoes, there was a much younger woman, with dark hair and a paisley-pattern one-piece jumpsuit and platform boots.

'I – can't see her face ...' Sam slurred sleepily.

'She keeps it covered when he beats her,' the Test Card

Girl said. 'But you don't need to see her face to know who she is. Come on, Sam – you're asleep, but you're still a policeman. Work it out. The answer's obvious.'

Sam felt ice run through his veins. Sleep fell away. He sat bolt upright, fully awake, fully alert.

'Make it stop,' he ordered.

'You can't change the past, Sam,' the Girl said.

On the screen, the appalling beating continued.

'I said make it stop!'

The Test Card Girl gently touched Sam's sleeve, as if to console him. 'He's a horrid man, isn't he. She should never have married him.'

Sam leapt to his feet, crazily lunging at the TV set to save the girl on the floor. He'd grab that evil, bullying bastard – he'd grab him and give *him* a beating – the biggest damned beating of his life! He'd batter him to a pulp! He'd stamp him into the ground! He'd kill him! He would really *kill him*!

But all at once, Sam found himself standing alone, in silence. Wherever he was, it wasn't his flat. He looked about him, saw drab, brown walls and a set of flimsy and quite obviously fake lift doors. To either side of him stood a couple of small shop counters with an array of suits and trousers behind one of them, a selection of ladies' undergarments behind the other.

'It's Grace Brothers …' Sam muttered in disbelief. 'I'm actually *in* Grace Brothers.'

It was as rickety and unconvincing in reality as it looked on TV. A cheap set, pieced together and dressed courtesy of the BBC scenery department.

'Just a set,' Sam said to himself. 'A set – with three walls ...'

He turned slowly towards the non-existent fourth wall. What would he see? An array of huge old BBC cameras, and the seats for the studio audience behind them? Or would there actually be another wall there, enclosing him, sealing him in?

Sam turned – and gasped. There was no fourth wall, but neither were there cameras or an auditorium. Instead, there was the universe. Stars – billions of them – swirling slowly and breathtakingly around the luminous hub of the galaxy.

The Test Card Girl appeared beside him and took his hand. Her skin was warm. Surprisingly warm. Together, she and Sam looked out across the glittering cosmos.

'Makes you feel very small, doesn't it?' the little girl said. 'A single life can't mater all that much, can it, Sam – not compared to all this?'

'It matters,' said Sam softly.

'The woman you saw being beaten, Sam – you know who she is.'

'Yes.'

'And you love her.'

'Yes.'

'But she doesn't matter, Sam. Look at all these stars. Too many to count. And what you can see is only a fraction of the whole. The woman you love is less than a grain of sand in the desert.'

'She matters.'

'But how?'

'Because …' Sam tried to think. He was just a copper, not a philosopher, not a poet. He was out of his depth. And the glittering panorama of stars and galaxies was making his head spin. 'She matters because she matters.'

'That's no answer, Sam.'

Sam freed his hand from hers and looked about him. He turned from the vastness of the universe to the confines of a bawdy seventies sitcom, and then back again. He couldn't help himself – he just had to laugh.

'Okay,' he said, forcing himself to get his head around things. 'Grace Brothers on one side, Infinity on the other. Very good. Excellent. Well done. Now – please – what the hell are you trying to tell me with all this?'

He planted himself squarely in front of the Test Card Girl and fixed her with a mocking, confrontational look.

'Spit it out. You're my resident Sigmund Freud. Let's have it. What the hell does all this represent?'

The Girl looked up at him, and her eyes went cold. She said flatly, 'It represents the System.'

'What system? The solar system?'

'No, no. The System you're trapped in.'

She used her dolly's hand to indicate the TV set, with its fake walls and prop dressing.

'It's not real, Sam, but even so you still can't escape it. These make-believe walls enclose you. They confine you – and they *def*ine you.'

'I – don't understand.'

'You think you can escape the System, Sam, but you can't. You can run around, kid yourself, score a few petty victories, tell yourself that you'll win in the end – but it's not so. Everything is fixed, set in place, unchangeable – like all those stars out there. You can more easily rearrange the universe, Sam, than alter the fate that awaits you – you and Annie.'

Sam took a step away from her and clenched his fists. 'I'm not accepting that.'

'There is a terrible power coming after Annie. It is linked to her, Sam. It is *married* to her.'

'No.'

'It was married to her in life and it's still married to her now it's dead.'

'None of this is true.'

'It's coming for her, Sam, and it *will* find her, and it *will* drag her down to somewhere very, very unpleasant. And there's nothing you can do to stop it. It's the System, Sam. It's all set. You can't change it.'

'You're showing me *dreams*! It's nothing! Pictures in my head! I know where I am. Right now, right *now*, I know exactly where I am! At home. Asleep. In a chair. With *Are You Being Served?* on the telly. Everything is *normal*! Whereas all this crap you're showing me here' – he angrily swept his hand to indicate the stars and the stage set about him – 'all this *bullshit*, it's just loony pictures you keep putting in my head!'

The Test Card Girl shook her head slowly, with mock sadness, and said, 'I'll tell you where you are, Sam – where you *really* are. You're lying in a coffin, six feet down in a Manchester graveyard.'

'That's the *future*!' Sam retorted. 'That's thirty years from now!'

'You're rotting, Sam. You glimpsed it yourself, remember? In the ghost train, in Terry Barnard's fairground?'

Sam froze.

'Tell me what you saw there, Sam.'

'I saw ...' he said, and he found himself trying to swallow hard in a dry throat. 'I saw something. I saw whatever it is that's after us, that's after Annie ...'

'Did you? Or did you just see *yourself*?' the Test Card Girl asked. 'You're a mouldering corpse, Sam. The worms have got into you. They're eating you from within. Your eyes are already gone. They're just two holes now, filled with maggots.'

'It wasn't *me* I saw, it was that devil out there!' Sam howled. 'I am *alive*! The here and now is 1973, and in 1973 I am *alive*!'

'No, Sam. You're dead. You're dead, and you're lost – not in one place, not in another – somewhere in-between—'

'I am *alive!*'

'You're fooling yourself, Sam.'

'If I *am,* then I'm happy with that! I came back here by choice. I came back here because I want to be here. I came back here for colour, and feeling – and Annie. I came back here for *life.* I don't understand what it all means, and I don't *want* to understand. I just want to live my *life.*'

'You have no life, Sam. And neither does your beloved Annie. Or that horrid man you work for, the one who smells of ciggies and is always shouting. Or any of you.'

'Bullshit! They're all alive! Of course they're alive! And as for *me,* I'm more alive than I've ever been!'

'If you're all so alive, Sam, then what are you all doing *here*? This isn't a place for the living, Sam.'

Sam wanted to yell at this little brat to keep her lies to herself, but deep down he knew that she wasn't lying at all. Indeed, he had long since suspected what she was telling him, though he had fought against the knowledge, suppressed it, blotted it out with his police work, with his clashes with Gene, with his feelings for Annie, with that constant internal mantra that said, *I'm just a copper, not a philosopher – I'm just a copper, not a philosopher – I'm just a copper, not a—*

'You don't need to be a philosopher to work it out, Sam,' the Test Card Girl said. 'A simple copper is more than able to see what's what.'

'I'm alive,' Sam declared.

'No, you're dead.'

'I'm alive, and so is Annie.'

'She's dead too. So's your horrid boss man. So are your friends in CID. All dead, Sam. You know that. You won't accept it, but you know it. Think about it, Sam. You *know* you're dead – you remember – you remember jumping from that roof and falling—'

Sam turned away, shaking his head, but the girl's voice would not stop.

'You remember, Sam. The others, they *don't* remember. They've been here too long. They should have moved on by now. And if you stay long enough, Sam, you'll start forgetting too. You'll forget you had a life before this one. You'll become like *them*. Lost, Sam. Lost.'

There were tears in Sam's eyes now. He dashed them furiously away, but more came. He was thinking of Annie, of the life she'd had before this one. Had she, like Sam, come from the future? Or had she come from a life even further back than 1973? And how had that life ended? How had she died?

'You know how she died, Sam. It was a horrible death.'

'Stop it.'

'Painful. Nasty.'

'I said stop it!'

'And it wasn't quick, Sam.'

'I don't want to be in this damned dream any more, you filthy little bitch!'

'Awake, asleep, whatever.' The girl shrugged. 'And calling me names won't help you, Sam. Look at that vast universe out there. You can't just wish it away. What will happen to you, Sam? Do you think you can carry on like this for ever, drifting in the gaps between this world and that one? You all have to move on one day. You, and your guv'nor, and your little friends in CID, and Annie too.'

'I'm not going anywhere! I'm staying here, in nineteen-bloody-seventy-bloody-three with Annie! I am staying! *We* are staying!'

'You think so? You think that you'll keep hold of your darling Annie when that thing drags itself out of the darkness and comes for her? Will you go with her to the horrid place he'll take her to? Could you even *find* that place? And, if you did, what then? Oh, Sam, it's all so complicated. So complicated – and so hopeless! Better to give up on it all.'

Sam's thoughts were crashing about inside his mind like waves tormented by a storm. Tears were flooding down his face now. He looked for answers, comebacks, words of defiance, but all he could find was a numb, silent horror deep within him. He knew the girl was telling him the truth. He knew that whatever it was that was prowling through the darkness towards his darling Annie was beyond his powers to defy. It would find her, it would drag her away – and there was nothing Sam could do to prevent it.

He felt small, cold fingers gently taking hold of his hand.

'I can help you, Sam. I can make you fall asleep so that all this nastiness and confusion is forgotten. No pain, Sam, just rest. Hold onto my hand and I'll lead to you to a place where you can go to sleep.'

'I'm asleep already.'

'Not deeply enough. Hold onto my hand.'

'I'm not going anywhere. I'm staying here. I'm staying with my Annie.'

'You know that's hopeless, Sam. Hold onto my hand. I'll take you away. And whatever happens to Annie – well, Sam, you'll never know. It'll be better that way. Better not to know, not never ever *ever*. Hold onto my hand, Sam. Hold onto my hand.'

But Sam had had enough. His mind was reeling from all this vertiginous metaphysics. He thrust the Test Card Girl's hand away and shoved past her, blundering into Mrs Slocombe's display of ladies' apparel. Comically huge brassieres and girdles fell across him. He dashed them aside and raced for the doors at the back of the set. Slamming into them, he felt them sag under his weight. They were just painted plywood, braced at the back and fixed down with stage weights. Sam battered at the doors, but they would not open. They shook and lurched and groaned and shuddered, but still they stood firm.

Sam hammered at them with all his strength. He began shouting. He was still shouting when he found himself face down on the floor of his flat in a pool of spilt brown ale, the TV grandly playing the national anthem and primly reminding him to please turn off his set.

CHAPTER FOUR

ANNIE CARTWRIGHT, GIRL DETECTIVE

Monday morning. Sam arrived at the grey, slablike building that housed CID. Reaching the concrete steps that led up to it, he paused, taking in the pale sky, the first rays of the sun, the high-up scraps of ragged grey cloud.

A normal sky. A normal Manchester morning.

He breathed in the air.

Car fumes – the whiff of distant cigarette smoke – normal, all so normal ...

He patted a concrete wall.

Normal.

He patted himself, felt his body solid and real beneath his leather jacket and slacks.

Normal. Everything's normal. If this is death, then death is normal. It's just normal.

And permanent? Would all this seeming normality last? And if so, for how long?

That's a question nobody can answer. Not knowing why you're here, and how long you've got – not knowing the answers to the big questions is well, it's just normal.

'Situation normal,' he said to himself. 'Everything might have changed for me but, in some ways, nothing's changed at all.'

The mantra started up in his head once again: *I'm not a philosopher, I'm just a copper. I'm not a philosopher, I'm just a copper.*

It blotted out the crazy dreams of the night before. It smothered Sam's suspicion that nothing about him was real, that it was all just illusion. It muffled the ice-cold terror within him that awful things were going to happen, that horror and pain were just over the horizon, that hell itself was drawing near.

I'm just a copper. I'm just a simple copper. I do my job and nick the bad guys and keep my head down because I'm just an oh-so-simple copper.

Up in A-Division, Sam found all the desks empty, all the phones unmanned. Everybody – Chris, Ray, a motley assortment of blokes from the department, and even Annie – was clustered together on one side of the room.

What had attracted them was a huge white contraption, about which a rep in a pinstriped suit fussed and tinkered.

'What's all this?' Sam asked.

'A new gadget, ordered in on trial,' said Annie. And then, looking intently at him, she frowned and added, 'You all right, Sam?'

'Bad night's sleep, that's all,' he smiled. Her eyes were bright and clear, her skin was gently flushed around the cheeks, her hair was glossy. Not bad, he thought. Not bad at all, seeing as she's supposed to be dead.

I'm just a copper. I don't understand these things. Annie's alive. We're all alive. That'll do for me – and to hell with the crazy bloody nightmares!

'They want to start sticking these new machines in the offices all over, Boss,' put in Ray, speaking without taking the fag from his gob. 'Not that the Guv's too keen on it.'

He nodded towards Gene's office, where the man himself was visible as a brooding, lurking shape behind frosted glass.

'I'm sure your guv'nor will change his tune when he sees what this little beauty can do,' said the rep. With a knowing smile, he pressed a button and the cumbersome device clanked and juddered, emitting a sudden sweep of light.

'Look out Boss, the bloody Martians have landed!' grinned Chris, turning to Sam.

'Not Martians, sir,' grinned the rep proudly. '*The future*.'

'The future's not always such a great place to be,' put in Sam.

The rep turned that oily smile towards him: 'Ahh – there speaks a man who's stuck in the past. But let me see if I can bring you up to date, sir. Look.'

The machine slowly disgorged a sheet of paper that reeked of chemicals. The rep swept up the sheet and flourished it proudly.

'See for yourselves, gentlemen, madam. Look at the quality of that reproduction. Pristine. Beautiful. Reliable. No more mucking about with messy old carbon paper or wasting time typing up duplicates. The Xerox 914 is the automated office secretary you've always dreamt of!'

'She's not the stuff of *my* dreams,' sniggered Chris. 'Secretaries are supposed to have – well, you know – a right ol' set o' melons.'

'In the ideal world, Chris, yes,' said Ray, and he smirked across at Annie. 'But we don't live in an ideal world. Do we, luv.'

'Not so long as it's got dopes like you in it,' Annie glowered back. Ignoring sniggers and jeers from the boys she added, 'And I'm nobody's flamin' secretary.'

'*This* office secretary doesn't need lunch breaks,' the rep went on. 'Or holidays. And she won't go and get married, leaving you all in the lurch.' He pressed the button again. The Xerox noisily and laboriously delivered another copy. 'It's a lovely model this, the 914 – but who knows, if you get on with it well enough then you might like to think about upgrading to one of our cutting-edge machines that actually makes copies *in colour*.'

'Colour?' exclaimed Chris. 'No way, give over!'

The rep nodded proudly. 'Full-colour copying at the touch of a button, right here in your office.'

Chris whistled through his teeth, genuinely impressed: 'It's Buck Rogers, ain't it.'

Mutely, the staff of CID stood watching the copies emerging one by one from the Xerox machine. They seemed almost hypnotized. Ray puffed smoke. Chris audibly chewed on his bubble gum.

'This ain't a church, it ain't a library, and it ain't a bloody undertaker's!' Gene's voice boomed out from the doorway of his office. Everybody jumped. 'It's too quiet in here! I want noise! I want activity! I want typewriters clacking and phones going ding-a-ling! Move it, move it! Mush, mush, you dogs!'

The gaggle of gawpers broke up at once as people bustled back to their desks. Gene gave the Xerox machine and its unctuous rep a sour look, muttered something about not wanting Robbie the Bloody Robot in *his* department, and vanished back into his office, slamming the door behind him.

All thoughts of the vastness of the cosmos, and the

terrible truths of ultimate reality, were pushed from Sam's mind. Mercifully.

'You got a moment, Boss?' Annie called to Sam.

'For you, as many moments as you like.'

Ray made smoochy kiss-kiss noises, but Sam ignored him.

'What is it, Annie?'

'I've been having a look at that letter you left for me, the one found on that lad who nicked the lorry,' said Annie, laying out a mass of paperwork on her desk. 'It was addressed to 'Derek', signed 'Andy', and sent from Friar's Brook borstal – we know because it's been stamped at the top, presumably to show it's been read by a member of staff and officially sanctioned. So I checked the Home Office files.' She plucked a sheet of paper from the array. 'Now – turns out there's a lad serving time at Friar's Brook borstal by the name of Andrew Coren. He's been in trouble on and off since he was a nipper – him and his brother Derek.'

'Andy and Derek,' mused Sam, nodding. 'Well spotted. Okay, so that would explain the names in the letter. What's Andy Coren in for?'

'Breaking and entering, handling stolen goods,' said Annie. 'Not for the first time, neither. And, what's more, seems like he's a bit of a slippery fish. He's twice escaped from open borstal, so they stuck him in Friar's Brook. Tighter security, apparently.'

'A name was mentioned to me last Friday. There's a

young lad in the cells called Barton. He's done time in Friar's Brook. He's absolutely terrified we're going to send him back there. He gave me the name McClintock. Did you come across that name at all?'

'Don't think so,' said Annie, leafing through the names of inmates she'd compiled. 'No McClintock amongst this lot. Do you think it's important?'

'I have no idea. Maybe this lad McClintock's been released – maybe he doesn't even exist.' He waved that line of enquiry away. 'Let's not get sidetracked by red herrings. Let's stick to what we know. Andy Coren's banged up in Friar's Brook. He sends a perfectly innocent letter to his brother Derek, and Derek violently steals a truck loaded with old fridges, making off with it like it's gold bullion. At the same time, we've got an unidentified white male fished out of the crushing machine at the same junkyard where Derek stole the lorry.' He sighed. 'Bits and pieces. And they *seem* somehow connected – but I can't see a pattern.'

'Neither can I,' said Annie. 'And I don't know if I'm complicating things by mentioning this, Sam, but there was a suicide recently at Friar's Brook. One of the inmates, a lad called Tunning. He hanged himself.'

'When was this?'

'Two weeks ago. I came across it looking for Andy Coren. And a month before that there was a lad died in the kitchens. Some sort of faulty cooker went off on his face.'

Sam looked at the arrays of papers on Annie's desk and sighed: 'If we're not careful here, Annie, we could get seriously bogged down in *data*. And *data* isn't the same thing as *information*.'

'That's true, but we can't afford to ignore details. If there *is* something weird going on here, and it's being concealed, then it might only be those seemingly unrelated details that'll reveal it to us.'

'Can I leave this with you, Annie? This needs some careful thinking about. It's all too Sherlock Holmes for the likes of *some* round here.'

He glanced over at Chris and Ray, who were discussing whether Xerox machines gave off radiation, and if they did was it enough to shrivel your nadgers?

'I'll call Friar's Brook and see if I can dig up anything new,' said Annie. And then, glancing over Sam's shoulder, she added, 'I think the Guv'd like a word with you.'

Sam turned and saw Gene's face scowling at him from his office.

Obediently, Sam went to him, choking on the thick smoke from half a dozen early-morning fags that filled the office.

'What's the matter, Tyler?' growled Gene. 'The air in here not to your liking?'

'It's fine, Guv,' spluttered Sam, waving his hand in front of his face. 'I love the smell of cheap tobacco in the morning.'

'Me too,' said Gene without irony, drawing heavily on a No. 6. 'But what I do *not* like is minions and skivvies carrying on behind my back.'

'Guv?'

'You've been talking to that nonce Barton. He's downstairs in the cells hollering that you promised to let him walk.'

Sam shrugged. 'There's no point holding him. He's just a kid.'

'He's an important link in a chain, Tyler.'

'A chain leading where?'

'To a den of pornographers,' said Gene dramatically, snorting smoke from his nostrils. '*Pansy* pornographers. You should see the pictures, Tyler. Lads in their Y-fronts with their bacon butties flappin' about fit to bust. It's bloody diabolical.'

'I *have* seen the pictures,' said Sam, dismissively. 'They're nothing. Small potatoes.'

'You reckon? Some of them boys had Hamptons like a Frenchie's loaf.'

'What I meant, Guv, was that Barton selling on mucky photos is hardly worth our while worrying about. He's done time already, and he didn't have an easy ride of it inside. He's absolutely terrified of going back.'

'My heart bleeds,' intoned Gene. He sparked up a fresh smoke, contemplated it for a moment, and then said, 'Okay. I'll let Barton go. We need the space down there in the cooler. But the point remains, Tyler, that you've been going behind my back. It's not for you to decide who gets to walk out of them cells.'

'That's what bothering you, isn't it, Guv?' said Sam. 'You don't give a stuff about 'the pornographer's den'. All that's bothering you is that you feel I've trodden on your toes.'

'Yes, I do. And, if there's one thing I have, it's sensitive toes.'

'Well, it might soothe your bruised tootsies to know that Annie's doing some nifty detective work out there. Looks like she's identified our lorry thief. Derek Coren. His brother Andy's doing time in Friar's Brook right now.'

Gene shrugged. 'That doesn't get us any nearer to identifying the bloke in the crusher.'

There was a demure knock at the office door and Annie appeared.

'Sorry to disturb you, Guv,' she said, 'but I've just picked up some information. Andy Coren was reported missing from Friar's Brook last Friday. He escaped.'

'Friday. The same day the body was found in the crusher,' added Sam.

'And the same day Derek made off with them fridges,' mused Gene. He was furrowing his brows, like a dog picking up the scent. 'All three incidents, all on the same day.'

'Those lorries at Kersey's Yard,' Sam said. '*Gertrude*

and *Matilda*. They were both bringing in junk from Friar's Brook.'

'There's major renovations going on there,' Annie explained. 'They're pulling down the old kitchens and boiler house.'

'And ten-to-one says they're using the inmates to help load up the lorries with junk,' said Gene. 'What you reckon, Sammy boy? Did our lad Andy Coren stow himself away on the back of one of 'em?'

'Kersey said it was a stack of old ovens he was munching up in that machine,' said Sam. 'It's perfectly feasible Andy Coren could have climbed into one when it was loaded up at Friar's Brook, and been carried out inside it.'

'Maybe easier to climb *into* one of them ovens than climb *out* again,' said Gene. 'Handy Andy's not quite the Houdini he thinks he is. He might have got himself out of Friar's Brook but he sure as shitty knickers didn't make it out of that crusher.'

'What if that was Derek's job?' suggested Annie. 'What if Derek turned up to get his brother out of the oven, but somehow got it all wrong?'

Sam nodded, seeing a pattern emerge. 'There were two lorries coming to the yard – *Gertrude* and Matilda. Andy was aboard Matilda – but Derek thought he was on *Gertrude*. That's why he made off with it like that – he thought he was rescuing his brother!'

'But instead all he got was a ton of old fridges,' growled Gene. 'Still, I know which is more use to society.'

'Guv, a young man has died,' Sam reproached him.

But Gene shrugged. 'What's the world lost? A thieving little tit. What you want me to do, drop big fat tears on my tie?'

'Perhaps you should for once, Guv, yes, instead of dollops of ketchup. Whatever Andy Coren did, he didn't deserve to die like that. He was just a kid.'

'A *flid*, more like,' Gene cut across him. 'And his brother Derek's an even bigger spastic than Andy. What a bloody pair. Not exactly *The Great Escape*, was it? Well, whatever. Case closed. There's nothing here for us.'

'You think so, Guv?'

'Of course. It's a ballsed-up escape attempt. Dopey Derek got the wrong lorry, and brain-of-the-week Andy Coren got put on the world's fastest diet. What you want me to do, nick the crusher and charge it with grievous? Leave it to plod, let them sort it out.'

Sam shrugged. In one thing at least Gene was right: it looked very much like nothing more than a bungled escape attempt. If so, their job here was done. But when he glanced at Annie he could see at once that she wanted to speak.

'Annie?' he said. 'Is there something you'd like to add?'

Annie looked from Gene to Sam to Gene again.

'Well …' she said.

'Well what, luv?' barked Gene. 'If you've got an opinion that you think's superior to mine then I'd love to hear it. It's Monday morning, I need a laff.'

'Well, if you really want my opinion, Guv,' said Annie, 'I reckon there's more to this than just Derek accidentally getting the wrong lorry.'

'Conspiracy, not cock-up, is that what you reckon?' asked Sam.

Annie shrugged, then nodded.

'And what do you base this supposition on?' said Gene, giving her a sour look. 'A hunch?'

'Something like that, Guv.'

'Hunches are for *real* coppers, luv, not for jumped-up secretaries. What you got ain't a hunch – it's called time o' the month.'

'For Christ's sake, Guv, that is bang out of order!' snapped Sam.

'Keep your hair on, Marjorie,' Gene said, examining his tie to see if it really *did* have ketchup on it. 'Sometimes, Tyler, I think you're like a bird an' all.'

'It's that letter, Guv, the one from Andy Coren to his brother,' Annie went on, keeping her cool. 'It's not normal. There's something about it.' Gene wasn't looking at her. He was picking at crusty bits of food stuck to his tie. She carried on regardless. 'You asked my opinion, Guv, and I've given it to you. There's something suspicious about that letter and I'm going to do my best to find out what it is.'

'Good for you, lass,' said Gene, examining the crust he'd just plucked.

'Look at the handwriting, Guv,' Annie insisted, holding out the crumpled sheet of paper. Silently, Sam willed her to stand her ground, make her point, break through Gene's macho carapace and make herself heard. 'Look how all the letters are nicely spaced out, dead neat. Andy Coren's barely literate, guv, he's never in school, he's always out thieving or getting himself nicked. You think he writes like this? And look how strangely worded it all is.'

There was a flicker of interest in Gene's face which he tried to disguise.

Sam took the letter from Annie's hand and studied it with renewed interest.

Dear Derek,
So brilliant you could make time for a visit.
Really good to get time with you again. Tell
Auntie Rose not to fret so much. Don't forget to
give Fluffy her special tablets – take her to the
vet in Lidden Street if she gets sick again. It's
very very important I can trust you to look after
her. See you again soon I hope.
Love, Andy

'It's very stiff and formal,' he said. 'No spelling

mistakes. Commas and full stops in the right places.'

'Exactly,' said Annie. 'I don't see Andy Coren being up to writing this.'

'Maybe he dictated it,' said Gene. 'Maybe he got some other inmate to write it down for him. It's what cons often do.'

'And how many cons use these turns of phrase, Guv?' Annie said. "Tell Auntie Rose not to fret so much' – 'Take Fluffy to the vet in Lidden Street if she gets sick again' – Guv, I just don't hear the voice of a borstal boy in these words.'

'Oh? And what *do* you hear?'

'A message, Guv. Not a message about Auntie Rose and Fluffy's tablets – a *hidden* message, one *behind* the words. Besides, there ain't no vet in Lidden Street. I checked.'

Gene gave her a long, level look, and then said, very slowly, 'Think carefully what you're saying, Cartwright. You're getting very, *very* close to saying you suspect this letter's written in secret code.'

'And why not, Guv?' Annie said, throwing caution to the wind.

'Why not? Because you ain't Nancy flamin' Drew, sweetheart! Secret bloody codes, my arse! This is *real life*!'

'This letter was rubber-stamped,' Annie kept on. 'Before it could be posted it was vetted by somebody at the borstal, somebody in authority. It had to be officially approved before it was sent. Now, if Andy wanted to get some message to his brother in this letter, and he didn't want the borstal authorities to see it, then he'd need to find a way of hiding that message behind something that looks totally innocent.'

'Codswallop!' barked Gene. 'You been reading too much Famous Five.'

'And what's more, one of the lads in that borstal hanged himself, Guv, just two weeks ago. And a month before that, a lad got his face burnt off.' Annie's voice was starting to become shrill. 'A death, a suicide, a dodgy letter, a body in the junkyard, the violent theft of a lorry that don't make no sense, and all of 'em connected to Friar's Brook. *Think* about it, Guv. It's not right! Can't you see? There's something *not right*!'

Her frustration had got the better of her, and she all at once realized it. Annie clamped her mouth shut and lowered her eyes, waiting patiently for her guv'nor's rebuke.

But Gene seemed calm. He wasn't about to be riled up by some bird. He smiled to himself, smoothed down his tie, and said, 'You know what I really miss right now?'

'No, Guv,' said Sam 'What do y—'

'Not you, Granny Clanger. *Her.*'

With a sigh, Annie said flatly, 'What do you really miss right now, Guv?'

'The whistlin' of a kettle,' said Gene.

Annie's shoulder slumped. With a muttered 'Yes, Guv, right away, Guv,' she turned and headed off.

'Not that we'll have time to drink it,' Gene said, getting to his feet and reaching for his jacket.

'Why not? Where are we going, Guv?'

'Where'd you think? Borstal.'

'Borstal? You mean Friar's Brook?'

'No, I mean one of the six dozen other borstals in the neighbourhood. Of *course* I mean Friar's bloody Brook, you spanner.'

'But I thought as far as you were concerned this case was closed and done with.'

Gene shook his head. 'Not quite. There's something iffy about this business of the boy in the crusher, something that needs resolving. That letter Andy sent to Derek, then Derek nicking that truck, and now some mention of suicide, and some lag's face going up like Guy Fawkes. It ain't quite right, Sam. It ain't quite right.'

'Wait a minute, Guv,' said Sam, indignantly. 'This is what Annie was saying just now and you pissed all over it.'

'It's them sensitive toes of mine,' said Gene. 'Sometimes the only way to stop 'em hurting is to at the very least *pretend* that's it me what runs this place, not you and twinkle-tits out there. I'm not about to let *her* start thinking she's leading this investigation. Slippery slope, Tyler, letting birds think they're in charge. Where would

71

all it end? You want to wake up one morning and find you got some bint *in charge*?' He bounced his car keys off his forearm and deftly caught them. 'Well come on, then, Sammy boy, don't hang about. Let's go and play with a borstal full of naughty boys.'

CHAPTER FIVE

KIDDIES' PORRIDGE

The borstal was situated well out of town, somewhere on the rugged moors north of Heponstall. Gene floored the pedal of the Cortina and took him and Sam hurtling through the outskirts of Manchester, through Rochdale and Littleborough, beyond the far side of Todmorden, until concrete began to give way to wide stretches of open country, and the buildings thinned out until there was nothing but isolated stone farmhouses beneath an oppressive, sullen grey sky.

Gene powered the car off of the main road, hurtling recklessly along smaller and yet smaller byways until at last they were bounding along what was little more than a dirt track that meandered across the landscape. Sam glimpsed forlorn trees forming tragic shapes against the clouds. He saw broken walls and derelict barns and here and there the rusting, overgrown hulks of long-abandoned pieces of farming equipment. In the far distance, a grey curtain of rain swept slowly across the horizon.

When at last they saw it, Friar's Brook borstal appeared as an assortment of squat, unfriendly buildings heavily fenced off from the surrounding countryside. The barred gate across the track and the barbed wire spiralling along the top of it made Sam think of concentration camps.

'It's so bleak,' he said. 'It's like something out of *Schindler's List*.'

'Schindler's list of what? Holiday camps to avoid? *I've* stayed in worse places.'

'All seems a bit tough, though, don't you think? I mean, for kids.'

'What's the matter with you, Tyler? You gone soft? It's a lock-up, it's *supposed* to be tough.'

'Half them lads in there, I bet they've never known anything in their lives but 'tough'.'

'Life ain't no picnic, not for any of us.'

'I bet they've never known what it feels like to be safe and warm and looked after,' Sam mused, peering through the high fence at the barred windows and heavily bolted doorways. 'What chance do they have? Parents who don't care, violence at home, violence at school, no job prospects, no education, no role models.'

'Well *I* did all right,' put in Gene, defensively.

'I wasn't referring to you, Guv.'

'And knock it off about 'no education'. I'm a walking encyclopedia, Tyler, you'd be surprised. Go on, ask me how to spell *silhouette*.'

But Sam's mind was still on that collection of low, mean-looking buildings and the unseen inmates entombed within. 'Just think of all the wasted talent, wasted intelligence just rotting away inside that place. There's boys in there could have been surgeons, or architects, or airline pilots, if only they'd been born a few miles across town where kids have a chance. Artists, writers – a future prime minister, who knows?'

'Future prime minister? From round here? There'll be a bird in Number 10 before there's a Northerner,' Gene growled.

'Maybe there *will* be a bird. And one who *is* a northerner. There's a thought for you, Guv.'

Gene snorted contemptuously and shook his head. 'I know what's going on in that grubby little brain of yours, Tyler. The only northern bird you want to see on top is your bit of prospective crumpet.'

'I take it that offensive epithet refers to our colleague WDC Cartwright? Guv, why can't you and the other boys in the department just get used to the fact that people sometimes have what the grown-ups call *relationships*?'

'Just keep your mind on the job we've come here

to do,' Gene barked. 'If we find a hint that Andy Coren's death *wasn't* an accident, and that he ended up in that crusher for any other reason than him and his brother being a couple of useless dopey donuts, then Annie's put us on the right track. She'll have earned her brownie points for the day. That should loosen her knickers, Sam – get you one step closer to the ol' pinball machine.'

'Jesus, Guv, the way your mind works.'

'Ain't no different from yours, Tyler, except *I've* got what it takes to make DCI.'

'So have I!'

'When you're old and grey, most like. But until then, Tyler, you're just my little trained monkey. Now, then – best behaviour. We've arrived.'

Gene brought the Cortina to the front gates and sounded the horn. They waited.

'It's like a picking up a date,' he observed.

'If *that's* our date, Guv, you're welcome to him,' said Sam, as a gate officer appeared, dressed in black warder's uniform with a fierce peaked cap. The man's face was hard and angular, with a flat, broken nose and small, unfriendly eyes.

Police IDs were flashed, and the gates were unlocked. As the Cortina nosed through, Gene stuck his head out of the window.

'What's going on there?' he asked, indicating a set of

roofless, broken buildings at the east wing. 'V-2 come down on you, did it?'

'Demolition,' said the gate officer in a surly voice. 'Pulling down the old kitchens and boiler house.'

'That's where the junk was coming from that ended up in Kersey's Yard,' said Sam. 'Andy Coren's escape plan wasn't bad, Guv. He saw a chance and he took it.'

'And then buggered it up,' Gene growled. 'Unless somebody else made sure it was buggered up for him.'

Gene parked the car outside the reception area and clambered out. Sam followed him. Beneath a weather-beaten sign that said 'HMP FRIAR'S BROOK' stood a heavy door, which the gate officer now began to noisily unlock with yet another key on his chain.

I don't want to go inside there, Sam thought suddenly. He felt icy panic, as if something terrible awaited him within those drab, grey walls.

'What's up with you, Tyler?'

'Nothing, Guv.'

'Got the fidgets? You should've gone before we set off.'

'I said it's nothing, Guv.'

'If you're going to get spooked by a spot of kiddies' porridge, Tyler, you should never have come along. I'd be better off with Ray.'

'Guv, just leave it.'

The gate officer rattled his keys and the heavy door

clanged open, revealing a hallway with a tiled floor and whitewashed walls. It reminded Sam of a public toilet.

'Get yourself ready, Tyler,' Gene boomed, slapping his palms together and rubbing them briskly. 'If you think the outside of this place is grim, wait until you breathe the air in them cells. *Parfoom de Borstal*. The heady aroma of BO, spunk and bunged-up khazies. And that's just the staff who work here.'

The gate officer glared at him from beneath his peaked cap. 'Watch it, plod.'

'DCI!' retorted Gene, patting at imaginary pips on his arm as he swept by. Sam hurried after him. Behind them, the door clanged shut, with a power and finality that sent a cold shiver running along Sam's spine. It was as if he himself were an inmate, arriving within the walls of this terrible place, doomed never to see the outside world again.

Get a grip, Tyler, for God's sake, he told himself firmly, and followed the Guv's lumbering hulk as it swaggered off ahead of him.

Sam and Gene were escorted by a warder along an interminable corridor. Far from reeking of filth and sweat, the air was thick with the pungent smell of detergent. Everything was scrubbed and polished, obsessively so.

Up ahead, they saw one of the inmates. He was a frail,

spotty-faced boy, dressed in denim dungarees. He listlessly mopped the floor. But, the moment he eyed the guard approaching, he made a show of working hard.

How old is he? Sam thought. *Fourteen? Fifteen? What sort of life's brought him to this awful place? And what kind of future has he got in store?*

As Sam approached, he noticed a ragged piece of brown cloth stitched unhandily to the front of the boy's shirt. But, when Sam tried to get a closer look, the boy turned away, averting his eyes and keeping his face towards the wall.

'This way, gentlemen,' said the warder, and he indicated an oak-panelled door. The sign on it read: 'J. W. FELLOWES, PRINCIPAL GOVERNOR'.

'I suppose we'd better knock,' said Gene, flinging the door open straightaway without warning.

Mr Fellowes, the borstal governor, sat behind his large desk. He looked up, startled. He was a balding man, rotund and soft-skinned, more at home with civil servants than hardened inmates.

'Don't wet 'em, it's just us,' said Gene, holding up his ID. He sniffed the air extravagantly. 'At least your office don't honk of Dettol.'

'What's going on here?' stammered Fellowes. 'Are you arresting me or something?'

'I apologize for my superior officer, Mr Fellowes,' Sam said, positioning himself in front of Gene to try to block him. 'This is DCI Hunt. My name's DI Tyler, Manchester CID, A-Division.'

From behind him came a tight, clipped, richly Scottish voice. 'A dramatic entrance, gentlemen. Ill mannered, unprofessional – but dramatic, I'll grant you.'

Sam and Gene turned to see a proud, stiff-backed warder standing in the open doorway. His black uniform was immaculate. At his waist hung two chains, a silver one bearing keys, and a gold one attached to a showy fob watch he kept tucked into his pocket. For some reason, that watch caught Sam's attention. He felt a cold shudder run through his body.

Mr Fellowes cleared got to his feet and said, 'This is our head warder, House Master McClintock.'

So this is McClintock, thought Sam. *He's not an inmate at all: he's the head warder. Is this the man I need to be watching? Was Barton right to tell me to keep my eye on him?*

McClintock stepped into the room and closed the door behind him. And, again, Sam found himself peering at the gold fob watch at his waist. What was its significance? Why did it demand his attention like this?

'And to what do we owe the pleasure of your company, gentlemen?' McClintock asked, eyeing them both suspiciously.

'We've just been fishing one of your lads out of a crushing machine,' announced Gene, eyeing McClintock right back. 'Andy Coren. Handy Andy. Name ring a bell?'

Fellowes and McClintock shot a glance at each other.

'It does indeed ring a bell,' said Fellowes. 'I regret to admit that we ... slipped up recently and permitted Andrew Coren an opportunity to escape. We were rather hoping we'd pick him up again without too much of a fuss. He's not violent, just slippery.'

'We have an excellent record here for security,' said McClintock in his clipped tones. 'None of us wish to see it besmirched.'

Gene shrugged. 'Your reputation might not be besmirched, Jimmy, but Andy Coren certainly is. Well and truly besmirched all over a load of old ovens in a great big crusher. Right old mess it was. Squashed, flattened, half his internal organs squirtin' out his arse. I can go into more details if you like.'

Fellowes sat down slowly and laid his hands on his desk. 'So. He got out inside one of the ovens. It's as we thought.'

'It won't happen again,' declared McClintock. 'I have implemented tighter security.'

Fellowes looked up at Gene and Sam, said, 'Thank you for coming out here to inform me of this tragedy – though I can't see why it took two experienced officers to come here in person, when a phone call would have sufficed.'

'We came here, Mr Fellowes, because of certain irregularities associated with Coren's death,' said Sam.

'What sort of irregularities?'

Sam found himself glancing nervously at McClintock, although the House Master was motionless and silent, his blank face unreadable.

I don't like that man. There's something wrong about him.

'Well, Detective Inspector? What sort of irregularities?'

'Hard to say at present,' said Sam, forcing his attention away from McClintock and back to Fellowes. 'Ongoing intelligence. We're in receipt of – scraps of information. We very much want to make sense of these scraps.'

Fellowes looked searchingly at McClintock, then shrugged.

'Very well,' he said. 'We'll help you all we can – *if* we can.'

'Your kitchen block and boiler house,' said Sam. 'They're being demolished. Why is that?'

'They were unsafe,' said Fellowes. 'The boilers were ancient and simply had to go. And the kitchen had been in a dire state for years. We'd struggled on with it, but then there was a terrible accident with one of the gas ovens. It went up like a bomb.'

'A boy was killed, am I right?' asked Sam.

'I'm afraid you are. After that, the Home Office had

no choice but to allocate us funds for a refit. Perhaps you'd like to see our brand-new kitchens?'

'I'd love to see your new kitchens more than words can say,' growled Gene. 'But, before you thrill me and my colleague with that particular emotional roller coaster, I want to know more about this boy what got barbecued. What kind of lad was he?'

Fellowes fumbled for something to say, but it was McClintock who answered. 'He was a young man by the name of Craig Tulse. Nasty little rogue he was. A lot of backchat. Insubordinate. A constant source of trouble to me and my warders.'

'So – a relief to be rid of him?' Gene said. His manner was confrontational.

McClintock gave him a very cold stare. 'The boy died. Burned. Horribly.'

'I'll bet. And what about this other lad, the one who topped himself a couple of weeks back? What's his name again, Tyler?'

'Tunning, Guv.'

'Aye, Tunning. What's the story with him, eh?'

'Tunning hanged himself in his cell,' said Fellowes. 'Unfortunately, these things do happen. But may I point out that our suicide rate is lower than the state prison average.'

'We're not casting aspersions, Mr Fellowes,' said Sam.

'Well, we *might* be,' growled Gene.

'No we're *not*,' Sam cut across him. 'We're just trying to make sense of all things. Mr Fellowes, is there any connection that you can think of between Tunning's suicide and Andy Coren's death?'

Fellowes shrugged and looked to McClintock for support.

'They were both inmates at this facility,' McClintock said flatly. 'What more connection could there be?'

'So – two deaths in two weeks is just a coincidence?' said Sam. 'Not to mention Tulse's death a month or so before?'

McClintock sighed. 'Faulty stoves which have been replaced. A suicide. A bungled escape attempt. That, gentlemen, is the whole story.'

'Are you sure of that?' Sam asked.

'You said just now that you were not casting aspersions, Detective Inspector,' McClintock said. 'Your tone suggests the contrary.'

'And *your* tone suggests you're hiding something,' snarled Gene, glaring at him. 'What's in the sporran, McTavish? Something nasty you don't want the world to see?'

'Detective Chief Inspector, I strongly suspect that you said that for no better reason than to get a rise out of me.'

'You're right. I've got this thing about Jocks. As soon as I come across one I just *have* to get a rise.'

'Then may I save you the bother of doing so by informing you now that you will get no such pleasure from *me*?'

'Any institution housing criminals will have its share of accidents and suicides and escape attempts,' put in Fellowes, keen to calm the tightening atmosphere. 'We do our level best to keep such things to a minimum, but you appreciate that we cannot prevent them entirely.'

'I recently spoke to an ex-inmate of yours,' said Sam. 'He suggested there were ... irregularities here. What do you think he might have been referring to?'

'I'm very surprised at you, Detective Inspector,' said McClintock. 'A man of your experience, giving credence to convicts' tittle-tattle. The inmates will always cry 'foul'. It is in the nature of inmates to do so.'

'True,' said Sam. 'But sometimes they have a point.'

'Not here, they don't,' McClintock said firmly. 'There is a system in place here. *The* System. And the boys within these walls will abide by that System. No negotiations. No compromises. The System is everything, and that's an end.'

'Perhaps a spot of negotiation and compromise is exactly what these boys need,' Sam suggested. '*Treat* them like adults and maybe they'll start *behaving* like adults.'

Mr McClintock fixed him with an implacable look. 'Whether you like it or not, young Detective Inspector, the boys here cannot escape the System. They can run, kid themselves, score a few petty victories, tell themselves they'll win in the end …'

Sam frowned. He'd heard these words before. But where?

'But it's not so,' McClintock went on, pulling out his fob watch and polishing its shiny casing with a pristine white handkerchief. 'Everything here is fixed, set in place, unchangeable – like the passing of time itself. You can more easily rearrange the hours of the day, Detective Inspector Tyler, than alter the System.'

I've heard that little speech before – in a dream – in a dream about stars and the cosmos and—

For a moment, Sam felt his head spinning, his thoughts reeling.

I'm just a copper – and I've got a job to do.

His gaze was drawn back to the gold fob watch in McClintock's waist pocket. Its polished surface glinted, and Sam felt a powerful, almost giddying compulsion to reach out and grab it by the chain.

He forced himself to stay focused.

'What can you tell me about this?' Sam asked, controlling his breathing as he placed the letter from Andy Coren on Fellowes's desk.

Fellowes peered at it, shrugged, and handed it to McClintock.

'Well?' Sam prompted.

'All correspondences between inmates and the outside

world pass by my desk,' McClintock said proudly. 'This letter bears my personal stamp. Thus, I approved it.'

'It was written by Andrew Coren and sent to his brother Derek, correct?'

'No, Detective Inspector, *not* correct.'

Gene's ears pricked up. 'Explain what you mean by that, Jimmy.'

'Like many inmates, Coren's literary abilities did not stretch to the writing of even a simple letter such as this one,' said McClintock.

'He was illiterate?' asked Sam.

'No, not at all. Just unhandy with the written word. This letter, gentleman – and I know this from the handwriting – was written by a lad by the name of Donner. He's an inmate here, although he shouldn't be, not with the quality of the brain between his ears. He's too intelligent to be indulging in crime. Perhaps he will mature in time and grow out of these criminal compulsions.'

'So, this lad Donner,' said Gene. 'It's him what wrote this letter on Coren's behalf?'

'It's a service Donner supplies,' said McClintock, passing the letter back to them. 'Many of the boys here make use of him. No doubt they repay the favour in kind. Do you wish to speak to him?'

'Yes, Mr McClintock, we do,' said Sam.

'With your leave, then, Mr Fellowes?'

'I have no objections, Mr McClintock,' said Fellowes,

shuffling papers in his desk drawers. 'But if you might excuse me, I have a great deal to get on with. An escaped inmate is a headache. A dead one is a migraine.'

'But the company of an uptight Jock is always a joy!' grinned Gene, looming over McClintock. 'Lead on, MacFanny.'

McClintock narrowed his eyes. 'It will do you good to see the System at work. And as luck would have it, Donner's on work duty in the new kitchen block. You can interview him *and* cast your eyes over our new facilities at the same time.'

'Stone me, I've just shat meself,' intoned Gene.

CHAPTER SIX

CRIME AND PUNISHMENT

McClintock led the way, striding trimly ahead of them, a straight-backed, jet-black figure in shiny shoes and sharp-peaked cap who carried himself with the self-assurance of Napoleon.

I don't like him, thought Sam, watching McClintock as he followed him. *The man's a jumped up, self-important control freak. I'll bet he's a bully, too – a tin-pot commandant strutting about his private empire, playing God with the inmates. And yet – it's not his personality that's getting to me. There's something else, something that turns my stomach.*

His eye was caught by a glint of light flashing across the gold fob watch at McClintock's waist. For some reason, Sam's attention kept coming back to it.

What the hell is it about that watch that's bugging me? And what was all that he was saying just now, all that talk about never being able to change the system? Didn't I hear all that in a dream not so long ago? Or am I losing my grip altogether?

No, he wasn't losing his grip. He knew, all too well, that there was something out there, something dark and mean and unspeakably evil, and that bit by bit it was closing in. Whatever it was, it had its sights fixed remorselessly on Annie, and yet it was attempting to reach her through Sam. It found ways of manifesting itself, ways of materializing in Sam's world, over and over; and every guise it took was a step closer, a step nearer, until, one day, one day soon …

One day soon we'll meet face to face.

A voice echoed though his memory: *'I make it my business to know my rivals. I'll keep coming at you, you cheating bastard. I'll keep coming at you until I've got my wife back –* my *wife –* mine.*'*

Sam clenched his fists. *We'll see, you little shit. We'll see.*

As he and Gene turned into another corridor, they were suddenly confronted by words in bright-red paint, three feet high, stencilled boldly along the wall.

SILENCE – RESPECT – DUTY

'Now *that*,' announced Gene, stopping and staring at it, 'is exactly what I never get from my staff.'

'And it's precisely what *I* expect from every single inmate in this establishment,' said McClintock. 'Without fail.'

'So you write it on the wall,' said Sam.

'And the boys see it every day. Perhaps, in time, these virtues might sink into their criminal minds.'

'Slogans on wall? Don't you think it's a bit Orwellian?'

Gene gave Sam a look of total incomprehension mixed with utter contempt. 'Doesn't he think it's a bit *what?*'

'It's like *Nineteen Eighty-Four*,' Sam said. And then, in an aside to Gene, 'It's a famous book, Guv.'

'I know what it is,' Gene snapped.

With a curt, controlled gesture, McClintock indicated at the red letters dominating the wall. 'Every boy here must learn silence, for it is golden. Then he must learn respect – respect for the warders, for his fellow inmates, for himself, and most of all for the System. And then – perhaps – he might start to grasp the concept of duty.'

McClintock touched the gold chain at his waist, running his fingers along it until they reached the fob watch in its little pocket. He patted it.

That watch – I bloody hate it! Sam thought. *Why? Why do I want to rip the damn thing out of his pocket and smash it to pieces?*

'Silence, respect, duty,' McClintock said, almost to himself. 'The three graces.'

And, with that, he continued along the corridor, Sam and Gene striding along in his wake.

'You put a lot of faith in your System here, Mr McClintock,' Sam said as they walked.

'Of course. The System is what holds this place together. It's what stands between order and chaos.'

Gene nodded. Despite his instinctive loathing of all things tartan, there was a lot of common ground between him and McClintock.

'It's all a bit draconian, isn't it?' Sam suggested.

Gene threw his head back in exasperation. 'Oh, knock it off with the bloody *Doctor Who* language, Tyler, will you *please?*'

'Running this place with a rule of iron,' Sam went on, 'slapping huge slogans on the walls. Doesn't it jack up the pressure round here? I'd say if you weren't careful, Mr McClintock, you're going to turn this place into a powder keg, ready to explode.'

McClintock snorted contemptuously. 'It's the System that keeps this institution firmly under control, young man. There'll be no disturbances here, no riots, not on *my* watch.'

'I'll tell you something, Mr McClintock. This place reeks of tension. I sensed it the moment we got here.'

'It's a prison, Detective Inspector, with a prison atmosphere like any other. That's all you sensed.'

'I think you're wrong.'

McClintock halted at a heavy door and waited for a warder to unlock it. He took the opportunity to turn to

Sam and say, 'I don't care for your manner, Detective Inspector.'

'And I don't care for yours, Mr House Master.'

'Settle it with a fight,' suggested Gene.

McClintock's gaze locked onto Sam, and Sam refused to be cowed by it. He stared right back, willing himself not to blink.

'What's on your mind, mmm?' McClintock asked in a low, threatening voice. 'Out with it.'

What is on my mind? Why does this man set my teeth on edge so badly?

McClintock stared at Sam.

Sam stared at McClintock.

Gene sniggered.

And then, the moment was broken by the clanging of the door as the warder opened it.

'I think we three should meet up socially,' Gene suddenly declared, rubbing his hands together excitedly at the prospect. 'Have a few drinks together, maybe go on a lads' night out. There's a real chemistry between us.'

Slowly, and in his own time, McClintock turned away from Sam and stepped neatly through the open door. Sam found he had been holding his breath.

Gene winked at him. 'Nice one, Sammy. Lovely to see you winding up the Jocks. Didn't think that was your bag.'

'I don't like that man,' whispered Sam.

'Well, no, he's Scottish.'

'No, I don't mean I don't like him the way *you* don't like him, Guv, I mean … I mean I don't like him because … because he's …'

He tried to explain, but he couldn't, not even to himself. It wasn't possible to put such deep, instinctive emotions into words.

Gene gave him a blokey nudge.

'You think too much, Sam. You don't have to analyse *everything*. And you know what? It's okay to hate the Scots. It's fine. It's natural. It's not like it's racist or nuthin'. Patriotic duty, ain't it?'

He pushed Sam ahead of him through the doorway after McClintock. They found themselves outside, in an enclosed yard beneath a sullen, rain-filled sky. On one wall, in huge letters, was the word SILENCE, on another RESPECT, and on the third DUTY. Hemmed in by these huge commands stood a metal frame, with a crossbar about seven feet from the ground. Two inmates in regulation dungarees were lifting themselves up and down, up and down, like lads working out at the gym. Their faces were screwed up in pain and shiny with sweat. They were clearly at the very end of their endurance, but still they hauled themselves up and down, forced on by the barking and bellowing of the uniformed warder who oversaw them.

'Exercises?' asked Gene.

'Punishment,' replied McClintock. 'These two young scallywags are being taught that fighting will not be tolerated, not by me, not by the System.'

The warder overseeing the boys barked at them like a drill sergeant: 'Say it! Say the System! Say the System you 'orrible little shits!'

And in unison, as they dragged themselves up, the boys struggled to say, 'Silence.'

They hauled themselves up a second time: 'Respect.'

And then a third. Their faces were so screwed up with agonized effort that they could do no more than grunt.

'Say the bloody System!' the warder shrieked, his voice breaking. He clashed at the metal frame with his baton. 'Say it!'

'Duty,' the boys managed.

'Right! Again! From the beginning! Silence, respect, duty, let's have it all over again! Up, up! Lift your 'orrible lazy arses *up*!'

'What are those bits of brown cloth on their uniforms?' Sam asked. 'The boy mopping the floor back there in the corridor had one on too.'

McClintock nodded. 'All the boys here wear them. I insist on it. I call it the 'Stain'. I have them stitch those tokens on themselves the day they arrive here.'

'The 'Stain'?' said Sam, incredulous. 'You mean, you make them boys wear a badge to mark them out as – what? Corrupted? Contaminated?'

McClintock nodded.

Sam's jaw dropped. 'Mr McClintock, this is a borstal, not Buchenwald.'

Gene rolled his eyes, lost once again by Sam's vocabulary.

Sam opened his mouth to speak again, but he was interrupted by a cry. One of the boys – a wiry lad with narrow, squint eyes – lost his grip and fell exhausted to the ground.

At once, the warder exploded, 'Capps! Get your lazy arse off the ground! Up! Up! Get your filthy self *up*!'

The other lad – a tall, red-haired boy with powerful shoulders – still managing to hang from the bar, glanced down.

'Don't you look at him, Priest!' the warder screamed, and he jabbed at Priest's ribs with his truncheon. 'Get yourself going up and down! Say the System! *Say it! Bloody well say it!*'

Priest screwed up his eyes again and tried painfully to lift his chin above the crossbar. His face was scarlet. The warder clashed his baton against the metal frame, making it ring.

'You can't treat these boys like this!' Sam announced.

'It's no worse than how they treat each other,' McClintock retorted.

'That's why you and your warders are here, to set an example. How many of these lads have male role models to look up to, eh?'

'My warders are here to punish and reform, not to

play surrogate father to a shower of young villains.'

'And that's your 'System', is it? Drill them with slogans, mark them out as corrupted, scream at them all day, punish them?'

'Aye, young Detective Inspector, that's about it,' said McClintock, and he looked down his nose at Sam. 'Clearly you're one of these new breed of do-gooders. Holiday camps and hand-outs of sweeties, is that your prescription?'

'Showing a bit of respect, giving these lads a good example to follow, *that's* all I'm saying,' Sam replied. 'Your precious System does nothing, Mr McClintock, except trap these kids in a cycle of beatings and hatred.'

'If these hooligans are trapped in such a cycle, they have only themselves to blame,' said McClintock. Primly, he pointed. 'That lad there, hanging from the crossbeam. Priest, his name is, though you'll not find a less priestly boy within these walls. He tried to blind another boy using an improvised weapon. A screwdriver, to be exact, pilfered from the woodwork shop.'

'The little tyke,' interjected Gene.

'And that other lad,' McClintock went on. 'Capps – beat another boy so badly his jaw was dislocated. Such brutes need to be made very aware of the seriousness of their actions.'

Gene nodded. 'I hate to side with a Jock, Tyler, but wee Jimmy's right on that one.'

Sam shook his head. 'Decency. Understanding. A little human compassion, for God's sake. *There's* the three graces you should be teaching them!'

Beneath the shadow of the punishment frame, Capps was trying to get to his feet, but his strength was exhausted. The warder overseeing the punishment lashed out at him, cracking the truncheon across the lad's elbow.

'I'll break your bloody arm, you lazy shite! Now get yourself dangling from that bloody crossbeam!'

'If we can instil in these villains fear of the law, then we've perhaps made the outside world a safer place,' said McClintock.

'Can't argue with that,' muttered Gene. He exchanged a look with McClintock. Despite their deep and mutual antipathy, they clearly stood shoulder to shoulder on one thing at the very least.

'Indeed – one *cannot* argue with that,' McClintock said. 'One cannot argue with the System.'

McClintock picked up his already brisk pace. A warder unlocked a doorway and McClintock trotted through it. Gene loped in after him, but Sam hesitated, glancing back at Capps and Priest in the yard. In agony, they slowly dragged their chins above the high crossbar, their shirts darkening with sweat.

In agony, he thought. *Just as that little brat in my dreams said Annie is doomed to agony – that it's her fate, and she can't escape it – that she can't escape the filthy, stinking System.*

He gritted his teeth.

You're wrong, McClintock. You can *argue with the System. And you can break it. You* can *damn well break it!*

'This is disgusting,' Sam snapped, fronting McClintock face to face. 'Have you tried actually *talking* to these lads, Mr McClintock? I mean really actually *talking*?'

'Have *you*, Detective Inspector?' McClintock came back at him, cold and self-assured. 'If you had, you'd know what you can expect from them.'

'Backchat and bollocks,' suggested Gene.

McClintock nodded tightly. 'Aye. I'd nae have phrased it that way myself, but that's precisely what you'd get from them.'

'Then you ignore all that and get to the real lad behind it,' said Sam. 'They don't know any better. You need patience if you want to turn these kids around. Your warders should act as role models, not torturers.'

'It's hardly torture, young Detective Inspector. It's the System.'

Suddenly, in a youthful, high-pitched voice, Priest cried out, 'It *is* torture! He's a torturing, murdering bastard, he is!'

At once, the screw lashed out at him with his baton.

Priest took the blow right across the ribs, and down he went, falling from the crossbar and hitting the ground hard. The warder struck the boy again and yet again, bellowing obscenities at him. The sight of it brought back to Sam his terrible dream from just a few days before, when he had watched Annie being beaten and kicked on his TV screen. He thought of the Test Card Girl telling him calmly, 'There is a terrible power coming after Annie, Sam – and it *will* find her, and it *will* drag her with it down to somewhere very, very unpleasant. And there's nothing you can do to stop it. It's the System, Sam.'

'Leave him!' Sam yelled at the warder as he strode suddenly back into the yard. 'I said leave him!'

The warder, baton raised for another strike, paused, unsure if Sam had the authority to issue orders.

Priest was lying in a ball, his knees drawn up, arms cradling his head. Sam positioned himself between the boy and the warder.

'This stops!' he declared. 'Right now!'

'For Christ's sake, Tyler, don't make a tit of yourself,' growled Gene.

'Back me up, Guv!' Sam barked back at him. 'Just for bloody once, back me up!'

Gene loomed over him. 'You're shrieking like a nancy-boy, Tyler, and I do *not* like it! You can wear your pants over your trousers all you like, Sam, but that still don't make you bloody Superman! You can't save the world!

Even if you *could*, why would you waste your efforts on a bunch of worthless shites like the lads in this place, eh? And I'm not just referring to the warders.'

'I'm not letting this continue!' Sam declared. 'This boy will *not* be beaten!'

Gene suddenly grabbed Sam by the lapels. 'Don't you show me up in here, Tyler, not in front of all these people!'

'I'm not your bloody missus, Gene! Now get your hands *off me*!'

But Gene tightened his grip, hauled Sam off his feet and shoved him against a wall, right under the huge painted word: RESPECT.

'I mean it!' he hissed in to Sam's face. And then, over his shoulder, 'Sorry you all have to witness this. My colleague gets like this sometimes, starts thinking he's Joan of Arc or summat, comes over all high-minded and preachy. Dead embarrassing. If I hadn't chucked the receipt I'd have taken him back to the shop long ago.'

Sam fought free of Gene's grasp and pushed him away. He stood for a moment, glaring at Gene's face, McClintock's face, the slow, stupid face of the warder with the baton, the wide-eyed face of Capps, and the flushed, blooded face of Priest as he peered out from behind the cover of his arms at this strange man who had, quite suddenly and out of the blue, stuck up for him.

I'm on my own here, Sam thought. *Gene won't back*

me up. And the warders'll close ranks. I'm on my own, doing this the wrong way, letting my emotions get the better of me.

He looked at McClintock, who stared back at him from beneath the razor-sharp peak of his black cap.

That man's corrupt. I know it. I sense it. I can smell it. There's things going on here – worse than what we've seen so far. Crimes – torture, even deaths – and that cold-eyed bastard's behind, covering it up, keeping it all contained and suppressed by his precious System. I know it. I know it!

McClintock's fingers momentarily skimmed the length of gold chain that glinted at his waist. The shiny case of the pocket watch was just visible poking above the line of his pocket, glinting dully.

'Enough of this,' McClintock suddenly announced. He indicated with a curt gesture towards the two inmates. 'Officer, return these boys to the dorm.'

'Yes, Mr McClintock.' The warder saluted, and he turned to Priest and Capps. 'Right, you two, get your shitty arses back through that door! On the double! One, two, one, two, pick them lazy bloody feet up you idle sods and get singin'!'

As they ran, the boys chanted, 'Si-lence. Re-spect. Du-ty. Si-lence. Re-spect. Du-ty. Si-lence. Re-spect. Du-ty …'

They bundled through an open doorway that clanged shut behind them, cutting off their voices. There were now just Sam, Gene and Mr McClintock standing together in the courtyard beneath the ominous shape of the punishment frame. Above them, the grey clouds rolled slowly across the dim circle of the sun.

'Let me explain something to you, young Detective Inspector,' said McClintock in a clear, patient voice. 'And to you too, Detective Chief Inspector. Friar's Brook is a borstal. It houses young criminals. It is not a boarding school, it is not a scout camp. It is a place of punishment and correction, and it is run accordingly. And, so long as I am House Master here, the System will be maintained. The System punishes. The System corrects. The System teaches young hooligans what it means to go against society and to go against the Law. The methods are not pretty, but nor are they unjust. Justice must sometimes soil its hands in the pursuit of its aims. Justice must sometimes be hard.'

'Can't argue there,' said Gene.

'So,' McClintock went on, 'let us all be in no doubt that my regime here – my System – exists to turn bad boys into good ones, and if it cannot succeed in that then it at least delivers retribution on those who deserve it.' He focused his attention on Sam and added, 'Put away your suspicions, young Detective Inspector. I do not oversee a murderous regime, nor am I covering up institutional crimes. Tulse died in the kitchens due to a tragic accident. Tunning died by his own hand. And

Coren died through misadventure whilst attempting to escape. There is no plot. There is no conspiracy. I am, like you two gentlemen, a servant of the law, and I play by its rules.'

And, with that, he offered his hand to Sam. It was then that Sam saw that skin on his palms was unnaturally smooth and misshapen, disfigured by severe burns.

At once, Sam thought of Craig Tulse, the inmate who had burned to death in the kitchens. Were the inmate's death and the House Master's burns connected?

Impossible. Those are old burns from many years ago, long since healed up. Tulse's death was recent.

Even so, there was something about McClintock that reeked of malevolence, of danger, of guilt.

Sam stared at that burned hand but made no move to take it.

'Tyler,' Gene growled, assuming Sam was making yet another moral stand. 'Just grow up.'

Gingerly, Sam reached out. He took McClintock's hand and shook. But, when he pulled his hand away again, he felt the compulsion to wipe the palm against his jacket. It wasn't the thought of having touched burned flesh that disgusted him: it was the thought of having touched McClintock.

'Very well, then,' said McClintock in his clipped tones. 'We are all united. We understand one another. We *trust* each other.'

'Careful, Jimmy, you're one step away from suggesting a communal shower,' warned Gene. 'Let's get moving before my high-spirited colleague goes off on another one of his bleeding-heart crusades. It's what he's like. You know, McClintock, I have to put up with this sort of bollocks every working day. Reckons criminals got more rights than victims. Reckons we should warm the handcuff before we slap 'em on in case their little wristies get nippy. I tell you, it's like being partnered with the bloody Messiah.'

'The Messiah would be on *my* side, were he to visit this institution,' McClintock said, straightening his already perfectly straight cap. 'Of that I have no doubt. Now, gentlemen, if you will follow me – we were on our way to the new kitchen block before we were momentarily diverted.'

CHAPTER SEVEN

COOKING WITH GENE HUNT

'The kitchens are just along here,' announced McClintock, striding briskly towards a set of double doors. 'The lad Donner will be on duty. I'll call him out so you can speak to him.'

'Don't be obvious about it,' said Sam. 'Do it subtly. Don't make it clear he's the one we want to speak to.'

McClintock gave him a quizzical look. 'And why *shouldn't* I make it clear?'

'Because if the other boys know he's talking to the police then they'll see him as a snitch. If he's frightened of being labelled a snitch then he won't say a word to us, even if he knows something important.'

'He'll say what he's told to say,' McClintock declared. 'It's not for him to decide what to reveal and what to hold back. The System controls *him*. It's nae the other way around.'

'Please, Mr McClintock,' Sam insisted, 'just do it my way. Trust me.'

Gene let out a theatrical sigh, said, 'I've been dead patient since comin' here to this kiddies' clinky. I've been really well behaved. I haven't moaned, I haven't played up, I've been as good as ruddy gold as far as I'm concerned. But now I'm starting to feel certain people are taking the piss with me.' He gave Sam a fierce look. 'So. If the fairies and faggots don't mind, instead of poncing about with secret signs and playing it low-key, I think the hour of the Genie has come. I'm going to go in there and do things *my* way. Toodle-oo.'

He turned on his heel and barged through the doors. Sam and McClintock hurried in after him.

The kitchen was large and functional, with two dozen boys peeling spuds, mixing gravy, and cutting up rock-like slabs of stale cheese, under the watchful scrutiny of five or six black-clad warders. Everybody looked up with a start as Gene crashed his way in and looked about.

'Very smart,' he boomed. 'Very smart indeed. Pity it smells like the bogs at central station.'

He glowered about at the boys, meeting their sly, sulky stares, using his copper's sixth sense to read their eyes, look into their hearts.

'Let me introduce myself. You know that thing that

scares you the most, that thing that keeps you awake at night, fretting, that thing you have nightmares about? Well, that's me, that is.'

Gene paced slowly about, his bottom lip stuck out, the corners of his mouth pulled down.

'Making tarts?' he asked a nervous-eyed young boy, sticking his finger into the lad's open jam pot and scooping out a mouthful. He grimaced at what he tasted and spat it sharply into the boy's face. 'Colgate and boot polish! My missus can do better!'

Under his breath, Sam whispered to McClintock, 'Do you want me to try and rein him in?'

'I don't see any reason to intervene,' McClintock whispered back. 'His methods are crude but he's showing a strong hand. The boys will respect that.'

Sam opened his mouth to argue, but gave up. Instead, he asked softly, 'Which one's Donner?'

McClintock nodded towards a boy over the far side of the kitchen. Donner was totally average: average height, average build, nondescript colouring, unremarkable face.

Sam began to wonder how to get him out of the kitchen so he could speak to him in private, but without the other inmates becoming suspicious.

But his thoughts were interrupted by Gene's booming voice.

'Right, girls, listen up. One of you lot escaped the

other day, as I'm sure you're aware. Very bright kid called Andy Coren. Genius, in fact. So bloody clever that he not only got himself chauffeur-driven out of this place on the back of a lorry, but he booked himself into a very exclusive hotel at the other end. It's a cosy little place, not big but family-run. For no extra charge you get to die screaming in the depths of a huge crushing machine. Which is nice.'

There was a ripple of movement among the boys as looks were exchanged, but nobody said a word. Every one of them kept his mouth shut. There was silence. And, in that silence, Gene paced slowly.

'Now. The question is, was it an accident, or did somebody here have a hand in it? Mmm? Did Andy Coren bugger his escape up – or was it buggered up for him? Well? Anyone got any suggestions?'

For no reason that Sam could see, Gene's attention suddenly fixated upon one of the boys. It was a tall, rather weasley lad who was standing next to an open oven, ready to grill an array of wretched-looking sausages. Gene loomed over him.

'You,' he said, his voice low and dangerous. 'Name.'

'Townsend, sir.'

'What do you know, Townsend?'

'Nuffing, sir.'

'I don't think that's right, Townsend. I think you know about Andy Coren. I think you know why he escaped on the back of one lorry, while his brother thought he was on the back of another.'

'Don't know nuffing, sir.'

He's fishing, Sam thought, watching Gene carefully. *He's still not sure whether or not Coren's death was just a stupid accident or not. Some part of him must suspect there's more to this than a fatal cock-up. And, if there is, I'm going to make damn sure he remembers that it was Annie who spotted it first.*

Gene drew closer to Townsend until they were practically nose to nose.

"Coz I'm such a nice bloke,' he said in a deep, growling voice, 'I'm going to ask you again without losing my rag. What happened to Coren?'

'Don't know nuffing, sir.'

'I really advise you change your answer to something a little more positive, Townsend, do you understand me?'

'Yes, sir.'

'Do you?'

'Yes, sir.'

'Do you *really?*'

'Yes, sir.'

'Okay, then. Tell me, young Townsend, what happened to Coren?'

The boy glanced about at the other inmates, then at the warders, then at Sam, then at McClintock. After a few silent moments, he at last said, almost inaudibly, 'Don't know nuffing, sir.'

Gene moved with lightning speed. Before Sam had a chance to react, Townsend was being thrust head-first into the open oven. Gene whacked up the grill.

'Start talkin' or start sizzlin'!' he bellowed.

From inside the oven, a muffled, metallic voice howled, 'I'm cookin', bloody 'ell, I'm cookin'!'

'With gas, son, you bet you are! Now talk! I said flamin' talk!'

Sam shot a glance at McClintock, expecting to see the House Master furiously intervene. But McClintock was silently observing what Gene was doing. In fact, he seemed to be enjoying the spectacle. What was it he had just told them? *'The methods are not pretty, but nor are they unjust. Justice must sometimes soil its hands in the pursuit of its aims. Justice must sometimes be hard.'*

Sam shook his head. McClintock and Guv – they hated each other, but they were peas in a pod.

Townsend was bleating, 'Lemme out! Lemme out!'

Gene hauled him out, slapped a chunk of rock-hard cheese on his face, and shoved him back under the grill.

'You know it's done when you can smell it,' he announced to the inmates, who were all watching, mute and open-mouthed. 'You know the smell I mean? That crispy, meaty, stinky, cheesy smell. It's getting my buds going just thinkin' about it.'

111

'I don't know nuffing!' Townsend wailed. 'Please, sir, I'm meltin'!'

'Guv, I think he's starting to char,' Sam put in.

A thin trail of black smoke was starting to emerge from the oven. Gene dragged Townsend out and threw him roughly to the floor. The boy squirmed and whimpered, clawing at the hot, sticky, napalm-like Cheddar clinging to his face.

The Guv glared about at the other inmates. 'Okay, lads, that was Gene's Cheesy Surprise. Who's going to help me demonstrate how to make a Boiled Bollock Pie?'

Sam decided to intervene, seeing that nobody else was going to. 'No call for that, Guv. There's only one lad in here we need to talk to. One lad who knows what's what. One lad who's in charge.' Sam walked around, looking into the faces of the boys. 'I want to speak to the daddy. Come on, guys, I'm asking you straight: who is it? Who's the daddy? Eh? Who's the daddy?'

He stopped in front of a potbellied boy with heavily taped spectacles.

'You, son,' Sam asked softly. 'Tell me. Who's the daddy?'

After some hesitation, the boy muttered, 'Ken.'

'Ken?'

The boy nodded, and readjusted his glasses.

Sam crouched down, bringing his face to the boy's level 'And which one's Ken?'

The boy glanced about, then said, 'He's the one who lives with me mummy, but he's not me real daddy.'

The inmates sniggered, but were silenced by a shrill command from one of the warders.

'You're wasting your time trying to reason with these dregs and ne'er-do-wells,' McClintock observed. 'Your DCI has the right idea. Brute force is the only thing these creatures understand.'

'I'll carry on, then,' said Gene, rubbing his hands together. He picked up an industrial-size cheese grater. 'Let's see what I can do with *this*.'

'Forget it, Guv, these boys won't talk,' said Sam. He walked past Donner, pretending not to be aware of him.

'You underestimate my culinary powers, Tyler. I'm a bloody wizard in the kitchen.'

'But I don't think they know anything, Guv. We're wasting our time. There's nothing for us to find out here. We might as well call it a day.'

Gene looked sideways at him. He could tell Sam was playing some sort of game here, but couldn't quite nail what it was.

'Come on, Guv. Let's get back to the station.'

Sam made his way towards the door as if to leave, putting his hands in his pockets as he went. And then he stopped. He delved deeply into one pocket, then into the other.

113

'It's gone,' he muttered. And turning to confront the inmates he said, 'Okay – which one of you took it?'

Silent faces stared back.

'I said *which one of you took it?*' Sam roared. He stormed across the kitchen, making straight for Donner. 'It were *you*, weren't it! You thieving little …!'

He grabbed Donner by the scruff of his neck and frogmarched him furiously out through a door, kicking it shut behind him.

Gently, patiently, Sam said, 'You know that was all just play-acting just then, don't you – accusing you of stealing and all that?'

He and Donner were alone together in a storage room, surrounded by tins of spaghetti hoops, cans of Spam and industrial-size plastic tubs of Stork SB margarine.

'I needed a pretext to get you out of there, to speak to you in private without your fellow inmates becoming suspicious. Do you understand me?'

Donner was looking at him rather strangely. The boy's face was hard to read. Perhaps his tough life and his time behind bars had given him a poker player's skill at concealing his true feelings.

'Well? Do you understand me?'

'Of course I understand you,' said Donner. 'I'm not stupid.'

114

'No. I can tell that. My name's Sam. I'm a policeman.'

'A policeman, yes, I figured that out already.'

'Andy Coren escaped from here last Friday. He hid inside one of the old ovens being shipped out to the junkyard, but died in a crushing machine.'

Donner didn't react.

Sam went on: 'I'm trying to find out if his death was an accident, or if – if there was something …'

He let it hang there, unwilling to put words into the boy's mouth.

'What makes you think *I* know anything?' asked Donner. 'Is it because I wrote that letter for him, the one to his brother?'

'I'm not accusing you of anything, Donner, I'm just trying to follow up what leads we've got. Can you tell me anything?'

Donner said nothing.

'The letter you wrote for Coren, did he dictate it you? Or did you word it yourself?'

Still Donner remained silent.

'There's mention in that letter of a veterinary clinic in Lidden Street. But there *is* no veterinary clinic in Lidden Street. Why would Coren make that up?'

Sam waited for a response, but Donner's face was motionless and impassive.

'Please, Donner, I'm asking you to help me. Can you tell me anything about this borstal that I ought to know?

Are things going on here? Have you heard anything? Rumours? Hearsay?'

'It's too dangerous to tell you what I know,' said Donner in a low, level voice. 'I'd be the next one to end up dead.'

'What do you mean by that?'

'I think it's obvious what I mean.'

'Who would kill you if you spoke to me, Donner?'

'Well, I can hardly tell you that, given what I've just said. You're not very clever for a policeman.'

'I'll protect you,' said Sam.

'How?'

'I'm a detective inspector with CID. I have authority.'

'Be specific. I asked *how*?'

Sam was a little taken aback by the boy's manner. It was cool, concentrated, self-assured.

'I could see about getting you moved,' Sam said.

'Where?'

'To another borstal. An open one. A nicer one.'

'When?'

'As soon as I can.'

'Not good enough. I need to be transferred at once.'

'I don't think that's possible,' said Sam. 'It'll take time.'

'Get me transferred, *then* I'll talk,' said Donner.

It was a manipulative move, a pressing-home of a tactical advantage. Donner had fully grasped the situation, that the information he had in his possession gave him leverage over Sam, and he was boldly exploiting it.

116

Sam resolved to regain the initiative. He could not afford to have his hand forced by this intelligent but devious child. He had to maintain his authority.

'Sorry, Donner. You've proposed a deal I cannot accept,' he said. 'Give me something – a clue, a direction to look in – and I'll see what I can do for you in return.'

'You have to do what I say,' Donner said flatly, his voice devoid of emotion. 'You need me. I can see that. Get me moved to another borstal, and I'll tell you what you want to know.'

'If you won't talk to me, then I'll just have to walk away. Trust works both ways, Donner.'

It was a gamble. This boy wasn't going to be easily bluffed or coerced. Sam went silent, and let Donner consider his next move.

But Donner said nothing. Was he stonewalling? Or was he just playing his cards close, seeing what he could gain from this exchange?

Sam decided to try a different approach.

'I was recently speaking to a lad who did time here. His name's Barton.'

'I remember Barton,' said Donner.

'He said he had a hard time here.'

'Not from me.'

'You were friends with him?'

'Not like *that*. Not the way you mean.'

'I didn't mean anything, I just asked if you were friends.'

'He looked up to me,' said Donner. His voice was as flat and emotionless as ever.

'What happened to him?' Sam asked. 'Was he getting it pretty rough?'

'Yes.'

'Who from? The other inmates?'

'One or two of them, maybe.'

'Barton's real trouble, it wasn't with the *inmates*, was it?' Sam said.

'Maybe not.'

'Donner, you know something. Please tell me.' Deciding to take the plunge, Sam came right out with it. 'Coren's death wasn't an accident.'

'And Tunning didn't commit suicide,' Donner added calmly.

He's offering me titbits. He knows what's going on here.

In a low voice, Sam asked, 'And what about Tulse, the lad who died in the kitchens?'

'I was there.'

'You worked with him?'

'On and off.'

'And you were with him when he died?'

'I was ten feet away. I saw everything.'

'What happened? Was it a faulty oven that killed him?'

Donner looked slowly about the room, but remained silent.

Sam drew closer to the boy and dropped his voice to the merest hint of a whisper: 'Somebody's killing inmates. Aren't they.'

Donner's blank face was Sam's only reply.

'Tell me, Donner, where should we be looking? Amongst the inmates themselves? Or – or should we be looking at the System?'

'It's obvious,' Donner breathed back.

Sam nodded to himself. His instincts were proven right. He'd known, right away, where the dark heart of Friar's Brook really lay.

'I didn't say a word to you,' Donner said quietly but firmly.

'I understand.'

'You'd better understand. You really had.' The boy's manner was almost threatening. 'And now, tell me – before I lose my temper with you – what are you going to do about getting me transferred?'

119

CHAPTER EIGHT

THROUGH THE ARCHED WINDOW

'I want to have a snoop about this place,' said Sam. 'I want to see what's going on here.'

He and Gene were together in a corridor, a few yards away from McClintock, keeping their voices low.

'*Is* there something going on, Sam?' asked Gene.

Sam shot a glance at McClintock, and whispered, 'I felt from the start this place was all wrong. And McClintock, he's all wrong too. Coren's death wasn't an accident. Nor was Tulse's. And Tunning didn't kill himself. It's a cover-up, I'm telling you, Gene. We need to start digging around here. We'll find skeletons in the cupboards, believe me.'

'What did that lad say to you in private?'

Sam's glance kept going back to McClintock. 'We can't talk about it here, Guv. Just trust me – we need to investigate Friar's Brook, *and* the people who run it.'

Gene chewed this over, nodded and said, 'Fine. We'll haul Jock McSporran down to the station, stick his caber in a vice, and get him singing 'The Thistles of Old Loch Lomond'.'

'No, Guv, that's *not* what we're going to do. What we're going to do is behave like policemen.'

'I thought that *was* acting like a policeman,' said Gene, without irony.

Sam got closer and dropped his voice even lower. 'I need to be free to have a nose around without McClintock looking over my shoulder. He'll only let us see what he *wants* us to see. Keep him busy while I head off on my own.'

'Keep him busy? How am I supposed to do that, engage him in a spot of Highland dancing?'

'If that's what it takes, Guv. For God's sake, you're a DCI, you're supposed to be able to handle situations like this.'

'And, being DCI, I'm also supposed to be the one who *gives* the orders, not *takes* 'em!' Gene growled. 'Why don't *you* go compare bagpipes with Donald-where's-ya-troosers while *I* have a snoop about?'

'Because, Gene – and let's be honest about it – you'll blunder about, cause trouble, piss people off, and most likely get into some sort of fight. And that, Guv, would be unproductive.'

Gene gave him a sour look. 'That's a hurtful résumé of my capabilities, Tyler. I have my qualities.'

'I know, Guv, you're absolutely smashing with dogs. Now *please*, Guv, keep McClintock busy while I have a prowl around. It'll be worth it. I'll dig something up, I know it. And what's more' – now Sam's voice was barely audible – 'if McClintock's as guilty as I'm guessing he is, you'll have the pleasure of nicking him later on.'

Gene pulled a pinched, thoughtful expression, and then, without a word, he clapped his hand on Sam's shoulder and strode manfully towards the House Master.

Sam headed in the other direction. Behind him, he heard McClintock's voice raised in protest, 'Now wait just one second. Where does that lad think he's off to unsupervised?'

Gene thrust his ID badge into McClintock's face. 'Wherever the chuff he pleases, Jock. We're CID.'

'No, no, no, no, this is something I will not allow, officers running hither and thither as they please.'

'Hard haggises, you can't stop us. Oh, don't pull that face, Jimmy, we're all on the same side. Now – why don't you and me go to your office and have a nice cosy chat about which one of the Bond lasses we'd most like to stick it to. Me, I'm up for that one on the double-decker who tells fortunes in Jamaica.'

Sam moved through a succession of whitewashed corridors, which all reeked of polish and bleach. Everywhere, he was confronted by those stark words stencilled in red: SILENCE – RESPECT – DUTY.

The atmosphere here, Sam thought, *it's stifling. I've seen the inside of enough prisons over the years – always rowdy, always full of backchat and course laughter and somebody singing away like a loon until a screw yells at him to shut up. But here – silence.*

Silence, yes – but respect?

Gradually, Sam began to get a sense of the layout of the place. The inmates were confined within a network of buildings, all connected with corridors. There seemed to be, by and large, free access within this complex, allowing inmates and staff to move from one part of the borstal to another, but nobody could get out without unlocking the stout, bolted doors that led onto the various open-air exercise yards. Sam had to show his ID to a passing warder and get him to open up one of these doors so he could have a nose about outside. He found himself standing in an open space hemmed in by a huge, wire-topped wall. The slogan of the System glowered down oppressively from it in bright-red paint. Beneath the six-foot-high letters stood rows of inmates engaged in synchronized exercises. Every move was accompanied by a grunted word. They turned left – 'Silence!' – then right – 'Respect' – then touched their toes – 'Duty!'

Every one of them wore a ragged patch of brown cloth.

The Stain, thought Sam, shaking his head in incredulity. He looked at the rows of young faces, all spots and puppy fat and beardless chins.

'Silence!' – turn – 'Respect!' – turn – 'Duty!' – bend.

Sam turned to the warder who had opened the door for him.

'Where do the lads play footie round here?' he asked. 'This yard's too small.'

'They don't play footie.'

'Course they do! They're *lads*!'

'House Master's rules – no football, no games.'

'No games? What about table tennis?'

'Not even telly,' said the warder. 'Bending and stretching, that's all the recreation they get. Rest of the time it's chores or else they're banged up in the their dorms.'

The boys turned left, turned right, bent over. 'Silence! Respect! Duty!'

'What's McClintock doing to these kids' heads …?' murmured Sam. 'No footie, no telly – little wonder this place feels like the calm before the storm.'

The warder opened another door for him, and Sam found himself back in the rabbit warren of bleached corridors and red, stencilled letters. He reached a hallway that was sealed off from the corridor by a barred gate and guarded by a fierce-looking screw in immaculate uniform. Clearly, this area was strictly off limits to the inmates.

'What goes on here?' Sam asked, showing his police ID.

'Punishment block,' said the warder. He indicated the heavy doors. 'Isolation cells for lads who kick off.'

'Let me see inside one.'

'What for?'

Sam went to reply, then hesitated. What, indeed, *was* he hoping to find here? Clues that would incriminate McClintock for crimes against the inmates? The chances of that were a million to one. And yet something within him compelled him to explore, drawing him deeper and deeper into this wretched place for reasons not at all to do with police work and a criminal investigation. It was as if his own life, his own Fate, was bound up with this place and the labyrinth of rooms, corridors and cells within it.

'Just unlock one of those doors for me,' said Sam. 'Let me see inside.'

The warder shrugged and rattled his keys. He opened the metal gate that sealed the punishment block off from the corridor, then opened one of the heavy cell doors and stood aside. Sam stepped through the open doorway. The cell within looked and smelt like a public toilet. The whitewashed walls were vilely stained. The single window was barred and gridded, the glass so caked in grime that it let in nothing but a sickly trickle of daylight. There was no bed, not even a cot or shelf, just the hard, filthy floor to lie on. The toilet was a stinking slop bucket sitting in the corner. It was all in sharp contrast to the bleach and carbolic soap elsewhere.

'You lock *kids* in here?' Sam asked.

'Well we don't use it for storing brooms,' the warder replied. 'It's called the White Hole.'

'It's medieval. What do you think it does to some fifteen-year-old boy's head to be banged up alone in a dungeon like this?'

The warder shrugged. 'The White Hole's better than the Black Hole.'

'The *Black* Hole? You have a punishment cell here called the *Black* Hole?'

The warder showed him. Unlocking yet another huge, solid door, he revealed a windowless cell. Peering in, Sam could see nothing beyond the splash of light coming in through the open doorway. The air was fetid and stank like stagnant pond water.

'For the *real* troublemakers,' said the warder.

'This is barbaric.'

'It's an education, that's what it is. A lad with nous will realize pretty sharpish he don't ever want to come back to a place like this in a hurry. He'll change his ways.'

'Change his ways, you reckon? Don't you mean end up harder and more despairing than ever?'

126

'It's the *punishment* block. It's for *punishment*. Don't want to get punished? Then don't go against the System. Simple.' He handed Sam a cigarette lighter. 'Have a look, if that's what you want.'

Sam flicked the lighter and stepped inside. By the dancing orange glow of the flame he made out crude messages carved into the walls. The spelling was all over the place and half the letters back to front. There were names – ROZZA, BLINKY, JOEY, BAZ – all crisscrossed, written over each other, making a chaotic register of the lads who had paced and shivered in this abominable hellhole. Other, more hopeful names cropped up here and there – BOBBY CHARLTON, BARRY SHEENE. There were rows of upright incisions, marking the passing of days, and sticklike depictions of men dangling from the gallows.

'The Black Hole ...' Sam muttered.

'They smuggle lighters in, or matches,' said the warder from the doorway. 'Don't know how but they do it. Then again, some of 'em just work blind, scratching away at the walls.'

'These lads should be graffiti-ing their schoolbooks, not the inside of a solitary-confinement cell,' Sam observed.

Some youthful budding Picasso, with more ambition than talent, had attempted to draw a full-length naked woman. And there, beside those obscenely spread but

127

anatomically confused legs, was – what? An egg-shaped oval with a round nose and blankly smiling face. What was it? Humpty-Dumpty?

'Lost childhoods,' Sam mused. 'Kids behind bars.'

And what about these? Two teddy bears of differing sizes, side by side.

'Big Ted and Little Ted.'

And then, with incredulity, he recognized yet more doll-like figures drawn on the wall. He knew them. He knew their faces. He knew their names.

'Hamble, Jemima ...'

To the warder outside in the corridor he called, 'What the hell is this, a mural depicting the toys off *Play School*?'

'A house, with a door,' said the warder in a mild voice.

Sam glanced round. The warder had changed. In the doorway now stood a man in beige corduroys and a colourfully striped jumper. Sam knew him at once, knew him from his childhood, just as he had known those dolls and teddy bears. He knew that friendly face with its fair hair and twinkly eyes.

He gasped and straightened.

'A house with a door,' Brian Cant said again. 'One, two, three, four. Ready to play. What's the day?'

Automatically, like a man speaking in a dream, Sam muttered, 'It's Monday.'

'Is it?' Brian Cant asked. He was still smiling, but the twinkle had vanished from his eyes. '*Is* it?'

And, with that, he shut the door. At once, the cigarette lighter went out.

Total blackness smothered Sam like a physical entity. Panicking, he rushed at the door – only to find himself groping blindly in empty air.

Where the hell's the door? Where the hell are the walls?

His hands clutched at cold emptiness all about him, searching in vain for the confines of the cell and finding instead only a void and intimations of infinity.

Shaking, panting hard, Sam fumbled with the lighter – and dropped the damned thing!

Shit! No! Please, no!

But it was gone. Vanished.

Sam braced himself. Reality had shifted and buckled and transformed about him so many times since he'd crash-landed into 1973 that he should, by rights, be thoroughly accustomed to it. But, of course, he wasn't. Far from it. How could he? How could *anyone*?

Don't get frit, Sam, told himself firmly. *You're an old lag at this. You've been through all this sort of crazy stuff before.*

Reality rarely sat still for him any more. Time and again it warped and ran like wet paint caught in the rain, like a stray TV signal bleeding across another channel – and behind it all lay the inscrutable, insufferable, blankly smiling face of the Test Card Girl.

I won't panic. I will keep my head.

But his heart was already hammering.

I'm just a copper. I'm just a simple copper. Sooner or later, I'm going to wake up from this.

To his relief, he made out a semicircle of a dim, orange light away to his left, like an arched window set amid infinite darkness. Warily, Sam tripped and stumbled his way towards it, groping ahead like a blind man, and as he drew closer he saw that it wasn't a window, but the mouth of a tunnel.

He stepped through the arch and found himself in a dark street, a solid black night sky over his head, a few street lamps glowing dimly in the misty air. Glancing around, he saw that the tunnel he had just emerged from ran beneath a railway bridge.

I know this part of town, he thought to himself. *I've been through here before – this bridge, those houses, they're familiar – and yet ...*

Something was different – something he could not quite define.

A large brick wall ran along the street to his left. It was covered in ripped and tattered posters. Sam drew closer, peering at the posters in the murky orange gloom of a fitful street lamp. He made out a black-and-white image of four men, dressed identically in pale-grey suits, clustered around a microphone stand, promoting their brand-new single.

The Four Seasons – 'Walk Like a Man'.

What the hell year did *that* come out? It was old even in 1973. That poster must have been up there for years. It should have long since decayed or been buried beneath layer after layer of newer posters over the years. And yet there it was, a little dog-eared and rain-beaten but looking fairly fresh.

He moved to the next poster along. Another four men, also in suits – but this time sporting instantly recognisable mop-top haircuts. Four men who were yet to embrace hippy culture, yet to become experimental, yet to fall out and go their separate ways. Above the frieze of smiling faces, it said, 'THE BEATLES – FROM ME TO YOU'.

Again, the poster looked brand-new.

Sam's blood ran cold.

Oh my God – What the hell year is this …?

The next poster along depicted a very young, very quiffed Cliff Richards singing 'Summer Holiday'. This blandly cheerful image of carefree youth struck Sam like the announcement of a death sentence. He felt the pit of his stomach lurch, as if he were in a suddenly descending lift. It was the same sickening feeling of vertigo, the same nightmare feeling of disorientation and homesickness, panic and loneliness that had flooded over him when he had first found himself lost and alone in 1973, like a long-distance space traveller abandoned on the alien surface of an unknown planet.

Please, please, I don't want to go through that all again. I don't want to fall through time yet again, please – please not again!

He stumbled against the wall, pressing his sweating, clammy forehead against the face of a slim and healthy Elvis Presley singing 'Devil in Disguise'.

'Feelin' rum, sport?'

A young man had emerged from a curvy little Austin A30 parked beneath the flickering street light. The car was a relic from a time before 1973, as was the fashion the young man was dressed up in: black suit, waistcoat, Slim Jim tie and swept-back hair, slicked down and shiny. He might have been a stockbroker, or an undertaker's assistant – and yet the orange glow of the sodium lamp revealed a youthful face, surely not much older than sixteen.

'Pissed, are we?' the lad said, winking but not smiling. 'You should've waited till we got to the club. I'm sure Mr Gould would happily give you a free drink or two.'

Sam stood dumb and motionless, not knowing what the hell to do or say.

The boy tapped his wristwatch impatiently. 'Time's getting on. Don't want to keep Mr Gould waiting. We'd best go knock.'

He headed towards one of the terraced houses, but then stopped, glancing back over his shoulder and flashing Sam a cocky, lopsided grin.

'You ever seen her?' he asked.

Sam looked at him blankly.

'His daughter,' the boy said. 'She's up there now. That's her light on.' He pointed towards an upstairs window, glowing dimly. 'She's tasty. Let's cop a look, yeah?'

Scooping up a palmful of grit from the road, the young man threw it at the first-floor window. After a few seconds, he threw some more.

A shadow appeared on the inside of the window. The curtains moved. A hint of a figure appeared – but at once, the front door of the house flew open and a man strode furiously into the street.

'You pack that in, Perry!'

The man marched straight for Perry, who ducked away, grinning.

'Keep your hair on, Mr Cartwright!' he laughed. 'Just wanted to wish her goodnight!'

'And the rest!' Cartwright snapped back. 'I know what you're after, you greasy little ferret.'

'I ain't after nothing,' grinned Perry. 'Just being civil.'

Cartwright turned and called up at the window, 'Back to bed! Right now! And turn that light out!'

The shadowy figure in the window disappeared at once back behind the curtains. Moments later, the window went dark.

When Cartwright turned back, he noticed Sam and acknowledged him with a curt nod of the head.

'So,' he said, flatly. 'You've shown up. Good. Very good.'

Sam stood dumbly, not knowing what to say, or where he was, or what the hell was going on. Even the name Cartwright hadn't quite impinged on his reeling brain as fully as it might.

Perry made a show of straightening his suit and checking his hair, then said, 'Shall we be on our way, then?'

He graciously indicated the little Austin. Cartwright strode towards it – and Sam, without any conscious decision to do so, strode after him, his legs moving under their own volition, as if somebody were operating his body by remote control.

This isn't my body, Sam thought, fresh waves of panic washing over him. *I'm looking out through somebody else's eyes. I'm a passenger inside somebody else's mind.*

And then, in horror, he corrected himself: *No, not a passenger. A prisoner!*

Where this stranger's body went, Sam was powerless to control it. He was witnessing events from the past, from somewhere back in the 1960s, through the eyes of a stranger. He was a voyeur, forced to witness and experience whatever this alien host body witnessed and experienced. But whose body was it? *Who the hell was he?*

Without warning, Perry suddenly called up to the dark, first-floor window, 'Sweet dreams, Annie!'

Cartwright took a furious swipe at him, but Perry ducked away.

'You want to watch it, Mr Cartwright,' he said, producing car keys from his jacket pocket. 'Mr Gould thinks very highly of me. I'm an appreciating asset in his organization – hear what I'm saying?'

'Just get behind that wheel and drive,' Cartwright growled. 'And keep your mind on the road, not on my daughter.'

And, with that, he disappeared into the Austin, and Sam – or whoever's eyes Sam was seeing through – clambered in after him.

CHAPTER NINE

HOUSE OF DIAMONDS

As he sat in the back of the speeding car, the street lamps flashing by, Sam's thoughts turned over and over on the silhouette he had glimpsed in the upstairs window.

Could that really have been her? Could that really have been Annie? And what year must this be? Nineteen sixty-three, or thereabouts? Then how old would she have been? Fifteen? Sixteen? And this man sitting beside me – is that really her father? And who am I? Who's life am I being made to witness?

Sam could not process what was happening to him. He was moving through this sunken dream like a sleep-walker, like man under the control of a hypnotist.

In front of him, he could see the back of Perry's head, held upright as he drove. From time to time Perry's eyes flashed in the rear-view mirror as he glanced at Sam and Tony in the back seat. He whisked them through the dark and almost deserted streets until suddenly he flung the wheel and bounced them recklessly down a tight alleyway. He hit the brakes, and the car came to a stop.

'We're here, gentlemen!'

The three men clambered out. They were in a mean, badly lit passage tucked in between large brick buildings that might have been factories or workshops. An illuminated sign read 'HOUSE OF DIAMONDS'. Beneath it stood an open doorway, very narrow and uninviting, and beyond this doorway ran a flight of steps, descending steeply into darkness.

Perry straightened his jacket, his tie, and then his hair. He rolled his shoulders and adjusted the gold chain of his fob watch. When he was sure he was immaculate, he clapped his hands together and rubbed them eagerly.

'Righty-righty, then! I'll run on ahead and let Mr Gould know you're here.'

With a cocky wink at Sam, the lad bounded down the stairs and vanished into the smoky gloom.

Sam supposed he was to go down that gloomy staircase too, but Tony hesitated. He caught hold of Sam's arm and looked very intently into his face.

'When you go in there, say as little as possible. Gould doesn't like blabbermouths. The less you say, the more he'll trust you. Understand?'

Sam tried speak, to get some sort of word back to Tony – even if that word was only a single, pathetic 'Help!' But his mouth was not his own, and it stayed firmly shut. Instead, he nodded – or rather, Sam felt himself nod – and said not a word.

'That's the spirit,' Tony said in a hushed voice. 'Speak when you're spoken to, and tell Gould what he wants to hear. Once he's accepted you, we'll get the hell out of there as soon as we can.'

Tony pulled Sam nearer to him, close enough for Sam to smell the nervous sweat of his armpits.

'Gould will be suspicious. He'll send somebody to keep an eye on you. They'll sit you at one of the gaming tables, give you drinks, encourage you to enjoy yourself. Play along. I'll be in the office with Gould, explaining that I need you in on our arrangement. Once he's happy with that, he'll send for you. Sweet Jesus, I'm sweating cobs!'

Tony fumbled a handkerchief from his pocket and mopped his glistening brow.

'It was never supposed to bloody come to this! A few extra on the side to make ends meet, that's all it was. But those bastards, they suck you in. I should have seen it coming – I should have smelt it, right from the start, what Gould wanted in the long run. I just didn't realize it'd be *me* who'd be the one tangled up in it! There's others on the pay roll working for Gould, it ain't just me. There's lads creaming it in! Uniformed coppers, boys from Special Branch, boys from CID – right across the board. All sorts. But the bugger goes and singles *me* out, wants *me* to get him off the hook for that whole bloody messy business of his!'

With shaking hands, Tony scrubbed at his face with the handkerchief then shoved it back into his trouser pocket. He took a deep breath, held it, let it out slowly.

'Right, then. Let's go.'

Tony indicated that Sam was to go first. Sam felt himself turn, head through the doorway, and plod down the staircase into the murky gloom. The reek of cigars filled his nostrils. He stepped into a shifting, suffocating darkness, felt a curtain made of dangling beads brush against him and pushed his way through it.

Figures moved through a smoky, dim light. Decorated lamps glowed. Light sparkled from the effervescence of champagne glasses. Cards were dealt and dice thrown across green baize. A roulette wheel spun, and a steel ball shot across it. Gambling chips clacked.

'Gould's office is back there,' whispered Tony. He indicated past the gamers, the girls, and the croupiers towards a set of wooden doors set deep in shadow, outside of which were stationed two sharply dressed, bald-headed bouncers. 'We'll wait here until he sends for me. God, I need a drink!'

He grabbed two glasses of champagne and downed them both, one after the other.

Then they saw Perry appear out of the wooden doors

of Mr Gould's office and come threading his way between the gaming tables towards them.

'Mr Cartwright, Mr Gould will see you now.'

Tony hesitated, and looked around for another glass of champagne.

'*Now*, Mr Cartwright,' Perry insisted.

Without a word, Tony headed towards the wooden doors. The heavies opened them for him, and he vanished inside.

Perry thrust a block of gambling chips into Sam's hands. All by themselves, Sam's hands accepted them. He could feel the weight of them, feel the smooth plastic surface of each chip, and yet he knew it was the hands of a stranger who held them.

'Compliments of Mr Gould,' he said. 'You're to enjoy yourself this evening.'

Through shifting bands of thick tobacco smoke, the wooden doors to Mr Gould's private office were just visible. They reeked of menace, like the doors to some terrible underworld of lost souls and perpetual torment.

Violence, Sam thought. *Violence and cruelty. Pain and betrayal. It stinks of death here! My God, this is an awful place.*

Sam suddenly realized his hands were trying to thrust the gambling chips back to Perry.

'A refusal often offends,' said Perry, smiling, refusing

to accept them. But Sam wouldn't take them. Perry's smile didn't falter for a moment. 'Let's get something straight. This is the House of Diamonds. You're a guest of Mr Gould. You understand what that means? And, while you're a guest, you're to have a nice time, right? You're to have a very nice time.'

Politely but firmly, Perry was manoeuvring Sam towards the bar. They sat together on narrow stools, side by side.

'On the house.' He winked, sliding a cocktail glass into Sam's hands. 'You can have a good life if you do the right things. Mr Gould looks after his own. He's looking after *me*. I'm on the up here. You are, too – leastways, now you're on the team. You're one of us. One of the gang.'

He clinked his own glass against Sam's and sipped his cocktail, smacking his lips. He looked intensely into Sam's face for a moment, leant closer, and spoke in a low voice.

'Mr Gould's got plans, you know. Not just for me and you. For *her*. Cartwright's daughter. Know what I mean?'

He nudged Sam with his elbow.

'It's going to be hard for her at first, of course,' he went on, whispering. 'You know – tears and all that. But he'll look after her.' He grinned and winked at Sam. 'And, with her daddy out of the way, there'll be a vacancy. You want to get in there. Annie's a chip off the old block, you know what I'm saying? Her mother's still a looker.

A *real* looker. And, besides, she's more your age than mine.'

Sam's thoughts reeled. Was he reading Perry's meaning right? He felt himself turn away, shift position in his seat, and as he did he caught sight of himself for the first time in the mirrored tiles on the wall behind the bar. What he saw made his blood freeze in his veins.

The face looking back at him was familiar, but it was not his own. A young man with cropped, reddish hair and a trim moustache was staring out at him. It was House Master McClintock's face, but ten years younger, and dressed not in the black uniform of a borstal warder but in a sharp suit with a narrow tie.

My God, this is McClintock's past I'm seeing. This is McClintock's life I'm witnessing!

He saw one of his – or rather, McClintock's – hands reach out and pick up the cocktail glass. The hand, Sam now realized, was unscarred. Whatever injury had so disfigured him still lay ahead, in McClintock's future.

'You seem very tense Mr McClintock,' Perry said. 'I don't think this casino is your sort of place, is it. It *is* a bit smoky in here. Tell you what' – he knocked back his drink and got to his feet – 'let's chat outside.'

As Perry got to his feet, Sam waited for McClintock to follow him, but instead he stayed put. Perry looked at him with a strange expression for a moment, then laughed.

'*You* got nothing to worry about, old sport! It's

Cartwright who's up shit creek – as well you know! C'mon, let's get some air.'

Slowly, McClintock rose and followed Perry across the casino and back up the steep flight of stairs. Together, they stepped into the narrow alleyway, where Perry's car was still parked. Perry lounged against his motor and fished out a packet of cigarettes. McClintock refused the offer of one with a shake of his head, so Perry lit up alone, making a show of it, acting like the big man.

'Don't feel guilty, Mr McClintock,' he said, breathing out smoke. 'Cartwright brought it on himself, you must understand that. All Mr Gould needed was a little bit of messy business tidied up. That's all. But PC Cartwright went and let his conscience get the better of him. He tried to – oh what's the expression? He tried to 'wear the white hat' – that's it. But white hats have gone out of fashion, don't you think? I mean, we wouldn't catch *you* in a ruddy great white hat now, would we?'

And with that, he produced a huge wad of bank notes from under his jacket and held them out to Sam.

'Take it,' Perry said. 'Mr Gould insists. Go on, stick in your pocket. And please don't say 'thirty pieces of silver'.'

McClintock betrayed Tony Cartwright, Sam thought, his brain working frantically to make sense of what he was hearing. *McClintock was on the force alongside Annie's father, and he sold him out to the gangster who runs this casino.*

143

And then, very suddenly, and with the utmost clarity, Sam thought, *Tony Cartwright's about to die. Annie's father is about to die. And it was McClintock who betrayed him.*

It didn't matter how he had come to be here, in this decade and in this place and in this unfamiliar body, seeing events from ten years before through eyes that were not his own. All that mattered was that he seize the initiative. If Annie's father was about to be murdered by this gangster, Clive Gould, Sam could stop it. He could save him. He could change history.

That's why I'm here. I've been brought here to rewrite the past. God knows how, God knows why, but that's why I'm here! But how the hell can I make this damned body do anything – it's not mine to control!

He screamed silently at the body he was trapped in, *Move! Move, damn it! There's no point me being here if I can't change things!*

But still he just stood there.

Up the steps, looming out of the darkness, came the two bouncers who had been guarding the entrance to Gould's office. They planted themselves menacingly on either side of McClintock, like prison warders with an inmate.

Perry acknowledged them politely: 'Charlie. Lewis. Good evening to you both.'

The bouncers said nothing. They stood with faces like

bulldogs, implacable and humourless. One of them nodded, almost imperceptibly, at Perry. It was a signal.

'Very well,' said Perry, and patted McClintock's arm. 'Mr Gould is ready to receive us. Follow me, if you'd be so kind.'

McClintock hesitated. The bouncers drew closer, nudged him to walk forward, but still he did not move.

'Don't be concerned, Mr McClintock,' Perry urged him. From the tone of his voice it was clear that he was enjoying himself, savouring the opportunity to show what he could do, how he could deal with tricky business matters, how he could give orders and take control. Mr Gould would hear of it. Mr Gould would promote him. 'You've done the right thing. Everything runs smooth if everyone behaves. Cartwright was rocking the boat. He was dangerous. But not any more.' Perry looked deep into Sam's eyes. 'You haven't betrayed a fellow copper – you've proved your loyalty to Mr Gould. And you've saved yourself from ending up like Cartwright. You'd be sharing the same sticky end as him if you hadn't played along like a good boy.'

A coward! Sam thought furiously. *McClintock's nothing but a stinking coward, selling out his colleague to save his own skin!*

McClintock began walking, obediently following Perry down the dark alley, the bouncers plodding along behind.

Sam struggled to somehow take control of McClintock's body, to override him, to force him to act like a copper and get back down those stairs and get his partner out of trouble. He tried to pour energy into McClintock's body, into his limbs, to wrest control of them, to clad himself in McClintock's body as if it were suit of armour. The effort of it was all consuming. Sam's vision blurred and darkened. He felt a sudden pain, like a migraine, and sense of nausea, and then he seemed to be falling backwards into an inky blackness that enveloped him utterly. He struck something hard that was a wall or a floor, he could not tell which, and found himself stumbling about, confused, his hands pressing against hard surfaces, something heavy and metallic clanging nearby, a sudden light falling across him and then a man's voice.

'What? Did you say something, eh?'

The warder was standing in the open doorway of the punishment cell, looking at him. Sam was standing flat against one of the graffiti-covered walls, so close that his nose was pressing against the filthy, black surface.

'I'm back,' he breathed, panting.

'You're *weird*,' corrected the warder.

CHAPTER TEN

A SIMPLE COPPER

Sam found himself stumbling back through the bleached corridors of Friar's Brook like a man in a daze. He felt adrift, dislocated, mentally jetlagged. The instability of Time – the suddenness with which he could slip from 2006 back to 1973, and then from 1973 to some point in the early 1960s – appalled him. He was like a man who had just survived an earthquake, shocked that the terra firma beneath his feet that he had taken for granted all his life was far from firma after all.

He leant against a wall, pausing beneath a huge painted slogan that demanded from him SILENCE – DUTY – RESPECT in big, red letters.

'Coward,' he muttered. He felt a red-hot anger rising within him. 'Pathetic, stinking coward.'

He could see it all clearly now. Clive Gould had been the big villain back in the sixties, with money enough to buy off the police. Tony Cartwright had fallen in with all that corruption and bribery, but only out of fear. He knew the consequences of trying to be the one good man in a rotten town. But his conscience had got the better of him, and he'd made his stand, looking to incriminate Gould and have him convicted. But he couldn't do it alone, he needed an accomplice – and that accomplice was McClintock, who back then must have been a regular copper just like Cartwright himself.

He trusted McClintock. He trusted him with his life. But he picked the wrong man to rely on. McClintock didn't have the nerve to go against Gould. He feared the consequences if they failed to nail him. And so he sold out his own colleague to save his skin.

That treachery was what Sam had sensed the moment he arrived here at Friar's Brook. Even before he passed the front gate, his heart had told him that something foul and corrupted resided within these walls. And then, at first sight of McClintock, he had felt an immediate sense of loathing, of repulsion. Instinctively, he had known that McClintock was rotten to the core.

He betrayed Tony Cartwright, sending him to his death at the hands of Clive Gould. Annie was left fatherless …

Perry had made it clear that, with Tony out of the way, Gould had his sights on Annie herself. Once he had washed her father's blood from them, he would get his hands on Annie for his personal pleasure.

Sam felt cold waves of sickness wash over him.

Annie was so young, just a child – she was just a child ...

He tried to make his way along the corridor, but he stumbled, nearly fell. His head was spinning. The glimpses of horror that the Test Card Girl had shown him were starting to make awful sense. Everything he had seen told a story of Annie marrying a brute, and of that brute beating her and abusing her and battering her until, one day, he went too far.

I know who that murderous brute is now. It's Gould. He killed her, and that's why she's here in 1973. She's dead – like me, she's dead. Like everyone else here, she's dead. Dead, we're all dead, everybody's dead!

He felt a nauseous vertigo as his brain started putting the jigsaw puzzle of his life into some sort of order.

I'm dead, he told himself. *I know I'm dead. I jumped from that rooftop in 2006. I fell. I died.*

It was the stark reality of his situation that he had continually avoided thinking about too deeply. Sam had fudged it, ducked it, hid behind deliberate ignorance and the mantra that it was all too much for him to understand, that he was just a copper, a simple copper.

But now, his head was reeling, and he could not blot out the thoughts.

Dead, we're all dead. Annie's dead. Ray's dead. Chris and Phyllis and all the others – and the Guv. The Guv's dead and we're all dead and everyone is dead!

So what did that make this place?

Sam looked around him at the cheerless borstal corridor, at the barred windows, the heavily bolted doors. He smelt the sharp reek of bleach in his nostrils. He looked up at the massive red letters: SILENCE – RESPECT – DUTY.

'Is *this* heaven …?' he muttered to himself. 'Or is it …?'

He violently shook his head to clear it.

Keep it simple, he ordered himself. *Keep it simple, or you'll drive yourself mad. You're here – this is 1973 – and an old murderous villain called Clive Gould wants to take Annie away from you. He killed her, and now he's after her again, wanting to claim her as his own for ever. He's reaching out for her, getting closer and closer. You must stop him. That's all there is to think about. That's the full story, as far as you're concerned. All the rest is bullshit. It makes no sense and it wouldn't help you even if it did. You're just a copper. Life and Death and whatever's in between, it's not your concern. Ignore it. Don't think. Stay focused. Keep it simple.*

It was all connected – Gould, McClintock, the threat to Annie. There was a line that ran through them, like a string through a necklace. The Test Card Girl saw it as Fate, McClintock saw it as his borstal regime – but both of them called it by the same name.

'The System,' he told himself. He was striding now, heading back to find Gene, fixed and focused, determined, resolved. 'I have to break the System ... McClintock and his System are behind the deaths here – and if I can break that System, I can break that Fate that has decreed Annie is to be dragged away from me. God knows how, but those two are related – this place, and Annie's future. I don't have to understand it – I'm just a simple copper – but I can change it. I can change everything. The System, and Annie's future – *I can change both of them for ever!*'

He reached the door to Mr Fellowes's office and burst through it. Fellowes himself leapt up, startled. Gene and McClintock turned to face him. Sam stood there, panting, glaring, the door still juddering from when he'd smashed it open.

'He's learnt everything about how to make a dramatic entrance from *me*,' explained Gene.

Sam looked down at McClintock's hands, scarred and disfigured from burns sustained long ago. Those pink, unnaturally smooth palms disgusted him. He was glad that McClintock had suffered, and that he still bore the stigmata of his suffering. It was the least he deserved.

'It was you,' Sam said, pointing straight at him.

'I beg your pardon, young Detective Inspector?' asked McClintock, primly running a finger along the gold chain of his fob watch.

Sam strode across the office squared up to him, eyeball to eyeball.

'I know,' he breathed. 'I know what you did.'

'You seem overwrought,' McClintock replied coolly. 'Has something upset you?'

Sam jabbed his finger into McClintock's chest: 'I'm not like you. I don't betray my colleagues. *I know what you did, you coward.*'

McClintock glanced across at Gene. 'Well, Detective Chief Inspector Hunt, are you going to intervene?'

Gene frowned, said, 'Dunno. I don't know what's going on. What *is* going on, Tyler? You winding him up or something?'

But this time Sam said nothing. He lashed out at McClintock. He couldn't stop himself. But McClintock shoved him away. Sam came back at him. There was a tussle.

'I know what you did, you bastard!' Sam yelled at him. 'And I'll get you for it! I'll break your bloody System and I'll break *you*, you Judas!'

And then, all at once, he found himself being hauled away by Gene. He fought, but the Guv'nor had him clamped in an armlock.

'What's going on here, Tyler? Tired and emotional? In need of a nap, eh? Little man had a busy day?'

Sam opened his mouth to shout something, but a powerful blow to the stomach knocked the air clear out of his lungs. He fell in a gasping heap upon the floor. McClintock and Fellowes stood staring mutely at him.

'Silence, respect, duty – the fast way,' said Gene, standing over Sam's prone body. 'Anyway, something tells me it's time we were going. Thank you for havin' us. We've both had a lovely time.'

They sat together in the Cortina, speeding back towards Manchester. Gene hunched moodily over the wheel, flooring the pedal. Sam brooded. Outside, a wet, wretched evening was settling over the moors.

'You disgraced yourself back there, Tyler,' growled Gene. 'And, more importantly, you disgraced *me*. What the hell did you think you were doing, going off like a tit on heat? You're worse than a bird, you are.'

Sam looked about at the miserable terrain outside. The light was fading, the sky was becoming dark and threatening. He looked at the heavy grey clouds and wondered what lay beyond them. Was there a solar system out there: planets, stars, the whole vast universe stretching away to impossible limits? Or was there something else: Heaven, Hell, angels, devils, or other things, stranger things, things Sam could not even begin to imagine?

I'm just a copper, he told himself yet again. *These questions are too big for me. I'm just a simple bloody copper …*

But he knew now that thinking like this was just an

act of denial. He could duck the big questions, but only for so long, because, sooner or later, those big questions would come looking for *him*. Whatever was out there, it would not be denied. One day – one day soon – Sam would find himself face to face with the hard reality of his existence. The Devil in the Dark was real. It was as real as the Cortina Sam was now sitting in, as real as the Guv, as real as Annie or Chris or Ray or any of them. And that devil was getting close, now. Very close.

'Why can't you just act normal?' Gene continued. 'Always the same with you, Tyler – talking crap, acting like a divot, coming up with stuff no normal bloke ever would. And then you go and kick off like some fairy with a ferret up his Khyber and make *me* look like a right nugget. Why? For God's sake, why?'

Sam let out a sigh. Deep within himself, he willed everything to be just simple. He wanted Annie, and 1973, and his work in CID. For all their faults and all the trouble they gave him, it was what he wanted. They were simple. They were good. They were his *life*.

But instead, it was all so impossibly complicated. Where was he? *What* was he? And how the hell was it all going to end? Was time passing? Would the years change? Would 1973 click over into 1974, on and on, into the future? Or would the same year start over again? Was he trapped in an eternal 1973, in an endless cycle, going round and round? And what if something were to happen to him here? What if he was killed in the line of duty, or if the Cortina left the road right now and went up in flames? What would become of him? Would he simply cease to be? Would he be catapulted into some other place, the same way he had been catapulted here? What were the stakes he was playing for here? Could he really save Annie by nailing McClintock? And, if he couldn't, how bad could things get? What was the price of failing to protect Annie from that devil out there that was coming for her?

'I'm just a copper,' he said feebly.

'You what, Tyler?'

'I'm just a simple copper. It's all too much for me.'

'I see,' said Gene, nodding to himself. 'Like that, is it? You're losing it, Sammy. You're having one them break-downs, aincha? Like Dougie Devon down in D-Division. Remember when he came in wearing a maternity dress and a load of lippy caked over his gob like Danny La Rue?'

Sam felt his heart labouring anxiously in his chest. A horrible, nameless panic was starting to settle over him. He felt a suffocating sense of claustrophobia – not physically, but in some deeper way, as if it were Fate itself that was enclosing him and from which he could not escape.

'Dougie had an excuse, though,' Gene was rambling on. 'He had problems. I met his missus, I knew what he was putting up with at home. A right bleedin' heffalump,

I can tell you. But *you*, Tyler, what's your ruddy beef, eh? Single fella, got a place of your own, got a bit of crumpet keeping warm on the side, got your health – now that in itself's worth its weight, believe me – and you got your Uncle Genie looking after you. What's to get hung up about?'

Sam found that there was sweat running down his face and the back of his neck.

'You should be 'appy as a sandboy, not talking shite and acting loopy.'

The Cortina felt as narrow as the inside of a coffin. The sky above him felt as solid and as heavy as lead.

'I don't feel right,' Sam muttered.

'You've *never* been right, Tyler, not since the moment you came waltzing into my department.'

Sam raised his hands to the side of his head. 'I *really* don't feel right. I need … some air …'

'You're not about to be sick, are you?'

'I – I feel—'

Gene shot him a ferocious look. 'Don't you *dare* chuck your chicken in my motor! Outside! Now!'

Gene stamped hard on the brake. The Cortina lurched to a stop, and at once Sam threw open the door and sprang out. He sprinted blindly, leaving the road and blundering away across rough terrain, water and wet mud flying up about him as he went. The wide horizon lay ahead of him, glowering dimly, a mass of sullen clouds bearing down upon it. A grey curtain of distant rain swept silently across the distant hills. The world seemed cold and dead, a dank prison, a prison without walls, an eternal prison, enclosing him in an endless nightmare.

'Where the hell are off to, you pukey wazzock?' he heard Gene bellowing. 'If you want to heave your carrots, you don't have to do it up the top of bloody Ben Nevis! Tyler! Come back here!'

Sam looked frantically about him. The world seemed to be spinning – the sky was rolling, the ground was heaving. Nothing was stable. Everything was illusion.

He fell to his knees and plunged his hands into the wet mud. He felt the cold, the moisture, the rough grass, the sticky mire.

'It *is* real!' he yelled out. 'I can see it! I can feel it!' He grabbed a handful of mud and thrust it against his mouth. 'I can taste it! It's real! It's really real!'

It only seems *real.*

Sam pitched forward and screamed into the earth, '*I don't understand!*'

A shadow fell across him. A hand in a black-leather string-back glove reached down and laid itself on his shoulder.

Gently, calmly, Gene said, 'All right, son. I've seen it before. I'm signing you off. No shame in that. 'Appens to the best of 'em.'

'I don't understand, Guv,' Sam said, turning his mud-smeared face towards Gene. 'I just – I just don't *understand*.'

'No,' said Gene. 'But *I* do.'

'You do?'

'Aye. I know what you need.'

'What, Guv? What is it I need?'

'What you need's a bit of time off, a few stiff sherbets, and plenty of leg-over. You'll be right as rain.'

And from the expression on Gene's face, Sam could see that he meant it. No sarcasm, no banter. He was talking man to man.

Sam's shoulders sagged. He felt disoriented, lost, and utterly alone.

By the time they got back to the city, Sam had wiped most of the mud from his face and hands, and regained his composure – at least on the outside. But Gene had made his mind up to sign him off as temporarily unfit for duty.

'What you need right now is some beer down your neck,' he said, stopping the Cortina outside the Railway Arms.

'I don't need beer, guv.'

'Oh yes you do. Booze, then home, then bed, and a bird if you can get it. And, if you're on your tod, watch tons of telly. That's your fitness regime, Tyler, until you've got yourself straightened out. No arguments. Dr Hunt's orders.'

'I don't need straightening out, Guv, I'm fine, honest. I just … lost it for a moment.'

'No kidding! Why did you have to be so bloody *public* about it?' But then Gene raised his hand, silencing any further discussion. 'Get your head down and get yourself sorted, Sam. Take a few days, as many as you need. We can manage. The department don't hinge around *you*.'

'Do me a favour, Guv. Don't tell the others why I'm off. Tell 'em I'm—'

'—down with the lurgy. Course I will. What do you take me for?' Gene fixed him with an intense look, very serious and narrow-eyed. 'You *will* get yourself sorted, won't you, Tyler?'

Sam nodded: 'I'll be right as rain, Guv. Scout's honour.'

'Now *that* is an oath not to be taken lightly.'

He jabbed a thumb at Sam in a gesture that said, Right you, get out of my bloody motor.

'Thanks, Guv,' said Sam. 'You know, for being understanding and that.'

'I hope that ain't the prelude to a snog, Tyler, I'm not that sort of boy. Now get in that pub and get bladdered. I'd join for a swift one but frankly I've seen enough of your face for one day, Sammy boy. Talk to Nelson. It's his job to listen to self-pitying twats like you mooing on about themselves over a pint glass.'

Feeling a sudden warmth for Gene, which was very rare indeed, Sam clambered out of the car. The Cortina's engine roared, the tyres screamed, and the motor shot away into the night.

Sam stood in the dark street, looking up at the blank sky. He was grateful he could see no stars. Stars would have sent his head reeling and spinning again.

He patted his chest. It felt real and solid. He looked at the drizzle falling against the orange glow of the sodium street lamp, felt it tingle coldly against his hands and face. He watched a cat slink across the road, its emerald eyes glinting bright green as it shot him a glance. He watched a car pass, swishing through water pooled over a blocked drain.

Details. Endless details. And all of them perfect.

At the far end of the street, he glimpsed a small figure – a girl, standing half in and half out of the glow from a street lamp. She was motionless, staring through the night at Sam, unblinking. He had seen that stare all too many times already.

She's never going to leave me alone. She's going to hound me for ever with her threats and her insinuations. Why? Why, for God's sake?

The windows of the Railway Arms glowed in the night, warmer and more inviting than they had ever seemed before. Repelled by the cold stare of the Test Card Girl, and unable to face going back to his cold, lonely flat, Sam pushed his way into the pub, like a moth drawn irresistibly towards the light.

CHAPTER ELEVEN

PORK SCRATCHING

Sam was at once cocooned by the warmth and friendly fag-smoke reek of the Railway Arms. His heart was still heavy and his mind was still reeling, but he at least felt safe here. Perhaps it was the familiarity, or the smell in the air, or the promise of booze. Or perhaps it had something to do with Nelson, the Arms' indefatigable landlord, who was stationed – as ever – behind the bar in readiness. Tonight, he was all togged up in his fineries: he had donned an extravagant shirt that depicted a rich Caribbean sunset (or was it a sunrise?) complete with sea, beach and wilting palm trees.

As Sam entered, Nelson looked up from behind the bar, where he was tucking into a bag of pork scratchings. He grinned massively, revealing chunks of pig fat between his white teeth and, turning his Jamaican accent up to eleven, declared, 'A customer at laahst! Yo savin' mah life, bro! I was tinkin' I was gonna be spendin' da whole naht alone wit' nuttin' but me scratchin's for company!'

Sam wandered uncertainly into the empty pub feeling lost and shell-shocked. He couldn't clear his brain of the turmoil of thoughts and fears that seethed there.

The guv was right to drop me off here. I need a drink – more than I've ever needed a drink!

Nelson leant over the bar and scrutinized him. 'What dat all over your face, Sam? You blackin' up to join de Minstrels?'

'It's mud,' Sam said.

'Is that so?'

Nelson passed him a tea towel used for drying glasses and watched Sam thoughtfully as he scrubbed his face.

'You wanna freshen up in de gents'?' Nelson asked. 'I tink at least *one* o' de taps in dere is workin'. But you might have to give de looking glass a wipe to see yo be-ootiful face starin' back atcha!'

'The looking glass,' Sam muttered. 'We're all through the looking glass …'

Through the looking glass. Wonderland. When he was a little boy, his dad would read him favourite passages from the Alice stories before lights out. 'The Owl and Pussy Cat'. 'The Red Queen'. 'The Jabberwocky'.

My dad. Vic. Vic Tyler.

A complex rush of emotions and memories came tumbling through his mind. He recalled his father's lean, boyish face, his impish smile, the rasp of his unshaven chin against Sam's cheek that always made him giggle and squirm, the sight of his jacket hanging on the banister, his silhouette in the bedroom doorway as he looked in to say good night, the signed Bobby Charlton cigarette card that his dad had presented to him one day and which had meant then – and still meant now – more to Sam than all the treasure in the world.

But there was more to Vic Tyler than this. There was the dark side that little four-year-old Sam had never seen or even suspected, but which the adult Sam had come face to face with here in 1973. There was Vic Tyler the crook, the liar, the pornographer, the ruthless killer. There was Vic Tyler the man who walked out on his wife and son without a word, never to return, because he knew CID was closing in on him. There was Vic Tyler who had tried to beat Annie to death just to evade arrest. There was Vic Tyler who had turned a gun on Sam, aiming the barrel straight between his eyes and pulling the trigger without a moment's hesitation, unaware that the gun was unloaded, that Sam himself had removed the bullets.

Sam screwed up his face and pressed his fists against his eyes, trying to block out the horror of the memory, the loneliness that had flooded over him as a child when he learnt that his father had walked out on him and his mum, all those years of daring to believe that in the next moment there would be a knock at the door and his dad would be there, out of the blue, come to kiss his wife and gather up his son in his arms.

Death. Loss. Blighted childhood. And that nameless, faceless threat emerging from the deep darkness to drag Annie away from him for ever.

'I can't cope with all this!' Sam growled through gritted teeth, driving his knuckles into his face as if he could crush the pain and confusion and fear he was experiencing. 'My dad tried to kill Annie, but I saved her! I thought it was enough! Damn it all, I thought it was enough!'

He felt that terrible panic rising in him again, that sense the world about him and the sky over his head was pressing in on him, crushing him, trapping, confining him. Unlike his father, he had nowhere to run to, nowhere to hide.

'I can't deal with this. I'm a copper! *I'm only a bloody copper!*'

'*Only* a copper?' said Nelson. 'Dere ain't no 'only' about being a copper, Sam. It's a high callin'.'

'I'm going mad, Nelson.'

'Not you, bro. You ain't goin' mad.'

Sam dug his fingers into his face: 'I – I … Ach, you don't understand, Nelson. How could you? How could anyone? Oh, God, I'm losing it, I'm losing it, I'm losing it big time!'

'Open your eyes, bro.'

'Nelson, I – I don't feel I can.'

'Open your eyes and look. That's all you gotta do.'

Sam dropped his hands from his face and saw Nelson opening the door behind the bar that led into the back room. But through the doorway, instead of the usual glimpse of piled-up boxes of crisps, discarded delivery invoices, old packing crates, and assorted heaps of junk, Sam saw a wide-open space, a vast shining plane beneath a glittering sky, all blazing with a cool, clear light.

In the next heartbeat, Nelson pulled the door shut and cut off the view. For a moment, pure white light blazed through the gap between the jambs and the lintel – and then, all at once, it faded out. Nelson stood with his back to the door, grinning his huge toothy, Cheshire Cat grin at Sam.

'*That* shut you up,' he smiled.

'What – what did I just see?' Sam asked quietly.

Nelson crunched on a pork scratching and flashed his eyebrows knowingly.

In little more than a whisper, Sam asked, 'Who are you, Nelson?'

'Me? Oh, I'm different from all you guys. *Very* different. I'm sort of like …' He thought for a moment, looking for the right expression. 'I'm sort of like passport control. Or maybe a bouncer at a club. Or something like that.'

'Are you … an angel?'

'Do angels eat pork scratchings?'

'It looks to me like they do.'

Nelson smiled. 'Angels, devils ... What's in a name? To you, I'm Nelson, the fella who pulls the pints and listens to your woes after you've had a hard day chasing bad guys. But maybe now you see what I was telling you: I *do* understand how you're feeling, Sam. Better than anyone.'

'Where am I?' Sam asked.

'Where'd you think? Your local boozer!'

'But the Railway Arms isn't really a pub, is it?' said Sam. 'And 1973 isn't really 1973 – I mean, not really.'

'It is and it isn't.'

'That's not very helpful, Nelson.'

'Well, it's not an easy question to answer.'

'I need to know where I am!'

'Then I'll show you.' Nelson placed an empty pint glass on the bar and pointed at it. 'This, Sam, is your Life. Your old life, the one you left behind. It's where you came from. And this' – about a foot from the pint glass he set down a virgin bottle of Johnnie Walker Red Label – 'this beautiful bottle of liquid gold is where you're heading to. It's your destination, all being well. But it's still far off. Right now, Sam, you're about here ...' He took a pork scratching from the packet and placed it carefully on the bar. 'That's you. Between the empty pint glass and the unopened whisky. That's where you are, Sam. In transit. On your way – to this.'

Nelson grinned and tapped the Johnnie Walker bottle.

Slowly, Sam said, 'So – I'm a pork scratching making my way to a bottle of Scotch.'

'Just a metaphor, Sam!' Nelson laughed. And, smiling, he cast his gaze about the pub. 'It's *all* a metaphor! This pub, those streets out there, all them villains you go chasing after.'

'It all feels – very real to me.'

'And so it should! It *is* real, Sam. It's as real as the life you left behind. The people here are real; your job is real; all the danger and the pain, the hopes and the fears – it's all as real as ever. But *here*, Sam, here between the pint glass and the whisky – reality has a twist. An extra dimension. Something more.'

'It has meaning,' said Sam. 'That's what you're telling me. Everything here has meaning.'

'Oh, yes.'

Sam picked up the pork scratching between his fore-finger and his thumb, examining it like forensic evidence. It was a lumpy, burnt, misshapen sliver of fried pig fat, as attractive and appetizing as a bogey. And yet it meant something. It had significance. And so did everything else in 1973. The stink and the squalor of this time and place – the fag ash and the filth. All the people – the Guv and Ray and Chris, and Phyllis and Annie, and McClintock and Fellowes and Donner. And Friar's Brook and even the Cortina. It all had significance. It was here for a reason, just as Sam was, just as the Railway Arms was, just as this little pork scratching was.

'I'm a copper,' Sam said softly. 'I solve crimes. That's what I do. But here those crimes mean something more. Don't they?'

'Very much more, Sam.'

'What do they mean, Nelson? Why am I here? What have I got to do?'

'Big questions!' laughed Nelson. '*Big* questions! Just keep doing your job, Sam. Keep nicking them bad guys.' And now his smile faded, and he fixed Sam with his eyes and said very seriously, 'Just do your best, Sam. It's important.'

'Help me,' said Sam.

'That's what I'm doing right now.'

'No, I mean *help* me. There's something out there, something in the dark. It's getting closer all the time. It wants Annie. It wants to … to hurt her.'

Nelson nodded, his face very serious. 'Yes, Sam. It wants to hurt her.'

'What is it?'

'A man from Annie's past,' Nelson said simply. 'They were together in Life. He killed her. And later he himself died. He died, Sam, but he still won't let her go.'

'It's Gould, isn't it? It's that bastard Clive Gould.'

'He's reaching out for her, trying to take her back. He

doesn't belong here – his rightful place is far away – but he never played by the rules in Life and he has no intention of starting now. It's taking all his strength to manifest himself here. Bit by bit he's piecing himself together here. You'll have glimpsed him first in dreams.'

Sam nodded. He was recalling when he had fallen into the fortified compound of the Red Hand Faction. Carol Waye, the public-school-educated revolutionary with the plaits like Heidi, had knocked him out with a blow from the butt of her handgun – and as he plunged into unconsciousness, he had seen a terrible, inhuman face leering out at him from the darkness. He had dismissed it later as a phantom of his reeling brain – but deep within himself Sam knew that what he has seen had been real. It had been all too horribly real.

'And then,' Nelson was saying, 'after the dreams, you'll have seen him in some other form. A picture in a book, maybe. A painting on a wall.'

'A tattoo,' said Sam. He was thinking of Patsy O'Riordan, the huge, bullet-headed, bare-knuckle boxer from Terry Bernard's fairground. 'A monstrous tattoo, like the face of a devil.'

Nelson nodded. 'He doesn't have the strength to come waltzing into your world and drag Annie away with him – at least, not yet. He has to take it in stages. Step by step, he becomes more real, Sam. And who knows what guise he'll take next? It might be something subtler, something more abstract. Whatever form he takes, Sam, it will always appear to you in the form of a crime, a case for you and your department.'

'The System,' said Sam, nodding to himself. 'McClintock's System at Friar's Brook. I knew it! I knew that I had to break that System! If I break that System, Nelson, then I break the other System too, the one that little bitch from the test card was talking about. She said Fate was a system that couldn't be broken, and that Annie's Fate was for that damned Devil in the Dark to get its hands on her! But I can change that! I can change it all and save her! That's right, isn't it, Nelson? That's what I've got to do?'

'Maybe it is – maybe it's not. *You're* the policeman, DI Tyler, not me.'

'Help me, Nelson. Help me do this job.'

'I can't do that, Sam.'

'Yes you can! You know the game round here, better than any of us. You understand what it's all about. You've got – you've got powers.'

'Powers, Sam? Do I look like Superman to you? Am I wearing my underpants on the outside, mmm?' He shook his head. 'I'm just Nelson the barman, the local colour, a bit of comic relief serving coppers in a pub.'

'You're more than that!' Sam insisted. 'I saw it for myself!'

'Yes, you saw. And, yes, I *am* more than just a barman, Sam – I'm a great deal more – but like you I got a job to do and rules to play by and a *very* big boss, bigger even than your DCI, who I've got to keep happy. So in this place, and in this time, as far as you are concerned I'm just the all-singin', all-dancin', pint-pullin' *Jee-may-kahn*.'

'You broke cover to speak to me this evening.'

'Broke cover?' For a moment, Nelson turned the words over in his mind. Then a broad smile spread across his face. "Broke cover'! Yes, that's a good, policeman-ish phrase. I like that! I 'broke cover', and spoke to my friend Sam, revealing more than I've ever revealed before!'

He laughed to himself, but Sam was deadly serious.

'You broke cover once, Nelson, now break cover again. Use what power you have. Help me save Annie. Help me face what's out there.'

'I'm not here to carry your burden for you,' said Nelson gently. 'That's for you and you alone. It's the rules, Sam, and I'll say no more about it. Just make sure you don't get yourself killed out there.'

'Then I can – I can *die* here?'

'Well of course, Sam! Just the same way you could in your old life. You're as much flesh and blood as you ever were. Cut yourself – you'll bleed. So will everyone else round here.'

'And what would happen if I – if I died here? What would happen, Nelson? Where would I go?'

'Don't think about that.'

'But – but I have to know what—'

'Be strong! It's the future that matters, Sam. *Your* future. Yours and Annie's. Because you two have a future, if you can reach it. You can be happy together. It's possible. It's all very possible.'

'But not guaranteed.'

Nelson looked at him wordlessly for a moment, and then, very subtly, shook his head, just once.

'But if I can stop this Gould …' Sam went on, gripping the edge of the bar. 'If I can stop him and get rid of him, then there really is a life for me and Annie? We can be together? Where will we go – to that place you just showed me? That place full of light?'

'Oh, that!' laughed Nelson. 'Sam, that's just the porch. It's much nicer once you get through the front door. Man, you should see the living room with the minibar!' His eyes sparkled for a moment, then his face became grave. 'But you've got a lot to do before all that, Sam. And I can't say if you'll manage it or not. There's everything to play for. Nothing's guaranteed. But if you and Annie make it through intact – if you defeat what's out there, and survive that confrontation – well then …' He edged the solitary pork scratching along the bar until it nestled against the bottle of Johnnie Walker. 'Don't forget this, Sam. Don't forget the whisky.'

'And is it worth it?' Sam asked. 'Is it worth all this effort, all this pain?'

'Is it *worth* it, Sam?'

Nelson smiled – a huge, broad, genuine smile – and set two small glasses on the bar, side by side.

'Let's see for ourselves, eh?' he winked, and twisted the cap off the whisky bottle.

CHAPTER TWELVE

READING BETWEEN THE LINES

Nelson sent Sam on his way, out into the night, pleasantly pissed and more at ease with himself and the universe than he had been in a long, long time. The turmoil of his mind was gone. All those unanswerable questions about reality and unreality, life and death, had receded.

I am flesh and blood – I am here in this city – I have a job to do, and I have a future with Annie. That's enough.

As he wended his way through the damp, dark streets, heading for home, Sam imagined that he could still feel the comforting glow of the Railway Arms about him, the reassuring presence of Nelson warming him like a camp fire. Patiently, knowingly, Nelson had listened to his clumsy attempts to explain the extraordinary events of that day, the sudden and horrifying lurch back through time that had occurred to him while he was inspecting the punishment block at Friar's Brook. Anyone else would have made Sam feel like a babbling lunatic – but Nelson merely nodded sagely.

'What did it all mean, Nelson? Why did it happen?'

'Let me ask *you* a question,' Nelson had said. 'Did you see something today – an object, perhaps just a very small one – that attracted your attention, made you feel ... odd in some way?'

'Yes. A watch. A gold-plated fob watch with a chain. It was in House Master McClintock's jacket pocket.'

'A watch,' Nelson mused thoughtfully. 'Mmm. And when you saw it, how did it make you feel?'

'Sick.'

'Really?'

'Oh, yes. Disturbed. Uncomfortable. I hated it the moment I clapped eyes on it. And I mean *really* hated it, Nelson. What does it mean?'

For a moment, Nelson's face was drawn and serious, his thoughts turned inward. And then he suddenly became aware of Sam again, grinned, and refilled both their drinks.

'We'll talk about it another time,' he said, raising his glass in a toast. 'There's only so much you can be expected to deal with it in one day, Sam!'

'That watch – was it connected to what happened to me? Was it the reason I started seeing things in the past, things though McClintock's eyes?'

'Yes, it was the reason for it.'

'Why? What does it *mean*?'

'Drink up, Sam, and clear your mind of troubles.'

But Sam had become insistent: 'It's because of that watch that I saw into the past, isn't it? I'm right, aren't I?'

'I said drink up, Sam.'

'That watch is a physical link to the past. I'm guessing pretty close to the truth, yes? It's a link to something that happened with McClintock and Annie's father ten years ago – and it's a link so strong that I sensed it at once, and it let me actually glimpse those events first hand!'

Nelson clanged the bell hanging over the bar. 'Time, gentlemen.'

Something in Nelson's manner, some invisible, indefinable aura about him – kindly, gentle, but strong – made Sam obey. To demand more answers and explanations suddenly felt impertinent, as if Nelson were a superior officer who far outranked him.

And, in a way, I think that's exactly *what he is.*

Sam was loath to leave the warm snug of the Arms and the mysterious and reassuring presence of its landlord. 'No chance of a lock-in tonight, Nelson?'

'Home and bed for you, Mr CID,' Nelson told him. 'Get some kip. You need it.'

'But we'll talk further, another time? You know, about – well, about …'

'Sure. Just do me one favour, Sam. Don't go blabbing

about our little chat here tonight. Best to keep it private, between the two of us. What happens in the Railway Arms *stays* in the Railway Arms, you hear me?'

Sam had paused, thought about it, then nodded. 'I hear you, Nelson.' And then, in the doorway, he had looked back and added, 'Thanks.'

'You're very welcome,' Nelson had replied. 'Safe home, Sam.'

I don't know who that man is – or if he's even a 'man' at all – but I do know he's a friend. A real friend. And that's enough, too.

When he got back to his flat, Sam's head was buzzing, but not with the booze. He felt curiously sober, given how much scotch Nelson had poured down his neck. What intoxicated him at the moment were visions and dreams, glimpses of some vaster reality than he could comprehend, and hopes of a future beyond what his imagination could conceive.

'I'm happy,' he said to himself. And he grinned. 'I'm actually really, bloody happy!'

Happy – and ravenous. He raided the kitchen, toasting himself a mountain of Mother's Pride and smothering it with Marmite. And, because he was still officially a bachelor, and therefore was perfectly at liberty to behave like one, he washed it all down with a couple of brown ales from fridge.

He was just on his third bottle when, from the hallway

outside his front door, came the one voice he most longed to hear: 'You awake in there? It's the girl of your dreams, Sam – and I've got something special for you!'

His heart leapt, and he instinctively went to open the door – then hesitated. He was officially off sick with the flu. That would be what the Guv would tell everyone, and that's what Sam wanted them to think, even Annie. Especially Annie. How could he explain that he had suffered a momentary existential breakdown brought on by too much involuntary time travel? He didn't want anyone looking at him sideways, whispering behind his back, diagnosing him over coffee in the canteen. It was the stuff of wildfire rumours.

'You can't come in, Annie,' Sam called back.

'Oh aye? And what's her name?'

'She's called influenza and I'm in bed with her right now. I'm on the sick, Annie. At home until I recover. Guv's orders.'

'You got the flu?' she called in to him. 'Poor Sam! Let me in, I'll play nursey.'

'I'm contagious.' And, to prove it, he coughed theatrically.

'Flippin' heck, Sam, you sound like you're at death's door!'

'Death's door. Yes, you could say that.'

'Oh *please*, Sam, open the door. I won't breathe in or nothing. It's really, really important!'

He couldn't resist. Sam turned the latch. There she was, in her beige overcoat and sensible outdoor boots. She beamed at him, her face flushed and excited.

'You don't look too bad to me,' she said.

'And you look like the cat who stole the cream.'

'I *feel* like it, too!'

She bustled in, throwing off her coat to reveal her muted paisley blouse and brown, chevron-patterned skirt.

'I've cracked it!' she grinned, pulling a couple of sheets of paper from her handbag and waving them in his face. 'I can't believe it, Sam! I've only gone and cracked it! I'm so excited! If you weren't snotty and contagious, I'd give you the biggest snog you've ever had!'

Sam inwardly cursed his cover story. Why hadn't he made up something about putting his back out instead?

'I've made sense of it!' Annie beamed.

'Made sense of what?'

'The letter! The one from Andy Coren! I *knew* there was something iffy about it. And I was right! I was bloody right, Sam!'

'There *was* a secret message in it?'

Annie nodded vigorously.

'And you've cracked it?'

Annie nodded even *more* vigorously.

'You're kidding me.'

Annie shook her head, most vigorously of all.

Sam grinned. 'Hit me with it!'

179

'Right! Look at this!' She thrust the crumpled, blood-stained letter at him. 'This is the original, right? Strangely worded, mentions a nonexistent vet in Lidden Street – but, other than that, innocent enough. Right?'

'Right.' Sam perused the letter closely. 'I still can't see anything.'

'No, you can't. And for ages, neither could I. I was going over it and over it, not getting any joy. I started to wonder if I was just driving myself potty over nothing. Anyway, as you can see, the original's getting pretty tatty. So, I decided to make a copy of it on that new Xerox machine and use that to work from instead.'

'And?'

'See for yourself.'

Annie proudly shoved a sheet of photocopier paper at him. Sam looked it over.

'I still don't see anything,' he said. 'It's just a copy of the letter.'

'Yes, but look! The Xerox sweeps a powerful light over what it copies – and that light shows up all sorts of marks and imperfections on the original. See how all the little rips and indentations show up as black speckles?'

'Yes. But I still don't—'

'Look at the individual letters! Here, and here, and here and here …!'

She pointed, and Sam looked. His eyes slowly widened.

DEAR DEREK,

SO BRILLIANT YOU COULD MAKE TIME
FOR A VISIT. REALLY GOOD TO GET
TIME WITH YOU AGAIN. TELL AUNTIE
ROSE NOT TO FRET SO MUCH. DON'T
FORGET TO GIVE FLUFFY HER SPECIAL
TABLETS - TAKE HER TO THE VET IN
LIDDEN STREET IF SHE GETS SICK
AGAIN. IT'S VERY VERY IMPORTANT
I CAN TRUST YOU TO LOOK AFTER HER.
SEE YOU AGAIN SOON I HOPE.

LOVE,

ANDY

'There are tiny marks beneath certain letters,' Sam said.

'Pinpricks.' Annie grinned. 'We'd have seen 'em straightaway if we'd thought to hold the letter up to the light! The pinpricks mark out a series of individual letters. Put them letters in order and you get *this*!'

She thrust a sheet of foolscap at him. On it, in her neat, schoolgirlish handwriting, it said, 'OLDFRIDGEGERTRUDEFRIDAY'.

And then, beneath it, 'OLD – FRIDGE – GERTRUDE – FRIDAY'.

'So this is how Andy Coren arranged his escape plans with his brother on the outside!' Sam said. 'They used a code. And *you* cracked it! Annie, you're a genius!'

'A genius? Me? Oh, no, no, no,' Annie simpered. 'Well – maybe just a bit.'

'You're a bloody marvel!'

He threw his arms around her, but she ducked away from him before he could land a kiss.

'I don't want your germs!'

'Oh. Yes. Of course. My germs.' Confounded, Sam turned his attention back to the letter. 'Andy Coren was a regular Houdini, escaping from one borstal after another. And this explains it. He must have had this code worked out with his brother all along. Derek could be there on the outside, helping him escape. They could communicate freely, right under the noses of the screws.'

'Yes, but something went wrong this time,' said Annie. 'The message says he'll be in a fridge on the back of *Gertrude*. But he wasn't. He was in an old oven that got brought in by the other lorry.'

'*Matilda*.'

'That's the one.'

'Which means,' said Sam, 'that either Andy Coren buggered things up and got in the wrong lorry, or—'

'Or somebody knew about his escape plan and buggered it up for him. Who might do that to him, Sam?'

'Well, what about House Master McClintock? He personally vets all the outgoing letters at Friar's Brook. He would have seen this letter before it was sent. He rubber-stamped it for approval and let it go out. But what if he spotted the code? Or was tipped off about it? Either way, let's suppose he deciphered the hidden message. He would have known what Andy Coren was planning.'

Annie nodded, then frowned. 'Yeah, but – if this House Master knew that Coren was planning to escape, why didn't he just scupper his plan right away?'

'Because that's not how McClintock operates,' said Sam. 'I met him today. He's a bastard, Annie. A *real* bastard. He runs that borstal like it's a concentration camp. You wouldn't believe the things that go on there, Annie.' He thought for a moment. 'Okay. Let's suppose that Andy Coren was a troublemaker. Let's suppose there was bad blood between him and McClintock.'

'Okay. Let's suppose that. What of it?'

'McClintock doesn't pull his punches when it comes to discipline. And he can't stand to have his precious System challenged. What if he somehow deciphered the message in that letter, but let it be posted anyway?'

'Why would he do that, Sam? It makes no sense.'

'But it *does* make sense. Because, once he's let that letter be posted, he changes the work detail! On the day of the escape, he shifts Coren from loading fridges onto *Gertrude* to loading *ovens* onto *Matilda*. He foils Coren's escape plan at the very last second, just to show him, just to really rub it in!'

'But he didn't *stop* him, Sam. Andy Coren did escape!'

'Yes. Perhaps Andy couldn't resist the chance. Perhaps he trusted to luck that his brother would find him anyway once he was at Kersey's Yard. But what really matters here, Annie, is that *McClintock knew he was inside one of them ovens*! He knew it, but he let that lorry carry him out anyway.'

Annie frowned. 'And why would he do that?'

'Because those ovens were destined for the crusher. It was his punishment, Annie. McClintock knew Coren was being taken to his death, and he let it happen. He let it happen!'

'That's a pretty big accusation to make, Sam. You sure that flu bug hasn't gone to your brain?'

'If you'd seen what *I'd* seen today, Annie, you wouldn't put anything past that bastard McClintock.'

'Well,' said Annie, glancing at her watch. 'Whether you're right or wrong, there's not much we can do about it tonight. And since you're supposed to be down with the flu, perhaps you'd best be in bed.'

'That bed's awfully cold – you know, for a man on his own.'

'I'm not sharing with a sick fella!' Annie exclaimed.

'I got too much to do, Sam. I can't catch your lurgy and go off sick an' all.'

'Don't leave just yet. We need to celebrate your new role as CID's very own Enigma machine! I'd open a bottle of champagne, but I haven't got one. So what about a bottle of brown ale? It's refrigerated.'

He waggled a bottle enticingly at her.

'I'm sold!' Annie smiled. 'But don't you start thinking you're going to get me tipsy enough for what *you've* got in mind.'

He poured them a glass each, and toasted her.

'You did some good work with that letter, Annie. I mean it. At this rate, you'll make DCI before I do.'

'Oh, yeah, Sam, I can really see that happening! A *bird* running a department!'

'Don't write it off. Who can say what the future holds? Just think how proud your parents would be!'

Her parents.

He recalled at once that modest little house with upstairs bedroom window all lit up, and a teenage Annie almost visible within in. And then he thought of Tony Cartwright, that anxious, frightened, troubled man, with his guilty conscience, his split loyalties.

'You never talk about your parents,' he said. 'What are they like?'

Annie shrugged, sipped her beer, and grimaced at it. But that didn't stop her taking a second swig.

'Are they still alive? Do they live in Manchester? Are you close to them?'

'Sam, you sound like you're interrogating me.'

'I'm just interested.'

'No. I know that tone of voice. *And* that expression. You use both of them when you're questioning suspects.'

'You can hardly blame me for asking,' said Sam. 'I mean, we're supposed to be – you know, getting closer to each other.'

'And so we are,' said Annie.

'Then why won't you talk about your family?'

'Why won't you talk about *yours*?'

'I never said I wouldn't!' Sam smiled. 'If you want to know, I'll tell you right now. I've got a mum. She's—'

He broke off. Sam thought of his mother, wherever she was now – a beautiful young woman, several years younger than he – and, at the same time, a woman in her sixties, somewhere in the future, mourning the tragic death of her only son.

Haltingly, he said, 'She's – a really great mum.'

'That's a bit vague, Sam.'

'It's complicated.'

'What about your dad?'

Sam swigged deeply from his beer bottle, gulped it down heavily, and said, 'My dad's even more complicated than my mum.'

'Well there you go!' laughed Annie. 'Family ain't easy.'

'But I know so little about you. Why won't you tell me anything about where you come from?'

Annie shrugged.

'Well?' Sam gently prompted her.

'Nothing to say.'

'Oh, come on.'

'I mean it.'

'It's like you're avoiding talking about it.'

'Knock it off, Sam.'

It was as if she was hiding something – but Sam knew that the real reason was quite different. It was as Nelson had said: she simply couldn't remember. She had been here too long, her old life had faded from her mind, she knew nothing outside of this strange facsimile of 1973.

Surely there's some scrap of memory remaining, Sam thought. *And, if there is, maybe I can rekindle it.*

'Annie?'

She turned and smiled, holding her bottle of brown ale.

'I want to ask you a question.'

'That sounds ominous, Sam.'

'It's difficult. I … heard something, saw something. Some information – about you.'

'Hey, Sam, it's me you're talking to. You don't have to be cagey. What do you want to know about me that's so important?'

Sam looked into her eyes and decided to come straight out with it.

'Does the name Clive Gould mean anything to you?'

'Not a thing.'

'Think. Think back. Think back to when you were a teenager. Was there a – a boyfriend? Or a *would-be* boyfriend? A fella who used to hang around?'

'What's on your mind, Sam? Checking out the competition?'

Once again, she was slipping around all questions of her past.

'It's important, Annie. Please think. Does the name Clive Gould really mean nothing to you at all?'

'Is it *supposed* to mean something to me?'

Could he jog her memory? Could he ignite a recollection of what once had been? And, if he could, would it help save her?

'There was a man,' said Sam. 'A villain. He was on the make, back in the sixties. Owned casinos. Bought off coppers. Bumped off rivals. He knew your dad – and he knew you.'

'Sam, I don't know what you're on about.'

'His name was Gould. He was – he was interested in you. Years ago, when you were just a girl.'

Annie laughed, then stopped. Her brows furrowed.

'He was determined to get his hands on you. But your father stood up to him, tried to put together evidence to convict him of murdering a rival. I think things went badly wrong.'

Annie carefully set down her beer and stood looking at Sam with a strange expression.

Sam hesitated, wondered if he should continue, and then decided to take the risk and keep talking. 'Your father was a police officer. The department was thoroughly corrupt. Most of his colleagues, and those higher up, were on Gould's payroll. That's how he literally got away with murder. But your father's conscience was deeply troubled by this. He tried to make a stand.'

The light had gone out of Annie's face. She had backed away from him, her expression hard to read.

'One of his colleagues tipped Gould off,' Sam went on. He wasn't going to even attempt to explain that that colleague had been McClintock, and that Sam himself had witnessed the whole thing first hand. 'Your father was betrayed. And I think – I think Gould may have – I think he may have …' Sam ran his hands over his face, took a breath, and said, 'I know how I sound.'

'You've talked like this before,' Annie said quietly. 'Stuff about the future.'

'And now I'm rambling on about the past.'

'No, Sam, it's not the past. It's certainly not *my* past, though you seem to think it is.'

'You must think I'm bonkers, right?'

'Do you *feel* bonkers, Sam?'

Sam nodded. 'Yes. Totally. Completely.'

'Well, that's a good sign. I mean, it's them who's most bonkers that think they're most sane.'

'Then why are you standing so far away from me? You're not frightened of catching the flu.'

'You ain't got the flu. That's not why you've gone off sick.'

Sam sighed. 'No. That's not why I'm off.'

Annie looked about awkwardly. 'Sometimes, Sam, I don't know what to make of you.'

Her awkwardness, her genuine discomfort at what he had been saying, told Sam that he had been wrong to try to stir up her past. Was this what Nelson had been warning him against? Was this why he had told him to keep all that he had learnt this evening to himself?

'I'm sorry, Annie, my thoughts sometimes run away with me,' Sam said. 'You shouldn't listen to me when I talk like that. I think about things too much sometimes. It gives me a distorted view.'

'You're not kidding,' said Annie. But her tone was softening. She drew a little nearer. 'Where do you get all this stuff? Do you make it up?'

'I probably do.' Sam laughed. He imagined how ridiculous he must look to her. 'Oh, Annie, my brain's like scrambled eggs tonight! And I've had too much to drink. What I need is to *sleep*!'

'Excellent plan,' Annie said, and now she touched his

arm and smiled warmly at him. 'And tomorrow you stay in bed, and you rest.'

'Oh, no. Tomorrow, I get back to work. Best thing for me. You'll see.'

'But you're on the sick. Make the most of it, Sam. You're getting paid to lie in bed and watch telly and that.'

'Just like a DCI!' He grinned. 'I'll see you tomorrow morning, Annie. Bright and breezy.'

There was no time to waste, not on this case. The stakes were too high. But he couldn't explain that to Annie.

'Well,' said Annie, 'you're a grown-up lad, you make your own decisions.'

She kissed him on the cheek. It was all the tonic he needed to get him back on track.

With her coat back on, she paused in the doorway. 'Sleep tight, Sam.'

'I'll be dreaming of you,' he replied.

'But of course!' She winked. And then she added, 'Oh, and Sam?'

'Yes?'

'Get yourself a bottle of mouthwash. You stink of Marmite.'

And with that she was gone.

CHAPTER THIRTEEN

OFFICE HUMOUR

It was morning at CID A-Division. Sam stepped through the doors and saw that the cigarette butts were already piling up in the ashtrays. Gene was lurking in his lair, visible as a looming shape behind frosted glass.

'I thought you was signed off on the sick,' said Ray, sitting with his feet up on his desk, reading the tit page of the *Sun*.

'Lucozade, Vicks VapoRub, and plenty of satsumas,' said Sam. 'Now I'm right as rain and all up for nicking villains.'

'*And* talking like a twat,' smirked Ray. 'Hey Chris, you still playing with that bloody whiz gig?'

Chris was hunched over the Xerox, pressing buttons and giggling at the copies he was making. Grinning, he lifted up a crude cut-and-paste job in which Sam's face had been photostatted onto the body of a naked young man engaged in the vigorous act of sodomy.

'Slapping on plenty of Vicks, is that what you said, Boss?' Chris sniggered.

'Suck on them satsumas, eh?' Ray grinned.

Sam took Chris's Xerox masterpiece and examined it. 'I see what you've done. You've cut out somebody's face and copied it onto a porno picture. Extraordinary. In all my life, I have *never* seen that done before, Chris. *Ever.* You're a pioneer. How on *earth* did you think up such an off-the-wall idea? Chris *Skelton*? I think we should start calling you Chris *Morris.*'

'Off *Animal Magic*?' Chris frowned. 'I don't get it, Boss.'

'No, well, my humour's perhaps not quite sophisticated enough for you,' said Sam. He grimaced at the intimate details displayed on the photo. 'Where the hell did you get this awful picture from, anyway?'

'From the files, boss. It's your official ID mugshot.'

'No, Christopher, I was referring to the homoerotica.' And, in response to Chris's utterly blank face, he clarified: 'The gay porn.'

'Oh, that. From Barton, the lad we nicked in the park,' said Chris. 'He were carrying tons of the stuff.'

'Chris is hanging onto it – just for safe keeping, mind,' Ray said, examining a whopping set of Page 3 knockers. 'He's got strangely attached to it.'

'Give over, I'm just using it for me artworks,' protested Chris.

'Is that what you're calling this stuff – your 'artworks'?' said Sam, picking up a sheaf of photocopies, all of which were variations on the theme of Sam's head crudely pasted onto the buggered boy's body. 'I hope you're not thinking of sending it in to Tony Hart.'

'Hey, there's an idea!' put in Ray. 'Send it to *Vision On*, Chris.'

Chris giggled. '*Vision Hard-On*, more like.'

'Pure comedy gold, Chris,' Sam sighed. And then, to no one in particular, he added, 'Why is it I feel worse at work than when I'm signed off sick?'

He confiscated Chris's portfolio of works in progress and ordered him to get back to policing the city. Sam headed over to Annie's desk.

'I hope you're not going to show that stuff to *me*,' she warned him, looking up from her work.

'I wouldn't dream of it. I'm just looking for a big enough waste bin. Or an incinerator.' He stuck the sheaf of grotesque copies under his arm. 'And, before you ask, the answer is yes, I'm feeling *totally* fine, and a lot better than last night.'

'I'll take your word for it. Just so long as you don't start talking daft again.'

He smiled at her. 'You look like you've been busy. What are you up to?'

'I've been digging up all the records I can on House Master McClintock.'

'And what have you found?' asked Sam eagerly. 'Anything we can use against him?'

'Nothing incriminating. He's pretty strait-laced. He were a regular copper back in the sixties, in uniform.'

A cowardly, treacherous, disloyal one at that, Sam thought, thinking how McClintock had sold out his colleague to Clive Gould. But he kept his mouth shut.

'What made him quit the force and join the prison service?' Sam asked.

'He got injured in a fire and was invalided out.'

'That makes sense. I saw his hands. They were burned. Any information on what happened?'

'It's all a bit vague,' said Annie. 'The records aren't very complete. It's like somebody's deliberately mucked about with them.'

Could it have been McClintock himself, covering his tracks for something? Or were police records from that time so corrupted by officers on the Clive Gould payroll that there was no way of disentangling the truth from the lies?

'Anyway,' Annie went on, 'after McClintock was discharged from the police he joined the prison service and ended up house master at Friar's Brook.'

'He runs that place like his own private empire,' said Sam. 'He's a cruel bastard, Annie. But we're going to nail him.'

'You've really got it in for him, haven't you? You don't think you might be letting personal animosity cloud your judgement, do you?'

'This isn't personal, Annie,' Sam lied. 'It's strictly business.'

'Are you sure about that, Sam?'

'McClintock's rotten to the core, believe me. He's like some sort of bad parody of a Nazi, all black uniform and shiny shoes.'

'But that don't make him a killer,' Annie said. 'He's a *suspect*, sure – but no more than that.'

Sam wanted to tell her what he knew. *That bastard sold out your father to gangsters, Annie – to murderers!* But he kept himself in check.

'If there *is* a case to be made against McClintock, we're going to need first-hand witnesses who are prepared to go on record,' said Sam. 'That's where we're in luck. We've got one already. Donner.'

'You think he'll testify?'

'I know he will. He just needs the right inducement. If we guarantee his transfer from Friar's Brook, he'll talk. And he's articulate, Annie. He's smart. If we prime him right, he'll make a fantastic prosecution witness in court.'

'But is he reliable?' asked Annie. 'How can we be sure he's not just stringing us along to see what he can blag out of us?'

'I trust him,' said Sam firmly. 'And he'll repay that trust, you'll see. He's a key witness to what's been happening at Friar's Brook. If we treat him right, if we're careful and smart and—'

At that moment, the sheaf of photocopied porn slipped from under Sam's arm and spilled all over the floor. He reached down and started to gather it up – then paused, his attention caught by one of the boys in a photo. Sam peered closer.

'Having new and unsettling urges, Boss?' asked Annie.

'Don't *you* start an' all.' Sam turned the photo towards her. 'Look!'

Annie at once grimaced and turned away.

'No, no, not the bottoms and what have you – the *face*,' said Sam. 'It's Barton. It's the boy Chris and Ray banged up for … whatever it was they banged him up for. He's the one who tipped me off about McClintock in the first place!'

Gingerly, Annie pushed the photo away so that she couldn't see it. 'You think he'll give us a statement?'

'He might. He took a bit of a shine to me. Maybe he'll talk.'

'And where is he now? He's certainly not in the cells any more.'

'I know where to start looking,' said Sam. 'He mentioned the Hayfield estate to me, said it was where they photograph all this stuff. I'll go there, ask around, see if I can pick up his trail. Don't tell the Guv about it, though. Let's keep it low-key. With Gene around, there'll just be trouble and shouting and things'll get broken.'

'I hear what you're saying.' Annie winked at him. 'Tell you what – while you're looking for Barton, why don't I do some homework on Donner. If he's going to be our star witness, we need to know who he is and where he comes from.'

'That would be brilliant, Annie. Oh, and could you do me a favour?'

'Yes, Sam?'

'Could you find somewhere safe to stash this lot?' He thrust the pages of porn at her. Annie acted as if he'd handed her a rat. 'Much appreciated!'

'Don't mention it, Boss,' she said, wrinkling her nose. 'And what shall I say if the Guv asks where you've got to?'

'Tell him ...' He paused, thinking for a moment. 'Tell him I've gone looking for a dishy young lad.'

Arriving at the Hayfield estate, Sam was confronted by stained concrete, smashed windows, graffiti, desolation. Music played from an open window – the slow, lugubrious beat of Gary Glitter's 'I Love You Love Me Love'. Somewhere, a furious dog barked and howled.

Sam headed up a stinking stairwell that led to a bleak, concrete balcony, along which stood a row of identical front doors, each with a mean, square, unwashed window beside it.

What should he do? Knock on a few doors, ask if anyone knew where the gay porn was being manufactured round here?

'What am I getting myself into here?' Sam muttered.

His attention was caught by a sudden flash of light from the window of one of the flats. Moments later, there was another. Then another. Sam sidled up to the window and peered through the filthy glass. Ranged along the windowsill was a grubby pair of Y-fronts, a tangle of unidentifiable leather straps, and a tub of Vaseline with hairs stuck to it. In the room itself he saw a man dressed in green corduroy trousers and a leather jacket adjusting a camera, giving muffled instructions, and taking another set of flash photographs. And then, just visible through the caked dirt on the window, Sam glimpsed very pale male flesh.

Sam barged at the front door. It came off its rotten hinges without putting up a fight. The photographer in the green corduroys jumped and spun round, revealing a narrow, beak-nosed face and unkempt greasy hair. Two naked boys, no more than eighteen, instantly disengaged themselves from one another and scrambled frantically to get away. One of the lads sported a curly mop of ginger locks, while the other had shoulder-length hair, well overdue for a wash, and a rough-skinned face that Sam recognized at once.

Bingo, he thought, and he flourished his CID badge.

'It's okay. Keep calm. I'm a copper, but this ain't a raid,' he declared.

But nobody was listening to him. The photographer grabbed a camera tripod and lunged with it as if it were a spear. Sam fell back against a wall, batting the tripod away, and caught a glimpse of green corduroy racing out of the door. Moments later, the boy with red curls dashed past, a T-shirt held over his crotch, skittering away frantically along the balcony, his bare feet slapping on the concrete.

And then Barton tried to get by. Sam leapt up and grabbed him, clamping both arms around that lad's naked waist. They crashed to the floor, and Burton struggled furiously, lashing out at Sam with surprising strength.

'Pack it in!' Sam yelled. 'It's me!'

The boy caught him a blow across the jaw, but Sam held tight.

'Barton, for God's sake, it's me, the copper with the kind eyes!'

But Barton was like a frantic animal, fighting tooth and nail to get away. Sam managed to clamp the boy face down in a half-Nelson, pinning his free hand to the floor by kneeling on it. And, even so, Barton kicked wildly with his pale, hairy legs.

From the open doorway came the sound of rough, childish laughter, "Ere, look out, that bloke's sticking it up his bum!'

200

'I'm a police officer!' Sam barked over his shoulder at the estate kids shrieking and hooting at him.

'You're a dirty ol' bugger!'

'No, I'm not! Now sling your hooks or I nick the lot of you!'

The kids went rampaging away along the balcony, yelling, 'He likes bums and arses' as they went.

Starting to lose patience with this situation, Sam got his arm around Barton's neck and clamped him in a fierce hold. Barton clawed helplessly at him.

'I've had enough of this, Barton!' he panted. 'I don't want to nick you and I'm not trying it on. I just want to talk! Now bloody well pack it in before them scallies come back here with a couple dozen more of their mates!'

Barton's wide, frightened eyes swivelled round and stared into Sam's face – and then, slowly, he recognized him. The struggling subsided. Sam released him.

'PC Brown Eyes,' Barton muttered.

'If you like. Here – get some trousers on and let's talk.'

Sam handed him a pair of unwashed jeans that lay discarded on the floor. Barton slipped them on, but delayed doing up the fly. He stood there for a moment, still exposed, and gave Sam a sly look. Sam shook his head. Barton shrugged, and zipped himself up.

'I never done this before,' Barton said. 'The photos, I mean. I just deliver 'em. But the regular lad didn't show

up, see? And the fella needed to get the shots done, and
– well – you know—'

'Barton, I'm not here because of that.'

'I'm not a fairy. I like birds and big tits and all that.'

Barton fished about for his T-shirt and slipped it on.
It was adorned with a gaudy image of the Bay City
Rollers, and at once it made Barton look very young,
very childish, and – despite everything – strangely
innocent.

What chance has this lad ever had? Sam thought,
looking at him in his boy-band T-shirt, standing here in
this concrete hellhole, making ends meet by selling his
body to lowlife pornographers? *I bet he's never known
anything else but this. Shitty flats, crime, being exploited
to earn a couple of quid. No education, no future, and
the fear of going back inside hanging over him like a
black cloud. For lads like him, it's like the Dark Ages
never ended.*

'I'm normal,' Barton said pathetically.

'I know you are.'

'Honest. I just need the money.'

'Barton, listen to me, I don't care what you do, I'm
only interested in what you can tell me about Friar's
Brook and what goes on there.'

'Friar's Brook? You're not – you're not thinking of—'

'Sending you back there? Of course not. I've been
there. I've seen what goes on.'

'You have?'

I've seen the punishment block.'

'The Black Hole!'

'Yes. Did they put you in there?'

Barton went over to the vile kitchen area and poured himself a glass of water. He downed it in one, holding the glass in both hands, like a small child. Water ran down his chin. He wiped it away with the hem of his T-shirt.

'I need you to tell me the truth,' said Sam, gently but firmly. 'I need you to tell me about McClintock.'

Hesitantly, Barton said, 'What – do you want to know?'

'Boys have died in Friar's Brook.'

Barton nodded.

'Why did they die? Do *you* know why?'

'McClintock,' Barton said vaguely.

'What does he do? Barton, I need to know. Do boys die because of McClintock's regime? Do they die, and does he cover it up so it looks like suicide or an accident?'

'Are you – trying to arrest him?'

'If he's guilty of something, then yes,' said Sam. 'And that's why I need you to tell me what you know.'

Barton thought for a moment, then said very quietly, 'Sometimes boys died because of the punishments. And sometimes – sometimes they died because they gave McClintock too much grief.'

203

'Too much grief? You mean that they upset his precious System?'

Barton nodded. 'Some of them lads, they'd stand up to him. Not me, I was too frit. And the ones who stood up, the ones who answered back, the ones who took him on, they paid for it. McClintock would put them in the Hole – for weeks on end, or even longer. He'd have the screws beat the daylights out of them. Or worse.'

'In what way worse?'

Barton glanced anxiously round the gloomy flat. He stared at a plug socket above the filthy Formica worktop for a moment, then said, 'Electric shocks.'

'*Electric shocks*? You mean, like in Abu Ghraib?'

'Not just in the Abu Ghraibs, sir, but *all over* the body – face, hands, you name it. And there were other things too, sir, like when they'd – they'd …' He ran himself another glass of water. 'They'd get a rubber pipe and stick it down your throat and pour water down it. Boys have drowned like that, sir.'

'McClintock has had boys *drowned*? Barton, I need to be one hundred per cent sure you're telling me the truth.'

'I am!' Barton exclaimed. 'Honest, sir, I'm helping you, I'm being good!'

'You're being good if you tell me the truth,' Sam insisted.

'That McClintock, sir, he's one of them psychos!' Barton exclaimed, his eyes wide and imploring. 'He can do what he likes in there, and nobody knows! And if a lad dies, he just puts it down as something else – he hanged himself, he got into a fight, he got burned—'

'Burned!' put in Sam. 'A boy called Tulse died like that. McClintock's report said that a faulty gas cooker exploded in his face. Is that the boy you're referring to?'

'What's his name again?'

'Tulse. Craig Tulse.'

'Craig Tulse, yeah, that's him! That's the one! It was McClintock, but he covered it up, sir, he covered it up and he lied! He's a psycho, sir. He's a killer. You need to do him, sir, you need to throw the book at him, 'coz *he's* the one should be banged up, sir, not lads like me, but *him*!'

Gales of cruel, childish laugher suddenly flooded into the flat. Sam spun round and saw the open doorway crowded with young faces – gap-toothed, narrow-eyed, jug-eared. It seemed that every scallywag on the estate was crammed into that doorway.

'That's the bloke! He was bumming that other one! Pervy! Pervy!'

'I've warned you lot!' Sam bellowed, and he strode towards them. 'Clear off!'

'Oooh! 'Clear off!' Get her!'

'I mean it! I'm a police officer pursuing an important case.'

'You're a *prat*!'

'I won't tell you kids again. I have the authority to charge you all with obstructing an officer in the line of—'

Sam found himself mobbed, jeered, pelted with gobbets of saliva and pink balls of gum.

'I am a *police* officer! Doesn't that mean anything to you?'

Sam tried to push the kids away, shouting at them, but they crowded him, treating it all like a game.

'I said bugger off the lot of you! I bloody mean it!'

Sam lunged at the kids, and off they ran, shrieking and hollering and hurling terrible insults over their shoulders as they went. The last kid to go was the obligatory fat boy, who cumbersomely picked up his bike, heaved his meaty arse onto the saddle, and shot Sam a venomous look.

'You're a bloody great buggering black bloody bastard, you are,' the kid spat at him. 'I'll get my dad round here and he'll kick your arse back to bloody wog-land, you paddy Jew-boy poof.'

And off he pedalled, slowly and unsteadily, away along the balcony after his mates, his head full of all the confused crap the adults in his life had filled it with.

When Sam returned to the filthy little flat that doubled as a porn studio, he found it empty.

CHAPTER FOURTEEN

BEAUTY AWAKES

On his way back to CID, Sam found himself – almost without realising it – taking a detour via the Railway Arms. The place now glowed in his mind as a refuge, a sanctuary, a place of promise and of hope. It was here, after all, that he could speak plainly and on the level with the one person in this world who would actually understand, who could show him glimpses of 'behind the scenes', of the secret reality behind the daily façade of 1973.

Walking into the Arms, Sam was confronted by a sorry array of lunchtime drinkers, unwashed, dishevelled men with nothing better to do than install themselves at the bar and avoid either work or the wife for as long as possible. Cigarettes burned silently between yellow-stained fingers. Bloodshot eyes scanned the racing pages of crumpled newspapers. And there, at the helm as ever, was Nelson, topping up the float in the till with change he emptied out of cloth bags. He glanced over his shoulder at Sam and acknowledged him with a grin.

'Ah, mah ol' pal Sam!' His Jamaican accent was back with a vengeance. 'Feelin' better today, are we?'

'Feeling better, Nelson,' Sam replied. 'Thanks to you.'

'Oh no, Sam – I tink it's *dis* you should be tankin'!' And he thrust a freshly poured pint of Courage Pride across the bar to him.

'It's a bit early – but what the hell! Cheers, Nelson.'

Sam sipped, wiped away a froth moustache and glanced about. The other men along the bar seemed lost in their papers or lost in their alcoholic haze, but still he resented their presence. He wanted to speak to Nelson in private, just as he had the other night. In fact, he found that he was jealous of anyone but himself taking up Nelson's time and attention.

'Can we talk?' he asked.

'No law against it – less you know udda'wize, Mr Copper.'

'What I mean is, can we talk in private?'

'I gotta pub to run, Sam, wit' fellas drinkin' in it. You wanna talk, we gotta do it here.'

'It's important, Nelson.'

'So's keeping me regulars happy! If I let dere glasses dry out dey kick up a stink fit to bust, Sam!'

'Nelson, please. I've got a million questions. I need to know more about ...' He dropped his voice and leant across the bar. 'More about what we were talking about before. That fob watch I was telling you about – what's the deal with it? And what's the story behind McClintock? I'm right to go gunning for him, yes?'

'Hey, bro, I just pull de pints round here.'

'There's a connection, isn't there? The fob watch, McClintock, Clive Gould? There's a chain that runs right through them, yes?'

'You been on de sauce *before* walkin' in my pub, Sam? You sure sound like it.'

'That watch, it's got something to do with my flashback to McClintock's past, hasn't it? Why? What's so important about it?'

But Nelson just looked blankly at him. His manner was completely different from how it had been last time. There was no knowing light in his eyes, no sense of 'breaking cover' and revealing hidden truths. Before, when Sam had stumbled in here on the verge of some sort of nervous breakdown, Nelson had been an administering angel. Today, he was just Nelson, the bloke with the phoney West Indian accent who ran the local boozer, with nothing more to offer him than a pint of Courage.

But, then again, it should have come as no surprise.

'I'm not here to carry your burden for you,' Nelson had advised him. *'That's for you and you alone. It's the rules, Sam.'*

Perhaps he had already bent those rules to reveal to Sam as much he had. What Sam had learnt from him that night – about where he was, where he was going, about the meaning of his existence in this strange place – would simply have to be enough.

'Okay,' said Sam quietly. 'I understand.'

'Oh, you do? Well, that's good, Sam. That's real good.' And then, as Sam turned to go, Nelson called after him: 'Surely you ain't slopin' off widout finishin' ya pint?'

'I need to keep a clear head, Nelson,' Sam replied.

'So you *is* sober, mmm?'

'Very sober, Nelson. More sober than I've ever been.'

Just for a moment, there was a look in Nelson's eye, a fleeting hint that he was about to say something, something important, something revealing. But then the moment passed.

'Stay sober, Sam – but not for ever, not if you don't wanna see your ol' china out beggin' in da streets!'

And with that, Nelson's attention left Sam and focused on the demands of the other drinkers. He watched as Nelson presented a hunched man in a trilby with a vodka and tonic. The man dropped coins into Nelson's palm. The simple, ordinary transaction – the buying of a drink in a squalid, gone-to-seed boozer – seemed in that moment to be as solemn and as charged as a holy sacrament.

It means something, Sam thought. *Like everything else round here.*

Back at CID, Sam found Annie still at her desk, dealing with an even greater mountain of paperwork than before.

'Sam, I think you ought to have a look at this,' she said, presenting him with a sheaf of official documents. 'I've been looking into the background of this lad Donner. He's got quite a history, Sam, and it don't look good.'

'What do you mean it doesn't look good?'

She held up a file of papers: 'These are his psychiatric reports. He's been assessed *five times* by psychiatrists – three times by referral and twice through the police when he's been arrested.'

'What's wrong with him?'

'According to these reports, just about everything.' She opened the file and skimmed through it, reading out salient points. 'By the age of six, he's discovered the joys of torturing animals. By the age of nine, he's figured out that you can blind cats with bleach, and a year later he brings a bottle of Domestos into school with him to see if it works on kids.'

'That's the behaviour of a disturbed little boy,' said Sam. 'Did he receive the appropriate psychiatric care?'

'He get expelled and moved to another school,' said Annie. 'He's there for a year, and seems to be doing well. Works hard, starts getting good marks – and then out of the blue he assaults a female teacher. This time, he gets put into care, and it's the same pattern: he keeps his head down for a bit, applies himself to his school work, and then, wallop, he goes off the deep end.'

'What did he do next?'

'Aged thirteen, he tries to burn down one of his foster homes in the middle of the night – but not until he'd locked his foster family inside. He's threatened with youth custody, but his psychiatrist gets him off the hook. His mother takes him back, and he seems to have gone quiet again until he was sixteen.'

'What did he do at sixteen?'

'Broke into an eighty-five-year-old lady's house, threatened her with a carving knife, and attempted to rape her.'

'Attempted? What stopped him?'

'The old lady's son turned up, let himself in with his key. This time, Donner gets sent down. And so there he is, in Friar's Brook, banged up for sexual assault of a half-blind housebound pensioner. Sam, I can see him causing us a lot of problems if we rely too heavily on him as a key witness.'

'We don't have much choice,' said Sam. 'He's the only boy in that borstal willing to testify. We need him.'

'Then we need to tread very carefully,' said Annie. 'All

these psychiatric reports talk about the same pattern of behaviour: he's quiet, he's intelligent, he's keen to help people out – and then, without warning.' She snapped her fingers. 'More than one of these reports describes him as a 'Jekyll and Hyde' character.'

'What kind of home life did he have before going into care?' Sam asked.

'Not good. There's a whole list of run-ins his mother had with the police. I think she may have worked as a prostitute. She was certainly a chronic alcoholic.'

'What about his father? Was he on the scene?'

'Not much, certainly not after Donner got to school age. There were no brothers or sister, neither. Just Donner and his mum, cooped in a council flat surrounded by bottles and the occasional client.'

'And yet the lad's got a first-rate brain,' said Sam, shaking his head. 'It's a tragedy. All he had to do was get himself born in a different flat on that estate and he'd be all set for university right now. And instead he's banged up in borstal, and clearly disturbed.'

'I think he's more than disturbed,' Annie suggested. 'I think he's got a real problem, Sam. A *real* problem.'

'Who can blame him? And, whatever's going on in his head, Friar's Brook isn't the place to sort it out. If we can get him out of there, get him transferred somewhere secure but decent, perhaps we can salvage him. He wants to cooperate with us, Annie. He wants to do the right thing.'

213

'Sam, I'm not sure I agree with you. I studied psychology, remember, I've read papers like these psych reports before. Donner's pattern of behaviour, it's not a one-off.'

'What are you implying? That he's some sort of psychopath?'

'The telltale signs are there,' said Annie. 'It's almost textbook. And at least two of the psychiatrists who've assessed him have openly said so.'

'But not *all* of them have said so.'

'No. But I'm inclined to agree with those who have.'

'I don't know much about psych-evaluation, Annie, but I know enough to say that you can't diagnose some-body from a distance. You've never met Donner, you've never spoken to him; all you know is what's in those reports. How reliable are these shrinks who've seen him? Are they biased? Have they been brought in by prose-cuting counsel to show Donner in a bad light?'

Annie sighed. 'I don't know, Sam. All I know is what's written here. And, if even *half* of it's true, there's more than enough grounds to at least suspect Donner of having psychopathic tendencies. Hurting animals as a kid, then graduating on to hurting people. The emotional coldness, the lack of remorse, the inability to make friends or connect with people. The high intelligence – a lot of psychopaths are very, very smart, Sam.'

'And a lot of kids who've had a crap start in life are smart, too,' Sam argued. 'And you know what happens to them? They get written off. By everyone: school, social services, the police, the prison system.'

'Donner's not gone out of his way to make himself liked,' said Annie, glancing at the police record.

'Oh, come on, Annie, you're smarter than that!' Sam retorted. 'Think it through. The lad's never been shown a scrap of love or affection – not from his mum, his dad, not from anyone. A lonely little kid with no friends. He's grown up watching his mother out of her head on booze and turning tricks with clients. And he's cursed with enough natural intelligence to pay close attention to what's going on in front of him, to think about it, analyse it. What the hell does that do to a lonely five-year-old kid, Annie?'

'I appreciate what you're saying, Sam. And I'm not trying to evaluate Donner at second hand. But his behavioural traits, they're classic symptoms of psychopathy.'

'And they're the classic symptoms of an emotionally disturbed child crying out to be loved! Yes, it comes out in violence and cruelty, but you know as well as I do, Annie, that there's a lot of youngsters out there whose criminal behaviour is a great big cry for help.'

'You don't want to let the Guv hear you talking like that,' Annie whispered.

'Balls to the Guv!' Sam snapped. 'You think I'm being soft on crime? I'm being *humane*. It takes more strength to understand than to condemn, and you know that.'

'You've been pretty quick off the blocks to start condemning McClintock. In fact, you've been hell-bent on nailing him right from the start. It's like you're blinkered to any other possibility.'

Blinkered? Yes. But with good reason. Sam knew what sort of a man McClintock truly was, that behind that clipped accent and obsession with rules he was a coward and a Judas. And, what was more, only Sam understood the importance of bringing down the System he represented. He could not be distracted from his purpose by suggestions of Donner's guilt. Donner was a red herring; everything hinged around McClintock and his System.

But how was he going to convince Annie of that? She was quite right to see Donner as a key suspect. Under other circumstances, Sam would have too. But this case was different. Sam knew things. He had seen things. Nailing McClintock meant more than just convicting a killer – it meant saving Annie from an unimaginable horror that was bearing down on her and drawing closer every day.

I have to win her over, get her onside with me. I have to convince her that Donner is nothing but a distraction, that it's McClintock we're after.

'If I'm coming across as blinkered, Annie, then it's with good reason,' Sam said. 'Don't forget, I've talked to both McClintock and Donner face to face. McClintock's a bully and coward. But Donner – I tell you, Annie, he's smart, he's cool, but he's frightened. Terrified. The real boy is hiding behind that cold exterior. He's damaged. He's screwed up. And what's going on in Friar's Brook is only going to screw him up even worse. And that's not just true for Donner, but for all them other boys in there who've never had a shot at a decent life. It's a vicious cycle. It's a *system*, and all it does is trap them lads in endless crime and punishment. And I tell you here and now: *it's going to stop*.'

'Sam, I really think that—'

'It's going to *stop*, Annie. You and me, we're going to stop it. We're going to show *trust* to these lads, perhaps for the first time in their lives. We're going to treat them with respect. We're going to play fair by them. It'll be the nearest thing to *love* half of them will have ever experienced. And in return, they're going to help us nail House Master McClintock for God knows how many deaths and how much abuse that's gone on behind those walls. We're going to break that System, Annie. We're going to break it, and we're going to do some *good*.'

He knew that he was raising his voice, that he was in danger of grandstanding, but he couldn't help himself. Seeing Annie there, looking so serious and so beautiful, with her bobbed hair and clear, blue eyes, Sam's heart ached to think of anything hurting her. He could sense, deep within himself, some echo of her past – a lingering residue of the beatings, the violence, the intimidation, the abuse that she herself could not now recall but that

Sam had glimpsed. A shadow seemed to fall across Annie's face as he looked at her – the shadow of the Devil in the Dark, looming up just outside of the window or on the other side of the door, close now, *very* close, and drawing closer still with every tick of the clock.

Sam glanced across at Chris, who was gawping at him. Ray was smirking, chewing his gum.

'Yes,' said Sam, confrontationally. 'You're right, boys. I spoke like a man instead of like a little boy. So that gives you all *carte blanche* to rip the piss out of me. Go right ahead.'

There was a tense pause of a few seconds. And then Chris said, with a frown, "*Carte blanche*'?'

'It's a kind of runny cheese,' Ray clarified for him. 'I've had it. It's a bit Frenchie but it ain't bad on a Jacob's.'

'Like Brigitte Bardot.'

'Yeah, Chris. Summat like that.'

Sam threw up his hands. How could these idiots understand what was at stake here? How could their silly, infantile minds grasp that this wasn't just about the case, or Sam's career, or showing off to impress Annie? It wasn't even about life and death. It was more important than *any* of that!

It was then that he noticed Gene lurking in the doorway of his office, scowling. A cigarette was burning in his gob, wreathing him in a cloud of smoke, out of which his intense eyes glared.

'Here, Guv,' said Ray with a grin. 'You hear the way Tyler's been carrying on? Sounds like 'e's been promoted. He ain't a DI any more: he's an avenging bloody angel!'

Gene glowered across at Ray, narrowed his eyes, and with the fag still wedged in his gob he growled, 'We're *all* avenging angels, you dopey bloody dumpty. Ain't you figured that, yet?'

He meant it. The room fell silent. For a moment, Gene looked out imperiously from his blue-white cloud – an unreadable, implacable face haloed with mist – before removing the cigarette from between his lips, hawking up a mouthful of phlegm, and swallowing it.

'Tyler!' Gene declared. 'I've just been on to the hozzie. Sleeping Beauty's alarm clock has gone off and she is most definitely awake at last!'

Sam frowned. 'Guv?'

Leaning forward, as if impatiently addressing a deaf simpleton, Gene boomed, 'Derek Coren has woken up. So what say you and me take him some tea and toast, eh, Tyler?'

'You again!'

As Sam and Gene strode alone the corridor towards Derek Coren's room, they were confronted by the same nurse as last time. She clocked Gene at once – and he clocked her. The two of them squared up.

'We've got some grapes for Dingley Del,' grunted Gene. 'Well, I say *got* some grapes, what I mean is we *would* have some if we could've been arsed. But it's the thought what counts, eh? He's through there, is he?'

'Yes, but he's in no state to see you,' the nurse said, folding her arms.

'But we came all the way special.'

'Then you can go all the way back again, because I remember only too well how you behaved last time.'

'I've learnt the error of my ways since then.' Gene winked. 'I've turned over a new leaf. Ain't I, Tyler?'

Embarrassed, Sam rolled his eyes and willed the Guv to stop behaving like this.

'Five minutes, luv,' Gene said. 'I'll be good as gold.'

'No,' said the nurse.

'Five minutes, and then we'll be on our way.'

'I said no.'

'It's a murder enquiry, luv. It's a bit more important than turning down the sheets and slopping out the crap pans, you get what I'm saying?'

'My patient is also important.'

'Are you being obstructive?' Gene asked, lowering his voice.

'Are *you* being threatening?' the nurse asked back.

There was a moment of tense, silent atmospherics between them. Sam decided to intervene.

'Guv, lay off. I'm sorry about this, Sister. It's completely uncalled-for behaviour from my DCI. But please, *please* can you let us speak to Derek Coren, just for a few moments?'

The nurse thought about it, and then gave her definitive answer: 'No.'

'Much obliged,' boomed Gene, and swept past her, shoving her aside like a battleship ramming a yacht. He went barging into Coren's room.

Sam made to help her, but the nurse shoved him away.

'That's it!' she snapped. 'I'm going to get the porters together and have the pair of you chucked out!'

'I'm genuinely sorry about what's just happened, Sister, I really am, I—'

'Oh shut up you little creep!' she spat, and away she went, striding off in search of reinforcements.

Sam sighed, rubbed his forehead wearily, then followed after Gene.

He found the Guv looming over the bed in which a very pale, very fragile-looking Derek Coren was lying propped up against a mountain of crisp, white pillows. Various tubes were attached to his arm, being fed from drip bags suspended about his bed. A mountain of crude-looking machines beeped and blinked, monitoring him.

'I've just been renewing our acquaintance,' said Gene

over his shoulder as Sam entered. 'Last time me and Derek met, it was all a bit rushed.'

'It's going to be rushed again, Guv. That nurse is getting the porters together to have us chucked out.'

'Oh my God, that frightens me so much I've just done a bit of poop in my drawers,' said Gene, casually lighting up a fag and dropping the spent match onto Derek's starched hospital bed sheets. 'I'll keep this succinct, then, Derek. Your brother Andy's brown bread, old son. Squashed. Flattened. You got the wrong lorry. He were on the one that rolled in half an hour previous. Bet you're gutted. Andy certainly was.'

Derek looked up at Gene with a hard, pinched expression. There were no tears.

'I'm sorry about what happened to your brother,' Sam put in. 'He died, Derek. He didn't make it out of the crusher.'

'What an obituary!' piped up Gene. 'Imagine knowing *that's* what they'd say about you after you snuffed it: 'He didn't make it out the crusher.' Personally, I'm hoping for something more like, 'Gene Hunt passed away, aged 103, humping two birds at the same time while a third one was getting her breath back.''

Derek sat against his pillows, clenching his jaw, staring daggers at Gene. But still there were no tears.

Expecting the door to fly open at any moment and a horde of furious porters to come barging in, fists flying,

Sam tried to get what information he could out of Derek as quickly as possible. It went against the grain to operate like this – *Hi Derek, glad you're out of the coma, your brother's dead, now answer our questions* – but he had no option. Gene, as ever, had pointlessly raised the emotional temperature with his oafish behaviour. If Derek had anything important to tell them, Sam had to get it out of him right *now*.

'We know about the code you used,' said Sam. 'Pinpricks on individual letters, spelling out a secret message. Very clever. Whose idea was it?'

Derek looked sullenly at him for a few moments, then seemed to slump. What was the point in holding out? His brother was dead, there was nothing left to lose.

'It was my idea,' he said at last. 'It's how we managed to work out ways of getting Andy out of bird. We could talk to each other, right under the screws' noses, and nobody ever spotted it.'

'Until now,' said Sam.

Without enthusiasm, Derek fixed him with a look and said, 'Well done, copper.'

'I wasn't referring to me. Somebody else spotted it. They knew Andy was planning to escape, and how. So they changed the work detail. They ensured that if Andy *did* get out of Friar's Brook, it would be on the back of the wrong lorry.'

Derek's expression changed. He raised his head, looked very intently at Sam, and said, 'McClintock ...!'

Yes! thought Sam. *It's falling into place! I'm right about McClintock – and I'm going to get the evidence together to bury him for ever!*

'What makes you think it was House Master McClintock?' Sam asked, controlling his voice to keep it impassive. 'Why not one of the other warders? Did Andy mention McClintock to you specifically?'

'It was McClintock,' muttered Derek, almost to himself. He was starting to breathe hard through his nose, like a bull preparing to charge. 'That bastard McClintock, he was making Andy's life hell in there. He wanted to wear him down, break him, just because Andy wouldn't be intimidated by that piece of shit.'

'Piece of *kilt-wearing, haggis-scoffing* shit,' Gene corrected him.

At last, tears began to well in Derek's eyes. He gritted his teeth, threw back his starched sheets and attempted to clamber out of the bed.

'I'll get that bastard!'

Sam grabbed the boy's shoulders and forced him back against the pillows. 'Derek! No! You're staying put, and there's nothing you could do anyway!'

'I'll get that bastard! I'll get that murdering bastard!'

Still grappling with him, Sam spoke very clearly and

224

forcibly into Derek's face. 'No you won't! But *we* will! Now get back in that bed and—'

But Derek's grief and rage had overwhelmed him. He fought against Sam, struggling to get free and get out of the bed, heedless of the drips in his arms and the machines he was rigged up to.

'Derek, for God's sake!' Sam implored him. 'Stay in the bed! You're going to pull your drips out!'

'I'll get that murdering bastard! I'll get him!'

'Derek! Stay still!'

'I'll *get* that *murdering* ba—'

Gene's fist flashed in like a thunderbolt. It struck Derek between the eyes. Derek fell back against the pillows, silent and motionless, his jaw hanging open, his tongue drooping out.

'He appears to have nodded off again,' opined Gene.

Sam piled Derek's limbs back into the bed and covered them with the sheets. Then he turned and glowered at Gene. 'Guv, just think what you have done.'

'I administered a sedative.' Gene shrugged.

'You have assaulted a grieving man who has just emerged from a coma!'

'He was going daft and noisy!' Gene protested. 'Didn't want him upsetting the other malingerers round here. Don't get your knickers in a twist, Sammy boy, he's snug as a bug now.'

The door flew open. Two middle-aged, potbellied men

and a gangly adolescent in specs, all dressed in porters' uniforms, bundled messily into the room.

'That's them!' cried the nurse from behind them. 'Now – chuck 'em out!'

Gene exhaled a plume of smoke, fixed the porters with a look, and said, 'Your move, lads. In your own time.'

There was a significant pause.

CHAPTER FIFTEEN

DECISIONS, DECISIONS

'Porters? I shit 'em!'

Gene gunned the engine of the Cortina as he powered it through the grey streets of Manchester.

'You behaved disgracefully back there, Guv,' sulked Sam. 'Sometimes, I'm genuinely ashamed to be seen in public with you.'

'Yeah, yeah. But that lanky one with the specs! I thought he were about to literally shit 'imself!'

'Those porters showed themselves to be real men, Gene, not like you!'

'*Real* men? Two roly-polies and a four-eyed beanpole?'

'Yes, Guv. Because they stood up to you and did the right thing. They were scared, but that didn't stop 'em.

They proved themselves, Guv, while all you do was act like a bully.'

'Oh put a sock in it, Deidre, you're making my lug'oles ache.' Gene flung the wheel and stamped on the gas.

'Still, it weren't a *completely* wasted trip,' said Sam. 'Derek Coren was pretty convinced that McClintock orchestrated his brother's death on purpose.'

'Mmm. But that don't count as evidence. It's conjecture.'

'Yes, but it does confirm what we already suspect.'

'What *you* suspect!' Gene corrected him. 'The Gene jury is still well and truly out on this one. I mean, I'm not the sort of a fella to balk at nicking a jock, but then again it goes against the grain to take the word of a bunch of pint-sized louts and lags. It's a difficult one, Tyler. I've got to weigh up my next move very carefully.'

They drove in silence for a few moments. And then, quite suddenly, Gene grinned. 'That fat one with the 'tache, I thought he were gonna have a flamin' coronary!'

Arriving back in CID, Sam and Gene were confronted by a mountain of photocopy paper.

'Bobby Moore on a bike, what's all *that*?' Gene demanded.

'Home Office reports,' said Annie, popping up from

behind it. 'Copies of everything that exists on file about the lads in that borstal.'

'You've been industrious!' said Sam.

'Well, I somehow managed to persuade the boys to help me, Boss,' she replied. She indicated Chris and Ray, who were at the Xerox machine, churning out copies from the original HO files.

'It's grand this!' Chris beamed. 'Just stick your thingy on the glass, close the lid, press the button, and fire photon torpedoes!'

He obligingly pressed the button and made laser-beam noises as the copier swept its light back and forth.

'I got to admit, Guv,' added Ray, 'it's sort of therapeutic.'

' 'Therapeutic'?' sneered Gene, appalled. 'I've just been single-handedly intimidating three grown men plus a gobby nurse, and I come back here and find you're doing *bird work*! You're meant to be *blokes*, not secretaries! Now get your arses away from that ruddy robot.'

Looking chastised, Chris and Ray carried over their copies and threw them on the pile.

'Donner was working in the kitchens with a lad called Tulse,' said Sam. 'Tulse got burned. What does the official report say?'

'Ah, I know where that one is,' piped up Chris, rummaging. 'Here we go! Craig Tulse. Coroner's report. Blah, blah, blah, load of old crap in Latin or summat

– here it is. Cause of death: gas explosion from a faulty stove resulting in severe burns to the face, neck and chest.'

'A faulty gas stove,' said Sam. 'Faulty on purpose, I reckon. If those ovens hadn't been shipped out and conveniently destroyed, we'd be able to check them for ourselves. We'd find signs of tampering. *McClintock's* tampering.'

'Conjecture, boss,' said Annie. 'And, even if there *was* sabotage, who's to say it was McClintock?'

'He was a bit of one, this Tulse,' said Ray, glancing through the report. 'Insubordinate. Answering back. Continually being reprimanded. A right gobshite, by the looks of it.'

'And he paid the price,' said Sam. 'Just like Tunning. What does it say about him?'

Ray dug through the paperwork for a moment, then read out, 'Barry Michael Tunning. Hard man. In for GBH. Whole list of disciplinaries while at Friar's Brook. Assaulting a warder, assaulting *another* warder, threatening the house master—'

'How did he die?' asked Gene.

Ray flipped some pages: 'Um, committed suicide in his cell during the night. He were found by the screws next morning, hanging from the end of his bunk bed.'

'Not much of a drop,' said Annie.

'Don't need no drop,' explained Ray, 'not if you're serious about topping yourself. Just get something round your neck, tie it off, and let your body weight do the rest. Slow, bloody painful, but it works.'

'How come you know so much about hangin' yourself?' asked Chris.

Ray shrugged.

'It happens in prisons all over,' said Gene. 'It's the way it's done. Horrible, but lethally effective. Like cider, or Ex-Lax.'

'The boys in Friar's Brook share cells,' said Sam. 'Who was Tunning sharing with the night he died?'

Ray thumbed through a copy of the relevant Home Office report. 'Um, a lad called ... Donner.'

Sam and Annie exchanged looks. Gene drew thoughtfully on his cigarette.

'The way I see it, there's three things might have happened,' said Annie. 'Number one: it's like it says in the report. Tunning hanged himself, and for whatever reason Donner didn't say anything until the cell was unlocked in the morning. Maybe he was asleep. Whatever. Possibility number two: Tunning *didn't* kill himself. The warders did. They either came into the cell and hanged him, or else Tunning died some other way – maybe undergoing one of McClintock's punishment sessions – and it was made to look like suicide to cover it up.'

'And number three?' growled Gene.

'Possibility number three is that it was one of the inmates

who killed Tunning,' said Annie. 'Which in turn would point the finger at his cellmate that night – Donner.'

Sam shook his head. 'I'm not buying that. My gut instinct says it was a McClintock cover-up.'

'And *my* gut instinct says it's time to drop a ton and half down the khazi while reading the paper, but that don't make my arse a copper,' opined Gene. 'Give me something better than a rumble in your belly, Tyler.'

'McClintock runs that place with a fist of iron,' said Sam. 'You've seen that for yourself, Guv. He's obsessed with discipline, order, his precious 'System'. He's a control freak. And it's not just the inmates he likes to control, it's everything – you, me, us, the law. He thinks he can punish inmates until they die, then cover it up and just keep on going.'

'Facts, Tyler!' Gene boomed at him. 'No more flowery speeches. Facts!'

'Every boy who died in that borstal was at odds with McClintock. Tulse was a born rebel. Tunning was a thug who refused to be beaten. Coren was the cheeky little Houdini determined to slip away. All three threatened to make McClintock look weak – and all three died.'

'All three were also connected directly to Donner,' Annie said. 'Tulse worked with him in the kitchen. Tunning shared a cell with him. Coren came to him to write that letter to his brother Derek.' She glanced at

Sam and said, 'I'm sorry, Boss, I've got to say it. I don't think it's McClintock we should be after.'

'Donner's not a big lad,' Sam said. 'Tunning was a bloody gorilla, in for GBH. Are you saying, Annie, that Donner somehow overpowered him at night after lock-up, and forcibly hanged him? Do you really believe he's physically capable of doing that?'

'If he attacked Tunning while he was asleep, then yes, Boss, I do,' Annie replied. 'Tunning would be half strangled by the time he woke up and realized what was happening – if he ever got a *chance* to wake up.'

'And what about Coren's work detail being changed at the last minute? How could Donner arrange that?'

'He couldn't,' said Annie.

'Well then!'

'But what if the work detail *wasn't* changed, boss?'

Sam gave her a look. 'We know it was changed. McClintock changed it.'

'And how do we know that? From McClintock himself? From one of the other warders? From the prison governor?'

Sam sighed. 'No. From Donner.'

'No, Boss, it weren't even from him!' Annie exclaimed. 'You're just assuming that! What if Donner wrote that letter for Coren, but *deliberately put the wrong information in it*? He's smart enough, he had the opportunity. It's perfectly possible. You got to think more clearly, Sam!' And then, after a heavily charged pause, she added, 'I mean Boss.'

Whistles and intakes of breath from Chris and Ray.

Gene scowled through his haze of cigarette smoke. 'Women's libbers in today, I see.'

Annie got control of herself and said with measured calm, 'I'm sorry I spoke like that, Boss. It's just—'

'It's okay, Annie, I understand,' said Sam, ignoring the kissy-kissy noises Ray was making. He turned to Gene. 'Guv, Annie went through Donner's psychiatric reports. She reckons he's a psychopath. She reckons he's the one killing inmates at Friar's Brook.'

'Motive?' growled Gene.

'No motive, Guv,' said Annie. 'He don't need a motive. He does it because he can. It makes him feel good. Makes him feel big.'

'But I don't agree with that assessment,' Sam countered. 'Donner's a badly disturbed kid, but so would any of us be growing up with the sort of life he's had. And let's not forget Barton, the lad who tipped us off about McClintock in the first place. He told me horror stories about what goes on in that place.'

'Ex-cons *always* tell horror stories,' suggested Ray.

'Electrocutions!' Sam exclaimed. 'Water forced down boys' throats! Some of them have *drowned*!'

'And this toerag Barton is the one what told you all this?' said Ray. 'And you believed it?'

'Barton accused McClintock of letting boys die in there and then covering it up,' Sam insisted. 'He named

McClintock. He *named* him, Guv. We *have* to act on this information. It's all stacking up – we got Donner, we got Barton—'

'All we got are the tall stories of a couple of borstal slags, that's what we've got,' interjected Ray.

'And who says they're just stories, Ray?' Sam asked.

'Lags always lie. It's a law of nature. And the biggest porkies they tell are about how badly they been treated. Every ex-con's got more sob stories than Quentin Crisp's had wangers up his flue.'

Chris winced. 'Steady on, Ray, I'm still digesting me sausage and beans.'

'I'm just saying, lads like Barton and Donner, you don't want to listen to a word they say.'

'It's that attitude that lets bastards like McClintock get away with murder,' Sam declared. 'I'm not saying these boys are angels, but if they're victims of human-rights abuses then we have a duty to take what they're telling us very seriously.'

'For the record, Guv, I think Donner's the one we need to be focusing on,' Annie chipped in. 'I don't think it's McClintock at all.'

'Choices, choices,' mused Gene. He peered across at Chris. 'What do *you* think, Chrissy-wissy?'

'I think it's disgusting, obviously,' said Chris. 'Wangers up the flue? I can't see what it's all about.'

Gene rolled his eyes. 'Ray? Your instincts are to collar the uptight Jock, I take it, even if it's just for the fun of it?'

Ray chewed his gum for a moment, then shrugged. 'Why not haul him in *and* the criminal nipper?'

'You mean question both McClintock and Donner?'

'Why not, Guv? Give 'em both the squeeze, see what comes up. Heads you win, tails you win an' all.'

Gene thought this through, then nodded.

'Makes sense,' he declared. 'And, what's more, it means that if McClintock *does* turn out to be in the clear, I'll have had the pleasure of giving him a right goin' over anyway.'

'A case of 'avin' your haggis *and* eating it,' Ray suggested.

'Exacta-flamin'-mundo!' Gene declared, slapping his chest heartily with both hands. 'Ray, Chris, Tyler – in the motor. Let's get rolling over to Friar's Brook.'

Sam saw Annie swallow hard, take a breath, and boldly say, 'I think I should come too, Guv.'

Gene, Chris and Ray all turned slowly and looked at her.

'I second that,' said Sam, backing her up.

'Sam sticks up for Bristols, what a surprise,' growled Gene. 'But the answer is no. A lock-up ain't no place for a dopey bird. Too much of a liability.'

'Seriously, Guv, I think I could be of real use to you,' Annie insisted.

Sceptically, Gene looked her over.

'Okay, Inspector Jugs, give me one good reason.'

'My background in psychology, Guv. I think I'd be – I *know* I'd be – the right person to question Donner face to face. And, what's more, I think he might speak more openly to a woman.'

'Or he might just get a stiffy and become distracted,' Gene intoned.

'Which might be exactly the best way to forge a connection with him,' Annie said. Gene thought about this, but before he could say anything Annie added, 'Besides, Guv, you're more interested in interrogating McClintock. You can have your fun with him while me and DI Tyler question the boy.'

Gene mused, nodded, shrugged. As he turned away, jangling his car keys, he said, 'For the record, I don't think it's right, a bird coming into an all-boy borstal. But, if she really must, she's your responsibility, Tyler. I'll leave her for you to look after. Me – I've got a kilt-wearing, bagpipe-sucking, sporran-shagging, caber-tossing tosser to break into pieces. C'mon, lads, let's take the high road.'

And with that he swept out, Chris and Ray striding along behind him.

Annie let out a shaky breath, then glanced at Sam. She was trying to suppress a grin. Sam patted her arm.

'That was a bold move,' he said. 'Well done.'

She beamed a smile at him, and then frowned. 'I'm sorry I went against you just now, Sam.'

'Don't apologize. You're a police officer, it's your duty to speak up.'

'I'm really convinced it's Donner we should be concentrating on. I don't see why you're so hung up on going after McClintock.'

Sam opened his mouth to tell her, but held back. How could he explain?

'I've got my reasons,' he said.

Annie looked at him for a moment, then said, 'Well, then. Let's get out to Friar's Brook and find out once and for all what's going on there.'

CHAPTER SIXTEEN

FEE FIE FO FUM

At the borstal gates, Gene thrust his ID badge into the face of the guard on duty.

'Open flaming sesame!'

As the gates opened, the Cortina swept in. Just behind it, at the wheel of a midnight-blue Alfa Romeo with Annie beside him, Sam hit the gas to keep up. The cars drew up at the main block and everybody piled out. Gene led the way, marching forward resolutely, with Chris and Ray a step or two behind. Sam and Annie followed along, watching as the Guv swept his way past any warder who dared to challenge him.

In the corridor that led to Mr Fellowes's office, they saw one of the boys mopping the floor, the brown patch of cloth – the 'Stain' – clearly visible on the breast of his denim dungarees. The boy glanced at them as they reached Mr Fellowes's office door, observing them like a wary, watchful animal.

'We'd better knock,' said Gene, and flung the door open with a resounding crash.

Fellowes jumped up from behind his desk, spilling tea over the paperwork he was reading. Monteverdi played serenely from the radio.

'Sweet Lord!' Fellowes cried, putting a hand to his chest as if he could forcibly still his suddenly pounding heart. His eyes widened as he recognized Gene's face. 'You again!'

'Me again! And this time I've brought the Party 7!'

Chris, Ray, Annie and Sam crowded in behind him.

Gene added, 'Not exactly Pan's People, I'll grant you, but we all have to make do.'

Desperately mopping up tea from ruined papers, Fellowes blathered, 'You're perfectly at liberty to ring ahead and make a proper appointment to see me! You don't have to keep barging in here like you're raiding a gin joint!'

'Well that's where you're wrong, porky,' said Gene, swaggering arrogantly over to Fellowes's desk. He was enjoying himself. 'Because, if I was to let you know my moves before I made them, I'd lose the element of surprise. And, in this game, the element of surprise is the maker and the breaker!'

'Detective Chief Inspector, we're all on the same side.'

240

'Ah,' said Gene, raising a wise finger. 'That's what we're here to find out. Raymond!'

'Yes, Guv.'

'Watch him like a hawk. Don't let him touch anything, move anything, *do* anything. He so much as sips that tea, cuff him! If there's evidence in this room – reports, paperwork, spunky tissues hidden in the drawers – I don't want him or no one else tampering with it. This place is on lock-down until I say otherwise. Christopher!'

'Yes, Guv?'

'Shut off that bleedin' racket.'

'Righto, Guv!'

Chris killed the radio. Monteverdi broke off in mid-cadence.

Fellowes stood behind his desk, staring aghast at the sudden invasion. He was speechless.

Sam decided to step in before things got out of hand.

'Mr Fellowes, it's really Mr McClintock my DCI needs to question,' he said. 'And, while he's doing that, WDC Cartwright here and myself need to speak to Donner.'

'You heard him,' added Gene. 'Make it 'appen.'

'I most certainly will *not*!' retorted Fellowes, his soft jowls wobbling in indignation.

'Look out, lads, Mr Toad's getting shirty,' said Gene.

'I am the governor of this facility and I will be treated with the due respect!'

'And I'm King Kong and I'm ten feet long and I gotta

big six-gun and everybody is scared!' Gene snapped back. And, when Fellowes looked blankly at him, he clarified: 'The Kinks, you opera-loving twat.'

'It wasn't opera, you oaf,' Fellowes came back at him, his fat cheeks flushed. 'It was a madrigal.'

Gene leant across the desk and glared into Fellowes's eyeballs as if he were aggressively trying to hypnotize him. 'Now listen up, butterball. I'm conducting a multiple-murder investigation, and it's getting on for teatime and my tummy is a'rumblin'. I do *not* want to be standing here arguing the toss when I could be tucking into my Captain Birdseyes and I do *not* want some jumped-up headmaster who play-acts at being a proper prison guv'nor giving me backchat worse than some bird. Now, I know full well I'm making you anxious – I'll bet right this minute you're squirting your Y-fronts with a gallon of frit piddle – so let's not pretend any more you've got the balls to stand up to me.' Gene leant closer, his eyes flashing with a barely contained fire. 'Start complying. Summon that jock house master or I'll nick you for obstruction and bang you up with Big Bill Bum Bandit in Cell Number 2. You getting what I'm saying?'

Fellowes looked like a small, harmless animal driven into a corner.

Gene barked at him. 'McClintock! Now!'

'I-I'll see if he's in his office,' he stammered, reaching shakily for the phone.

'For he's a jolly good Fellowes!' beamed Gene, watching him nervously dial and wait for a reply.

Fellowes spoke into the phone. 'Mr McClintock, would you be so kind as to come to my office straightaway? ... CID is here again, and they want to speak to you ... Well, I *could* ask them to come back tomorrow' – he glanced over at Gene, who was slowly and with great deliberation shaking his head – 'but on second thoughts, Mr McClintock, I think right now is the perfect time to clear up this matter ... Thank you, Mr McClintock.'

He hung up and gave Gene a pathetic look that seemed to say, *See? I did what you wanted. Now please don't hurt me.*

'Right – we'll wait,' said Gene.

He thrust his hands into his pockets and began pacing innocently about. The clock on the wall ticked. The atmosphere became tight and awkward.

'Guv?' piped up Chris.

'Yes, young Christopher?'

'What's a manderinal?'

'Madrigal,' sighed Fellowes.

'It's one of them porcelain troughs you piss in at the boozer,' said Ray.

Fellowes looked at him like a man who has just seen his prize petunias trampled.

'It's a type of nancy-boy music,' Gene explained. 'It's for ponces. Tyler's probably got a soft spot for it. And, by a strange acoustical anomaly, it's actually even more boring than it sounds.'

'*O tempora! O mores!*' muttered Fellowes, closing his eyes.

From outside came the sound of clipped, prim footsteps.

Gene's ears pricked up. 'Fee fie fo fum, I smell the blood of an uptight highland sausage-muncher who's about to get his sporran squeezed.'

Mr McClintock appeared in the doorway, his uniform immaculate, his peaked cap tucked under his arm military-style. He paused, perusing the scene in Mr Fellowes's office, turning his tight, narrow face from Sam to Annie, Annie to Chris, Chris to Ray, and from Ray at last to Gene Hunt himself.

'I see,' said McClintock coolly. 'The impertinent detectives from CID have returned – and this time in force.'

Sam found his attention drawn to that gold watch chain glittering at McClintock's waist. He felt an inexplicable urge to grab it, rip that fob watch from his pocket, and smash it on the floor. He also felt the urge to smash McClintock's self-satisfied face.

House Master McClintock neatly settled his cap back onto his head, straightened it with his scarred hands, and stepped into the room. Gene at once squared up to him, but Sam decided to get in quick before the Guv's mouth opened fire once again.

'You've had your time, Mr McClintock,' he said. 'You've run this borstal your way long enough. But now it's over. We're here to break your precious System, Mr McClintock. And we're here to break *you*.'

'Are you indeed?' said McClintock, primly arching an eyebrow. 'Let me guess. You're going to attempt to make the recent unfortunate deaths of inmates appear to be foul play, with *me* as the foul player, mmm?'

Sam nodded, slowly and deliberately. 'And, what's more, I received first-hand testimony of severe malpractice being carried on within these walls. Not just the beatings I've seen for myself, not just the totally unacceptable punishment block with its so-called 'Black Hole'. I'm talking about *torture*, Mr McClintock. I'm talking about electrocutions.'

'Electrocutions?' repeated McClintock, incredulous. 'And *where*, pray, did you garner your evidence, young Detective Inspector? Or may I be permitted to make a guess again? You've been speaking to the boys.'

'I have,' said Sam firmly. 'Not the current inmates, of course, because under your regime they're too scared.'

'Ah,' said McClintock, 'then it's not even *fresh* tittle-tattle you've been gathering but stale old nonsense from ex-cons. And what else did you hear, mmm? Have I been murdering the boys and cooking their flesh for my dinner? Do I drink their blood, and turn into a bat every full moon?'

'A wolf,' Chris corrected him severely. 'It's a *wolf* every full moon. Get your story straight, McClintock.'

'Is that what you're going to charge me with?' McClintock asked. 'Lycanthropy?'

Ray let out a breath, taken aback and somewhat angered by use of such a long and baffling word. He looked to Gene for support.

'It's all right, Ray,' Gene comforted him. 'He's not messing with *my* head. Now listen up, McClintock. It's nothing personal – well, actually, it is, but that's just a happy coincidence. Point is, Jimmy, there's a case building against you. The death of Craig Tulse, the death of Barry Tunning, the death of Thingy Coren.'

'Andrew,' Sam prompted him.

'Andrew, aye,' said Gene. 'Three deaths. All on *your* watch, with *your* fingerprints all over 'em.'

'Conjecture,' declared McClintock.

'That remains to be seen. And that's why we're here, me and my boys.' He indicated Chris and Ray beside him. 'We're going to have serious words with you. We're going to see what's what and get to the bottom of all this. As for Bootsy and Snudge over there' – he jabbed a thumb towards Sam and Annie – '-they're off to play KerPlunk with that lad Donner and see what *he's* got to say.'

'I see,' said McClintock. 'You really are determined to build a case against me, aren't you?'

'You bet we are!' Sam suddenly put in, stepping

forward and confronting McClintock up close. 'You've had the run of this place for too long. But that's over now. The boys in this borstal might not be angels, but that doesn't give you the right to treat them like scum. They're human beings! Damn it, McClintock, they're just kids! You have a duty of care to these boys!'

'And I exercise that duty!' McClintock snapped back. 'I teach them right from wrong!'

'You teach them nothing!' Sam shouted back. 'You reinforce the cycle of violence and revenge that these poor bastards have been born into! And when they won't be battered and cowed into submission, when they stand up and refuse to be destroyed by your precious System, you'll stop at nothing – *nothing* – to prove your so-called authority. Young men have died because of you! But not any more. We're going to shine a bloody great spotlight on you and this place, McClintock. And we're going to break your filthy, damned System into pieces!'

Was it House Master McClintock he was confronting, or was it Fate itself? In his mind, Sam was thinking as much about Annie, McClintock's betrayal of her father and about the Devil in the Dark as he was about Coren and Tunning and the others. What he was pitting himself against was something far greater, and far more dangerous, than a corrupt and sadistic borstal House Master and his murderous regime.

'You're finished!' Sam spat, jabbing his finger into

McClintock's chest. 'You're going down for what you've done here. Your System's history and so are you.' And then he whispered harshly, right into his face, 'I know things about you. Your past. *What you did.*'

Furiously, Sam turned on his heels and marched towards the door.

'Annie, let's find Donner,' he ordered, and Annie fell into step behind him. Over his shoulder, he declared, 'Break him, Guv, if that's what it takes. The bastard deserves it.'

He strode out into the corridor, and at once walked straight into the boy with the mop. The boy stumbled back from where he'd been eavesdropping, stepping into his bucket and toppling it. Water gushed all over the floor, and the boy splashed through it as he fled, chucking aside his mop and belting away along the corridor.

Sam marched resolutely ahead, Annie hurrying along after him.

'Sam, calm down, keep a clear head.'

'My head's perfectly clear, Annie. Never been clearer.'

'You're sounding like the Guv! Get a grip of yourself.'

'That boy there!' Sam declared, pointing at the lad running away and disappearing round a corner. 'You see what he had on his uniform? A brown patch of cloth. A 'Stain' to mark him out as corrupted, as less than human. McClintock's orders. It's like bloody Auschwitz in this place! But not any more. Not any more!'

'Sam!' Annie reached out and caught his arm, stopping him. 'Just stop and think. Don't go swaggering about like the Guv. That's not the way and you know it. You're *Sam* – so act like Sam.'

He looked at her, at her serious, round face, her searching eyes, her brown, bobbed hair that danced lightly above her shoulders as she walked. He wanted to shield her from everything, from every dark and malignant thing out there that would do her harm. He wanted to sacrifice himself, if that's what it took, so that the terrible Fate decreed for her was averted and her future became her own once more.

Break the System, he thought. *Break the System, break Fate, and break that damned Devil in the Dark. I can do it. I* know *I can do it.*

Behind her, stepping out of Mr Fellowes's office doorway, appeared the Test Card Girl, clutching her bandaged dolly and fixing Sam with a look of infinite sadness, infinite despair.

I have *to do it!* he told himself. *I don't have a choice. The stakes are too high. They're way too high.*

'Come on,' he said, taking Annie's hand and marching with her along the corridor. 'Let's find Donner and get this case wrapped up.'

When he glanced back, the Test Card Girl was gone.

'Where do you think he'll be?' asked Annie as she strode with Sam down the long, bleach-stinking corridors.

'There can't be too many places,' said Sam. 'Donner tends to work in the kitchens. But I think there are dormitories just along here somewhere. We could try there first.'

As they reached one of the dorms, a boy in dungarees rushed out, glanced at them, and then raced off again.

'That was the lad who was mopping the floor,' Annie whispered. 'You think he's spreading the word about what he's overheard?'

'I bet the rumour mill's in full swing.' Sam nodded. 'That could work to our advantage. If the boys know McClintock's under arrest, they might be more willing to cooperate.'

Together, they approached the dorm. It was a bleak room of whitewashed brick, lined with neat, grey beds. A dozen or so boys, all dressed in regulation prison overalls and bearing their brown 'Stain', were whispering intensely among themselves, but at once fell silent. They turned and stared silently, but not at Sam. All eyes were on Annie. The atmosphere became charged with a menacing sexual tension.

Sam held up his ID badge. 'My name's DI Tyler. Don't worry, lads, we're on your side, believe it or not.' He was answered with a tense silence. 'We're looking for Donner. Anyone know where he is?'

Looking around, Sam spotted a tall, red-haired boy with powerful shoulders amongst the other lads. His face was familiar. It took a moment, but then the memory came back to him: when he and Gene had first come to Friar's Brook, this lad had been one of those they'd seen being punished out in the yard.

'Priest,' Sam muttered, recalling the boy's name.

The boy's face tightened suspiciously. He, too, clearly remembered Sam striding up and refusing to let the warder carry on beating him. Did the memory rankle with him, that he had been seen in such a helpless and victimized state? Did it hurt the lad's macho pride? And now, to be recognized and named by a copper in front of his fellow inmates, did that tar him in their eyes, make him suspect? He certainly seemed to be looking at Sam with an expression that was as resentful as it was suspicious.

A uniformed warder suddenly loomed into the open dormitory doorway.

'What's going on here?' he demanded. He eyed Annie insolently.

Annie stood her ground and fixed the warder with a look. 'My name's WDC Cartwright. Me and DI Tyler want to speak to Donner.'

'Oh, really, love?'

Sam's temper flared within him. But Annie kept control of herself.

'Donner,' she repeated. 'Where is he?'

The warder smirked, and looked across at Sam. 'Do

you speak an' all, or do you let your crumpet do all the talking?'

Sam was ready to give the smug little bastard a straightener, right there in front of the boys. But, before he could do anything, Annie took a step closer to the warder, planting herself aggressively in front of him, speaking clearly and forcibly.

'I am a police officer conducting a serious investigation. I have asked you a question, *sir*. If you choose not to answer that question I will arrest you, *sir*, I will arrest you for obstruction, and I will have you hauled out of here in handcuffs and I don't mean in a fun and kinky way, *sir*, and by the time my DCI has had words with you in your cell down the station you will be regretting, *sir*, you will be deeply regretting your refusal to cooperate, I assure you of that, *sir*, I most sincerely assure you of that. So if you don't want your balls busted back down the station I advise you answer my question when I ask. *Where is Donner?*'

The warder stared at her for a moment, open-mouthed. She wasn't bluffing. He *knew* she wasn't bluffing. And she knew that he knew.

'You'd better follow me,' he muttered, and led the way.

Annie strode confidently after him, her head high, her jaw firm. She had clearly watched the Guv in action. She had watched, and learnt. Sometimes, and in moderation, Gene's methods had their uses.

Sam hesitated, shooting a glance back at the boys in the dorm. Their expressions were hard to read. They had heard the rumour, that McClintock was being given a going-over by CID, and now they had seen a copper – a *female* copper – fronting out one of the screws. Did they sense the end of the oppressive regime here at Friar's Brook? Did they see the System starting to crumble?

If they did, their faces betrayed nothing of their emotions. They had learnt too well to keep their feelings well hidden.

Sam looked once more at Priest, but the boy's face was as unreadable as a carved Easter Island head.

Without a word, Sam turned away and strode from the dorm.

CHAPTER SEVENTEEN

DONNER SPEAKS

Donner was at his usual place, in the kitchens peeling spuds. He looked up at Sam without surprise or interest, his face as bland and unreadable as before. He seemed barely even to register Annie at all.

'We need to speak to you,' said Sam.

Donner meekly set down his peeling knife, wiped his hands on a dishcloth, and let them lead him down one of the bleached and polished corridors.

'You can speak in there,' said the warder, opening a door onto a small room containing nothing but rows of folded-up plastic chairs.

'Thank you,' said Sam curtly. 'Now leave us.' And, when the warder hesitated, Sam added severely, 'I said leave us. This is a CID matter.'

Unsettled, sensing that something was up, the warder headed back to the kitchens. Donner watched this whole exchange with unblinking eyes, taking it all in, but revealing nothing in his expression.

'Here,' said Sam, unfolding a chair for Donner. 'It's all right, it's not a trap.'

Everybody sat down – Sam and Annie on one side, Donner on the other. The lad gazed blankly at them with pale eyes.

Sam said, 'I want to start by saying that if you cooperate with us, Donner, I guarantee I will do everything in my power to get you transferred to an open borstal far from here. Is that a deal?'

'Have you arrested Mr McClintock?' Donner suddenly asked.

Sam had to admit that he was impressed. The boy had read the situation perfectly. The sudden arrival of CID, Sam's curt dismissal of the warder, the urgent need to interview Donner formally – he had at once fitted the pieces together and seen what was happening.

'We've arrested him.' Sam nodded. 'Near as damn it.'

'Then you *haven't* arrested him,' Donner corrected him.

'He's being interviewed by other officers at this very moment. With your testimony, we can formally charge him.'

'And then you'll have me transferred to an open borstal?'

'Yes,' said Sam emphatically. 'I promise you that. Will you cooperate?'

Donner thought about it, and then said at last, 'Yes,
I'll cooperate.'

'You trust me?'

'I trust you.'

'And you trust my colleague here, WDC Cartwright?'

Donner looked over at Annie as if he had only just
noticed her existence. After a moment, he nodded. Yes,
he trusted her.

Excellent, Sam thought. *We've got the boy on side. I
knew he'd respond to fair treatment.*

'Then we can do business together,' he said. 'Let's talk.
And remember, I want nothing but the truth.'

'Of course.'

'Craig Tulse, the boy who was burned in the
kitchen?'

'It was Mr McClintock who killed him,' said Donner
simply.

'Go on,' prompted Sam.

'Tulse was always goading him, answering back, trying
to make a fool of him. One morning in the kitchens Mr
McClintock just snapped. He grabbed Tulse and shoved
his face towards one of the gas rings. Maybe he didn't
mean to go as far as he did, but ...'

Donner shrugged.

'You saw this happen?' asked Sam.

'Of course I did. How else would I have known about
it?'

'You might have heard that story as a rumour,' Annie suggested.

'I don't listen to rumours.'

'Okay,' Annie said, 'then you might be lying.'

'Like I said, I'm telling you the truth.' Donner's voice was flat, almost uninterested. 'I was in the kitchens. I saw Mr McClintock kill Tulse, and then I helped him cover it up.'

'You?' asked Sam. 'Why?'

'Because I was the only witness. I was in danger. So I told Mr McClintock what I'd seen – that it was a faulty gas stove, that it had blown up in Tulse's face. What else could I say? That cover story saved my life. And Mr McClintock used it to gain more funds to rebuild the kitchens, claiming they were dangerous – so it all paid off for him in the end.'

Sam glanced at Annie, saw from her expression that she was far from convinced. But he decided to plough on anyway.

'And what about Tunning?' he asked. 'The official report said he hanged himself in his cell.'

'He didn't hang *himself*,' Donner said, without a flicker of emotion. 'Mr McClintock turned up in the middle of the night with a few other warders. They held him down while Mr McClintock strangled him, then hung up the body to make it look like suicide.'

'And once again you just happened to be there and witness it all?' Annie asked.

'Of course I happened to be there. I was sharing a cell with Tunning when it happened.'

'But I thought you boys slept in dorms,' Annie went on. 'I saw one myself. There were a dozen beds in there.'

'Special privileges,' Donner replied. 'Two to a cell for good behaviour. Better than the dorms.'

'But Tunning was a troublemaker,' Annie said. 'Why would he be rewarded with a double cell?'

'McClintock wanted to punish him, good and proper. But he didn't want a dozen witnesses. So he moved him in with me, so it'd be private. And he knew from what happened with Tulse that I'd keep my mouth shut.'

Annie shook her head. 'This all sounds very far-fetched.'

'You asked for the truth,' said Donner.

'But that's not what we're getting, is it?'

Fearful that Annie's attitude would alienate Donner and make him clam up, Sam interjected, 'We're not here to judge you, Donner. We just want to hear what you have to say. Okay – you're telling us that Mr McClintock was directly responsible for the deaths of Tulse and Tunning. What about Andrew Coren – what can you tell us about him?'

'He tried to escape,' said Donner. 'Not that it was *his* idea. It was mine.'

'Yours?' Annie frowned.

Donner slowly turned his head to look at her. 'Of

course. Who else in here would have thought of it?'

Sam tried to shush Annie, but she ignored him.

'You came up with the idea of getting smuggled out on the back of one of those junk lorries?' she went on. 'Why didn't *you* make use of that plan yourself?'

'How could I? I work in the kitchens. I'm rostered to work in the kitchens. It was Coren and them others who were on labour duty, not me.'

'Labour duty,' said Sam. 'You mean clearing out the old fridges and ovens?'

'Of course that's what I mean,' said Donner. 'I could see them breaking up all that stuff and loading it onto the lorries, and I realized at once that if you could get inside one of those old fridges you could get yourself carried out of this place right under the screws' noses. You'd be well away before anyone knew you were missing.'

'Would you?' asked Annie, sceptically. 'What about roll call? Surely they take a name check at the end of the shift to make sure everyone's accounted for?'

Donner's mouth pulled into a tight smile, just for a moment. 'I thought of that. It's simple. You just get somebody to answer 'sir' for you when the screw calls your name out.'

'We sometimes pulled the same trick at school with the morning register,' said Sam.

'Then you see it's possible,' said Donner.

'Oh, grow up,' Annie cut in. 'There's a world of difference between a borstal and a comprehensive.'

'Not the one *I* went to,' muttered Sam under his breath.

Annie ignored him. 'Somebody saying 'Here, sir' on behalf of somebody else? I don't see the warders here falling for a cheap, Bash Street Kids trick like that, Donner.'

'Do you not?'

'No. No, I don't.'

'That just shows what you know, then, doesn't it?' And with that Donner sat back and stared ahead, thinking his own thoughts.

'I think what Donner means to say, Annie, is that the warders *did* fall for it,' said Sam. 'If they hadn't, Coren wouldn't have made it as far as Kersey's Yard, and we wouldn't be sitting here now.'

'Aye,' said Donner. '*He* gets it.'

A telling remark. I think he's starting to warm to me. Is that what Annie's doing – playing bad cop to my good cop? Maybe she's right to be hard on him after all. Perhaps I should play along.

'So,' he said, leaning towards Donner with an expression of openness and honesty. 'You figured out your escape plan, but you couldn't make use of it yourself.'

'I would have to have got myself transferred from the kitchens to the labour detail,' the boy said. 'And to do that I would have had to have applied to Mr McClintock. He'd have wanted to know why. He'd have been suspicious.'

260

'Because of what you know about him, the things you've seen him do?'

Donner tilted his head and looked slyly at Sam. '*And* because he knows I'm not like the others. I'm smart. I play chess.'

'Play chess? On your own?' asked Annie, raising an eyebrow.

Donner paused for a moment, then said mildly, 'I cut out chess problems from magazines.'

'Which magazines?'

'Any magazines.'

'Such as? Name one.' And Annie fixed him with a look. She waited.

Donner turned to Sam. 'Is she always like this?'

'She's a police officer,' Sam shrugged.

'*Isn't* she just?'

'I think we're getting sidetracked,' Sam said. He was concerned that Annie was overdoing it. If Donner clammed up or got stroppy and retracted his statement, they were stuffed. 'You worked out an escape plan, but you couldn't make use of it yourself. But why did you give that plan to Coren and not one of the other boys?'

'Coren was perfectly suited to make the attempt,' Donner said flatly. It was almost as though he were speaking lines committed to memory. 'He had the right mentality to escape – he'd escaped from borstals before. He was small enough to fit inside one of those fridges.

And he had a brother on the outside who could meet him at the other end. You see, I figured that you'd need help getting out of the fridge at the other end. It might be stuck under a load of heavy junk, or chained up, or you might get grabbed by the workers in the scrapyard when they saw you suddenly appear.'

'You've really thought this through,' said Sam.

'Of course I have.'

'I'm impressed.'

Donner looked flatly at him, a curious expression that Sam was not sure he could read, and then, without warning, he said to Annie, '*The British Chess Magazine* if I can get it. *The Guardian* – that prints chess problems. And, if a screw brings it in, *The Times,* but that's rare.' And after a pause he added, 'Or I recall them from memory. I have a good memory for chess problems. And other things.'

He's showing off, thought Sam. *He's preening himself. Maybe he's even flirting. Either way, it's all to the good. He's talking. Let's keep him at it.*

Sam went to ask another question, but Donner began speaking, unprompted.

'I saw the opportunity to escape in one of the old fridges. I worked out how to get marked down as present on the roll call. I foresaw the need to be met by a trusted contact on the outside – the real problem, as I saw it, was making the necessary arrangements with that contact.

I needed a way to get messages to them in secret, without the screws being aware. So I worked out a code.'

Sam frowned. Derek Coren, lying in his hospital bed, had told them how he and his brother had been using that code for years, that they had worked it out between themselves.

'*You* worked out that code?' Sam asked. 'Are you sure?'

'Of course I'm sure, you idiot,' Donner said, his voice flat. 'Who else round here could work out a code like that?'

'But – Derek Coren told us that *he* was the one who created that code.'

'Oh, well, he would say that, wouldn't he?' Donner said dismissively. 'You asked for the truth, and that's what I'm giving you. It's his word against mine.'

Annie leant forward, looking at Donner intensely.

'Let's assume you *are* telling the truth,' she said. 'Let's assume for now that you *did* work out that pinprick code. It took me a long time to crack that code, Donner, and then it was as much through sheer luck as anything else. How would Derek Coren have known how to read the hidden message?'

'I told him how to do it,' Donner answered simply.

'How?'

'When he was here on a visit to see his brother. I whispered to him, 'Hold any letters you receive up to the light.''

'And then you worked a letter that was supposedly from Andy, encoded it with information about the escape, and even got it personally approved by Mr McClintock.' Annie shook her head. 'And you did all that for Andy Coren out of the goodness of your heart?'

'I hate to see a good idea go to waste.'

'But it *did* go to waste!' Annie countered. 'Because the escape failed. Andy Coren died.'

'Mr McClintock must have spotted the code,' Donner said. 'He *must* have done, because at the last minute he changed Coren's work roster, he moved him from loading up old fridges to dealing with the ovens. But Coren took a gamble and made an escape attempt anyway. His brother on the outside was looking for the wrong lorry, and the wrong consignment of scrap – and that's why Andy ended up in the crusher.'

'And do you feel guilty about that?' Annie asked.

'Why should I feel guilty?'

'It was your plan.'

Donner shrugged, thought for a moment, then said flatly, 'It was Mr McClintock who killed him, not me.'

Annie turned to Sam and asked for a word in private. Together, they stepped outside. As Sam shut the door behind him, he saw Donner sitting quietly in his chair, unmoving, hands folded in his lap, looking up at the ceiling as if patiently waiting for something to appear there.

'He's lying,' Annie whispered. 'Everything he's telling us in there, it's lies.'

'I can't accept that,' said Sam. 'Maybe he's stretching the truth a little, here and there.'

'Stretching the truth? Sam, it's all fairy stories what he's spouting!'

'He's just swinging the lead. God knows, he's a bright enough lad. This is probably the most intellectual stimulation he's had in months.'

Annie shook her head. 'It's not about swinging the lead, Sam. Can't you see what he's like? '*I* figured out a plan, *I* worked out how to do it, *I* can play chess problems from my head, it's all *me, me, me*, the screws know *I'm* the smartest one in this place.' That lad's ego is practically bursting out of him.'

'So?'

'I kept pricking that ego of his,' Annie said, leaning close, her voice low. 'I was goading him. He'd barely respond. A flicker, nothing more. And then he'd come back with an answer, minutes later. Like when I pushed him about which magazines he got his chess problems from. He carried on talking, but he was working out an answer in the back of his mind – and he wouldn't have rested until he'd given me that answer, Sam. He just *had* to put me in my place, no matter how long it took him. He's cold, Sam. He's ice cold. He's like a machine. Yes, he's smart, and, yes, I've no doubt he's a wizard at chess

265

problems – but I also see a cold, razor-sharp mind with three dead bodies associated with it. I was right about him, Sam. The boy's a psychopath.'

'I'm not buying that, Annie. It's McClintock, *he's* the psychopath.'

'Proof, Sam!'

'Barton's testimony,' Sam replied. 'The things he told me about – the torture, the electrocutions—'

'Oh, he was just telling you what you wanted to hear!' said Annie, waving her hand to dismiss the whole matter. 'He was terrified of going back. And he knew you were a soft touch if he made himself appear vulnerable enough.'

'The System is rotten, Annie. McClintock's System stinks!'

'Of course it does, Sam, anyone can see that. But it's not Nazi Germany. McClintock's not killing anyone. *He* is.' She pointed back at the door, beyond which sat Donner.

'And what if he corroborates what Barton told me?' Sam asked.

'He's bound to, Sam! And I'll tell you what else he'll do – he'll go further. It won't just be electrocutions or whatever, it'll be bloody firing squads and branding with hot irons and a ruddy great medieval rack down in the dungeons, and there in the middle of it all, using his Godlike intelligence to win over McClintock and control him, will be our wonder boy, Donner. Go back in there and speak to him, see if I'm not right. And what's more, Sam, he's seeing a soft touch in you. He knows you're playing along, lapping it all up. He's controlling you.'

'Nobody's controlling me!'

'Oh yes they are. That boy in there, he's stringing you along. Have *you* seen any evidence of these so-called torture chambers, eh?'

'I've seen the punishment block. A solitary-confinement cell, Annie, all blacked out, pitch dark.'

'That's cruel, but it's not what Barton was telling you. It's not boys being plugged into the national grid, is it. Think about it, Sam.'

Sam shook his head. 'It's McClintock and his System that's behind these deaths. I – I have my reasons to be sure about that.'

'And why won't you tell me what those reasons are?'

'And why won't *you* just trust me on this, Annie?'

Annie threw up her hands. 'Sam, you're not making sense! Evidence, proof – you know better than anyone that's what we need, not just some hunch!'

'It's not a hunch,' Sam insisted. 'We need to nail McClintock.'

'Oh, Sam, forget McClintock, can't you? McClintock's just a uniform and a set of rules. That boy Donner, on the other hand, he's dangerous.'

'Rubbish!'

'I don't think it is rubbish.'

'Donner's a victim, not a suspect. Oh, for God's sake Annie, if only you knew!'

Sam turned away from her. When Annie touched his arm he brushed her off.

'Think clearly, Sam,' she said. 'I don't know why you're so hung up on nailing McClintock for all this.'

'Because he's guilty!' Sam hissed back. 'Him and his System! They both need breaking!'

'Maybe they *do* need breaking, Sam, but that's not why we're here!'

'That's *exactly* why we're here!' Sam cried.

Annie stared at him, frowning.

'Tell me,' she said softly, but without warmth. 'Tell me what game you're playing here, Sam. It's like the other night at your flat, when you started talking daft and telling made-up stories about my dad. There's something going on inside you, and I want to know what it is.'

Sam ran his hands over his face. How the hell could he explain everything to her? How could he tell her the danger she was in? How could he make her understand that everything he was doing he was for her and her alone?

'Sam? What's the matter with you? Why can't you see Donner for what he is?'

Because Donner was irrelevant! It was *McClintock* he needed to destroy! It was McClintock and his System that needed to be broken, and, in breaking them, a blow

268

would be struck against the Devil in the Dark that was drawing closer all the time. Perhaps it would be the fatal blow, the one that would break the stranglehold of Fate and release Annie from the terrible destiny that awaited her. That lad Donner was nothing. Nothing. But McClintock – he was *everything*.

And what if I'm wrong? What if Annie's right? Have I misunderstood everything? Damn it, damn it, it's all too much for me!

Sam dug his fingers into his scalp, as if he could gouge out the confusion and turmoil in his brain. In his mind's eye, he saw that gold-plated fob watch nestling in McClintock's pocket, its slender chain forming a link through space and time to Perry – and then from Perry to Annie, connecting them all one to the other, yoking them altogether in some terrible web of Fate that defied even death and the grave to ensnare them.

I'm just a copper, for God's sake – I shouldn't have to be dealing with this – I'm just a simple bloody copper.

'I'm feeling very confused,' Sam muttered, his back to Annie.

'You should have stayed off sick like the Guv said.'

'I'm not sick. I've just … seen too much. I'm … confused, and it's all so … big.'

'Sam, I don't understand what you mean?'

'I—' He swallowed, and turned to face her. 'I'm here to save you. If I can. It's more important than you can

269

imagine. Somehow – and I just know this, Annie – it's McClintock. He's the one, he's the one who—'

'Forget McClintock!' Annie yelled at him, her patience suddenly snapping. 'It's Donner! We need to nick Donner!'

And at that moment, they both realized that Donner was standing in the open doorway, staring at them. There was a still moment of silence. Donner tilted his head, almost imperceptibly, then said quietly, 'Time for the endgame.'

And, with that, he hurled himself at them.

CHAPTER EIGHTEEN

IT ALL KICKS OFF

Donner's fist slammed into Sam's jaw. He fell back against a wall, stunned, Annie leaping to his defence as Donner rushed into the kitchens yelling, 'McClintock's gone! Now's our chance! McClintock's gone!'

Annie dragged Sam to his feet.

'You okay?'

Far from scrambling his brain, the sudden blow had miraculously cleared Sam's thoughts. The fog of confusion and metaphysical turmoil that once again threatened to swamp him had vanished. Everything became very clear. It made no *sense*, but it was clear.

I got it wrong. McClintock's not the danger here. It's Donner.

In the kitchens, boys were standing dumbly, staring at

Donner as he shouted at them, 'McClintock's gone! The System's fallen apart! We can do what we want!'

The warder came striding furiously towards him, glaring fiercely from beneath his peaked cap. 'Oi, you! Shut your face, you little shit! And all the rest of you, get back to—'

Donner grabbed a huge metal saucepan and smashed it against the back of the warder's head. As the man went down, Donner clubbed him, over and over, expressionless and dead-eyed, until the pan handle snapped.

'We can do what we want now,' Donner declared. 'They can't stop us. *They can't stop us!*'

The mood of the room suddenly shifted as the boys standing around the kitchen sprang into life, and all at once there was chaos. Instinctively, Sam grabbed Annie and hauled her away. All about them, knives were flashing, cooking utensils and food were being hurled about, windows were being smashed. Donner, having adjusted his grip on the shorter pan handle, was still mechanically bludgeoning the warder, stopping only when the handle broke off completely. By then he was standing in a slowly spreading pool of red.

Reaching the corridor, Sam shoved Annie through and glanced back. The whole kitchen was in uproar. The boys were going crazy, smashing everything, trashing the place. And there, in the middle of it all, calm and controlled but by far the most dangerous of them all, stood Donner, his face speckled with blood, his pale, unreadable eyes staring slowly about at the tinderbox he had just ignited.

Boys roared out of the kitchen, howling and shrieking. They burst into the dorms, spreading the contagion of the riot. From every side now, windows were breaking, boys were howling, warders were screaming.

We're surrounded – overwhelmed!

Sam grabbed Annie's hand. He would not let go of her. Nothing – *nothing* – would make him let go of her.

That little bitch from the test card tricked me. She made me think the System here was what needed to be broken – when in truth it was the one thing holding back this tidal wave of violence.

Still clutching her hand, Sam dragged Annie out into a corridor, trying desperately to recall which way led to the front gates.

So this is how that damned Devil is reaching out for Annie. It's through Donner. It's through this riot!

Tearing along the corridor, disoriented and lost, they raced past rooms and dormitories that were filled with chaos. The boys were smashing everything – beds, furniture, windows, and the skulls of any warders they could get their hands on.

Will we be surrounded and attacked? Is this how Annie will be dragged away from me?

He renewed his grasp on her hand, even though he was crushing her.

I'm sorry, Annie – I was wrong. I would never have let you come here if I'd known how wrong I was.

Whichever direction the two of them were going in, it wasn't leading them out. Up ahead, the corridor ended in a row of bars and a stout metal gate. Sam recognized it at once as the entrance to the punishment block where the Black Hole was situated.

'No getting out that way!' Sam cried. 'We've got no choice but to double back.'

But at that moment, haring along the corridor towards them, came Chris, his hair flopping wildly about his pale and terrified face.

'Keep going, keep going!' he howled, and raced past them towards the punishment block.

Moments later, Ray appeared, sprinting along behind him.

'It's all kicking off back there!' he cried. 'This way, quick!'

He too ran past them. Together, Chris and Ray bundled through the metal gate and peered anxiously back through the bars.

'Don't fanny about, Boss!' Ray called to them. 'In here, sharpish!'

From somewhere back along the corridor came a succession of crashes and thuds. Windows shattered. Boys' voices shrieked and howled wildly.

'They're ripping the place to shreds up there!' Chris grizzled. 'There's millions of 'em! *Billions* of 'em!'

'No way out, Boss! Our only hope is to hole up in here, lock the door, and wait for reinforcements!'

'Where's Gene?' asked Sam.

'And what about McClintock and Fellowes?' put in Annie.

At that moment, a figure in a billowing camel-hair coat came pounding up the corridor, his face red and shiny with sweat. Hot on his heels roared a furious mob of boys, hurling debris and howling for blood.

'Keep moving, you nonces!' Gene bellowed at them.

At once, Sam grabbed Annie and pushed her towards the punishment block, where Ray pulled her though the gate. But when Sam turned back he saw that Gene had halted and was reaching under his coat.

'Guv, let's go!'

Gene ignored him. He drew the Magnum. The huge barrel glittered dully. The horde of boys clattered to a sudden, chaotic stop and stared at the monstrous firearm aimed at them.

'Now then, kiddiewinkies,' Gene intoned. 'Say hello to Uncle Genie's big bad boom-stick.'

The boys filled the corridor, but they neither retreated nor advanced.

'You wanna rush me?' Gene challenged them. 'Then rush me.' He cocked the hammer with his thumb. 'That's right, lads. Grown-up toys.'

Keeping the Magnum levelled at the boys, Gene backed up along the corridor. Out of the corner of his mouth he hissed at Sam, 'Move.'

'Where's McClintock and Fellowes?' Sam whispered back.

'God knows, we lost 'em in all the fun and games.'

'We can't just abandon them, Guv!'

'I don't think we've got much say in the matter, Tyler. Now, don't just stand there, dopey bollocks, shift yourself! Now!'

Together, Sam and Gene turned and ran. The borstal boys came crashing after them. Sam felt Gene thrust him through the open metal door that sealed off the end of the corridor, and then bundled in right after him. They slammed the gate.

'Lock it!' Gene ordered.

'With what?' Ray yelled back, bracing the door with his own body.

'We ain't got no key!' Chris howled in despair.

A barrage of missiles rained down and crashed against the bars. Ray fell back, pelted with chunks of broken furniture. Chris threw himself against a wall and covered his head with both hands. Sam positioned himself in front of Annie, ready to die to protect her if that was what it took – and, at the same time, he cursed himself, over and over, for having brought her here, for not seeing the danger where it really lay, for letting himself be lured into a trap.

Gene strode forward and pointed the Magnum, but, without warning, a huge metal filing cabinet crashed against the metal bars like a battering ram. The gate burst open with a resounding clang, slamming into Gene's hand and sending the Magnum skittering away along the polished floor. All in a split second Sam glimpsed Gene stumbling back against a wall as the boys poured in. He saw Ray swinging a punch, and Chris howling in terror. Annie turned to Sam, her face ashen, her eyes wide.

I'm so sorry, Annie, I was wrong, I was wrong.

And then something large and heavy crashed down on him with a shuddering impact. Sam lost his footing, fell, slammed into the floor – but at that very moment he felt strong hands pulling him up again.

'Don't damage him!' a youthful voice ordered. The tones were familiar.

Sam felt himself being gripped tightly, his hands forced up his back, an arm clamping itself around his neck.

'Easy!' the young voice said. 'This is Mr Gould's new purchase. He doesn't want it broken before he's had a chance to play with it.'

The clamour of the riot had stopped. Cool night breeze brushed across Sam's face.

Oh, no – oh, no, not again!

The realization of where he was struck Sam suddenly, right in the guts, making his stomach heave and lurch as if he were in a suddenly plummeting aircraft. That

277

was Perry's voice he could hear – and those arms clamped around him were not the arms of borstal boys on the rampage, but two huge, bald bouncers dressed in immaculate 1960s suits. In front of him stood an open doorway, with a staircase plunging down into darkness. Above him shone a sign that said: 'HOUSE OF DIAMONDS'.

He tried to call out to Annie, but a huge, hairy hand was clamped over his mouth. Other hands gripped his arms and pinned them behind him. He couldn't move or speak.

Idiot,' Perry muttered, shaking his head. 'What did you think you were playing at just then? We're all on the same side now, Mr McC. You're just going to have get used to that fact.' Then, with a sigh, he said, 'Right, let's go. Can't keep Mr Gould waiting.'

Perry strolled away along the dingy alley, while Charlie and Lewis, the two bouncers, hauled McClintock along behind him, dragging his feet along the ground. They moved through a brick arch into a gloomy courtyard that seemed to be used for motor repairs. Several cars were parked in the shadows, waiting to be fixed. As Sam passed by, he caught a reflection of himself in one of the perfectly polished windscreens. It was House Master McClintock's. Younger, smoother, less grey, less lined, with a bouncer's hand clamped over the mouth, but unmistakably McClintock.

Perry patted him on the back.

'Don't fret yourself,' he said with a wink, and ushered him along. 'It's not *you* who's for the chop. PC Cartwright on the other hand ...'

They came to a large building with tall metal doors. The bouncers let go of McClintock and shoved him roughly inside. There were tools, old tyres, engine parts, bottles of engine coolant, and all the usual paraphernalia of a working garage lying about.

But there was something else, too.

Wrapped in chains, hanging by his ankles, and ready to be lowered head first into an open barrel of congealed sump oil, was Tony Cartwright. His face was flushed and red, his bloodshot eyes bulging with terror.

CHAPTER NINETEEN

PUNISHMENT BLOCK

'Jim! Get me out of here!' Tony Cartwright cried. 'I'll do what they say! I'll do anything they say! Tell 'em, Jim, tell 'em I'm on side with Gould! *Tell 'em!*'

McClintock spoke up in a strong, clear voice. He said, very firmly, 'Get that man down from there. Do it at once.'

Nobody moved.

McClintock turned angrily towards Perry. 'You heard what I said, Laddie, now get that man down!'

He's standing up to them, thought Sam. *Have I misjudged McClintock? Is he no Judas at all? Is he being a copper – a* real *copper – trying to do the right thing from himself and his partner despite all the odds against them?*

'I gave you an order, laddie,' McClintock intoned.

But Perry just winked at him. The two bouncers took up position in the open doorway, folding their arms and fixing McClintock with an implacable stare.

And then, emerging slowly from the shadows, came Mr Gould himself. He was dressed in a Nehru suit which, for all its fine tailoring, failed to disguise the broad, thuggish body lumbering beneath it. Jewellery flashed on his fingers. At his wrists glittered solid silver cufflinks.

I've seen that man before, Sam thought. And then, in horror, he corrected himself. *I've seen that* suit *before – with a mouldering corpse inside it.*

It was the same figure he had glimpsed in the ghost train of Terry Barnard's fairground, back when they had pursued tattooed bare-knuckle fighter Patsy O'Riordan in there. Disoriented, confused, Sam had found himself blundering about amid the cotton-wool cobwebs and plastic skulls – all of which had, at that moment, not felt fake at all, but genuinely grotesque and menacing – and he had glimpsed in the shifting, coloured lights a figure dressed in a Nehru suit identical to this one. But, as it turned, it had revealed a cadaver's rotting face, the eye sockets alive with maggots, the grinning skull teeth caked with grave soil.

That monstrous dead thing and this man in front of me now are one and the same. They are both Clive Gould. This is the Devil in the Dark.

Gould sauntered forward a few more steps, then

stopped. He tapped his expensive, patent-leather Chelsea boot on the hard floor, and let the echo die away.

'The time has come,' he said, 'for us all to draw a line under this tedious business concerning Philip Noyes. And you, Mr McClintock, are going to help me.'

He smiled, and as he did he revealed a chaotic jumble of huge, yellow, uneven teeth. It was the same snaggle-toothed face Sam had seen tattooed on Patsy O'Riordan's belly, and leering out of the dark at him after Carol Waye of the Red Hand Faction had clubbed him unconscious with the butt of her pistol.

'Philip Noyes was a close friend of mine,' Gould said. 'We were business rivals, that's true. And we had our ups and downs. But his sudden and tragic death was a terrible personal blow to me. Wasn't it, Perry?'

'A terrible personal blow, Mr Gould,' piped up Perry. 'I can vouch for that.'

'You saw what happened that night, didn't you, Perry?'

'I did, Mr Gould. He left the road and went into the canal.'

Gould paced towards where Tony Cartwright was hanging, but his attention was fixed on Sam. Or, rather, on McClintock.

'He should have bought his motor through *me*,' Gould said. 'I'd have seen that the brakes were properly checked. *And* the steering. But he insisted on buying Italian.'

Gould shrugged. Casually, he felt into his jacket pocket,

and pulled out a delicate gold chain. From it hung a fob watch. Sam saw it, and knew it at once. It was the very same gold-plated fob watch that nestled in the pocket of House Master McClintock's uniform.

'Philip Noyes died in an accident,' Gould announced. 'That's the truth. That's what happened. Except certain people who should know better think otherwise. Isn't that so, Cartwright?'

Tony stared back at him, his eyes wide and terrified.

'Certain people have forgotten they're on the payroll,' Gould went on. 'Certain people have got it into their nutty heads that I'm somehow responsible for Noyes's death, and that this here gold watch once belonged to him, and that I took from it just before I had him killed. As if I would do a thing like that!' He dangled the watch on his finger, letting it sparkle, and said, 'Certain people think this watch links me to the murder of Philip Noyes, and, not only that, but they can use it as evidence to convict me. Now who on earth would think such a thing!'

'Not me, Mr Gould,' put in Perry.

'And not our friend Mr McClintock,' said Gould. 'Which only leaves ...'

Gould reached up and nudged Tony's shoulder, making him spin slowly on his chain, first one way, then the other.

'Mr Gould, I'm sorry,' Tony said, his voice now

strangely calm and level. He was pleading for his life, but his tones were those of a man apologising to his boss for a minor misdemeanour. 'I made a mistake. An error of judgement. You can't blame me, Mr Gould, I'm a police officer, it's in my nature. But I see now I did wrong. And there was no harm done. You're in the clear for Philip Noyes's death; we can't touch you for it. And killing me, Mr Gould, it'll cost you money. Think of all the bribes you'll need to pay out – to my fellow officers, to my superior officers, to the coroner ...'

'Oh, it's not about money!' Gould smiled, waving his hand dismissively. 'There's more to life than that, Tony. There's things that *really* matter. Loyalty, trust, that sort of thing.'

'And you've got those things from me, Mr Gould, I swear to you.'

Gould pulled a theatrical wince. He shrugged, drew in breath, slowly shook his head. 'The thing is, it don't work like that. The way a fella behaves, the choices he makes – these things define him. And some things, once they're done, stay done, you know? You can't unring the bell, Tony, you hear what I'm saying?'

All at once, Tony's manner changed. He strained his scarlet face towards Gould and screamed at him, 'I got a wife! I got a daughter! Think of them! *Think of them!*'

'I am!' Gould told him, grinning. 'Believe me, I'm thinking of them. Especially your daughter.'

Sam felt revulsion and fury rise up like bile from the pit of his stomach. He stared at Gould's flat, broad face, at those cruel eyes, and that snaggle-toothed mouth. With Tony Cartwright dead, Gould would take Annie for himself.

Without warning, McClintock lunged forward, grabbing hold of the watch and snatching it from Gould's hand. He stumbled back, holding the watch aloft.

'Listen to me, Mr Gould!' McClintock's voice bellowed into the harsh space of the garage. 'I've got Noyes's watch here. It links you to the murder of Philip Noyes, just like my colleague PC Cartwright says. It's evidence, Mr Gould. Evidence I can use against you in a court of law! You're implicated, and I will see that you go down for life.'

I got McClintock all wrong, thought Sam. *He's a copper. He's the real thing.*

But Gould was unimpressed by McClintock's display. He laughed. Perhaps he thought it was all a joke.

McClintock thrust the watch into his inside pocket and stood firm. 'You will not bribe me. You will not intimidate me. You will let down my colleague unharmed *right now*, or, so help me, I'll see you put away for the rest of your miserable life!'

'Don't, Jim!' Tony Cartwright cried. 'Please! Mr Gould's the boss, just do what he says!'

'Silence!' McClintock snapped back at him. 'You are a serving police officer, as am I. You will not grovel to scum like Gould, nor will you cut deals with him. You will show respect not to *him*, but to the law that you have made it your duty to serve!'

'Jim, please, *please*, I'm begging you, think of my wife and kids!'

'Silence!' McClintock ordered fiercely. 'Respect! Duty!' And turning to glare at Gould he added, 'And, as for *you*, you're under arrest. I suggest you give me no trouble.'

Gould looked at him, his face expressing disappointment. He sighed, said, 'Back in the day, coppers had a sense for business.'

He shrugged, and gestured to one of the bouncers. Lewis obediently picked up a blow torch and ignited the flame. Calmly, like a man with a chore to do, he strolled towards McClintock.

Is this it? Is this how McClintock got those burns?

But it was Sam, looking out through McClintock's eyes, who suddenly thought, *Oh, my God, it's me who's going to feel this! It's me who's going to endure that pain!*

Sam was McClintock, and McClintock was Sam. The agony inflicted on one would be felt by the other.

He looked from the hissing blue flame of the approaching blowtorch up to Tony Cartwright's terrified face. At that moment, Gould reached out and threw a lever. Noisily, a gear whirred up in the rafters, and Tony descended head first into the oil. Sam caught one last glimpse of his face, bright-red, wide-eyed, utterly despairing, before it slipped beneath the thick, black ooze.

McClintock rushed forward. But at once he felt his legs being brutally kicked out from under him. Down he went down, hitting the floor hard. Charlie grabbed him, hauled him upright, and smashed him square in the face with a fist the size of a mallet. It was McClintock's body that took the force of that blow, but Sam sure as hell felt it, too. The impact went through him like an explosion. As his head shot back, he felt blood splatter over his face and pour down his chin. Another blow powered into his stomach, and, through the haze of his spinning, reeling brain, he was dimly aware of blood and vomit splattering over his shoes.

He heard Gould say, very calmly, 'Shove that torch in his face, Lewis.'

Dredging up a wild and desperate strength from somewhere, McClintock kicked out with both feet simultaneously. Sam felt McClintock's boots strike Lewis, good and hard, right in the crotch, and then he felt himself and Charlie tumbling chaotically to the floor.

There was a sudden whoosh of noise and a blaze of light. Lewis was tumbling heavily into the barrel of oil in which Tony had been submerged, but now the barrel was blazing furiously, ignited by the blowtorch. It was burning, and so was Tony.

McClintock went crazy, lashing out wildly, driving blows into Charlie's face and windpipe, and then he found himself back on his feet, grabbing a crowbar and glaring about. He saw Perry, standing there in the light of the exploding oil barrel, staring in mixed horror and fascination at Tony Cartwright's burning body. The boy seemed oblivious to everything except that spectacle of horror. Sam lunged at him and brought the crowbar down on the back of his skull. Perry pitched head first against the blazing barrel, over-turning it. A torrent of flaming oil swept across the garage floor.

McClintock grabbed one of the chains suspended from the ceiling and hung on, lifting his feet clear of the inferno beneath him. He saw the rolling wave of fire engulf Charlie, who rose up from amid the flames and ran, screaming and flailing. Lewis, also ablaze, came floun-dering towards him. They collided. The two bouncers rebounded off each other and fell back, consumed by fire.

The chain McClintock was hanging from was red hot now. Sam could feel the skin of his hands burning. But still he hung on, keeping himself clear of the lake of fire beneath him. Agonized, he turned his head and saw Tony Cartwright hanging as a piece of charred meat suspended amid blackened chains. Perhaps, for him, the fire had been a mercy. Perhaps he had died far more quickly then he would have done in the filthy black ooze.

Where was Perry? Presumably he was already dead, lying face down in the burning oil, his skull cracked like an eggshell.

Gould! he thought, gritting his teeth against the searing pain in his hands. *Where's Gould? Please let me see him burning – please let me see him dead. Please!*

Through the fire, he caught sight of Clive Gould, standing in the open doorway of the garage, very much alive. His face was lit manically by the leaping flames, his eyes glaring, his teeth bared. Did he see McClintock clinging like a monkey from his chain? Or did he see only Tony Cartwright, who had escaped the worst of the punishment owed to him? Did he see only the burning bodies of his minders? Did he see only the loss of Perry, his youthful driver and runaround, who'd need to be replaced? Or was it just the loss of his garage that this cold, evil bastard mourned?

Whatever ran through his subhuman, reptilian mind, Sam could not read it. Billows of black smoke blinded him for a moment, and in the next instant, he looked and saw that Clive Gould was gone.

I still have the evidence. That fob watch – it's in my pocket.

And then he corrected himself: *It's in McClintock's pocket – right now, as McClintock dies – and it will still be in his pocket years from now, in the life after this one.*

There was a riddle here, a riddle Sam felt on the brink of solving, but he was unable to think any further. More smoke swept across him, engulfing him, choking him, smothering him in total blackness.

CHAPTER TWENTY

LIKE CAMPING BUT WORSE

The black smoke blinded him. It filled his lungs. He gasped and spluttered for breath – and then found himself being hauled and heaved about.

My God! One of those damned bouncers is still alive!

Feebly, utterly disoriented, he tried to fight back.

What if it's Gould? What if he's that damned Devil in the Dark?

'I'll kill you!' Sam choked, thrashing blindly. 'I'll kill you, I'll kill you!'

'Only through the boredom of your company, Tyler,' a familiar gruff voice growled back. 'Even so, I'm moderately glad to see you ain't quite snuffed it yet.'

Sam looked about him – and saw nothing. Blackness. Void.

'Gene?'

'Who else, dum-dum?'

'I'm blind!'

'No you're not, you twonk. We're in the punishment cell that ain't got no windows. I got us both in here and slammed the door. It was either that or a lynching.'

'The Black Hole? We're locked inside the Black Hole?'

Sam felt about in the darkness. His fingers brushed against the Guv's face.

'*Naff off!*'

He ran his hands over himself. He felt his shirt, his jacket, the familiar contours of his face.

'I'm me,' he breathed.

'Oh, God, he's gone Tonto again,' Gene muttered.

Sam groped about and found a wall. He could feel the rough texture of the carvings and graffiti.

'Annie!' he cried. 'Annie, can you hear me!'

'Knock it off, Tyler!'

Sam's head was spinning with the terrible things he had witnessed: Tony's death, the fire, McClintock's agonizing demise in the flames. But, more than that, his mind was branded with the ugly, hard face of Clive Gould, the man who would take Annie as his own, brutalize her, murder her.

He felt an overwhelming need to find Annie, to put his arms around her, protect her from the terrible things of this world. But she was alone, somewhere out there in the murderous madhouse that was Friar's Brook in meltdown, while Sam was trapped in the dark.

'We got to get out of here, right now! Right *now*, Guv!'

'Well *I* ain't stopping you.'

'For God's sake, Gene, they could be raping her, they could be killing her, they could be—'

'I said it weren't no place for a dopey bird!' Gene barked from out of the darkness. 'I didn't want her along. *You* wanted her along.'

'She's one of the team, she's one of us!'

'She'll *never* be one of us, Tyler, 'coz she don't drink pints and she don't stand up when she takes a wazz.'

'What the hell's that got to do with anything?'

'In this game, Tyler, it's got *everything* to do with *everything*! And before you say 'no, it ain't', tell me why you're more worried about drippy-knickers right now rather than our boys? You know as well as I do, Tyler, that this were a job for *blokes*. Bringing a bird in here, it was asking for trouble!'

'This isn't the time for this argument, Guv!'

'I'd say it was the *perfect* time. There's stuff all else to do!'

'Annie is out there, Guv. God knows what's happening to her. We need to get that door open and find her.'

'She's probably with Chris and Ray. I reckon Raymondo managed to get his hands on the Magnum. He's smart like that. He'll have held off them scallywags long enough to get him and Chris and Bristols to a place of safety. They're all holed up somewhere, like us.'

'But we don't *know* that!'

'No, we don't. And for the time being we ain't gonna find out one way or the other. So until we get out of here, we have to *trust* them Tyler. You know? They're all serving officers, even that soppy tart Annie. They know how to look after 'emselves, they know how to handle trouble. So – have a bit of faith, Sam.'

Hopelessly, Sam battered at the solid door, dragging his fingers down it the way countless terrified inmates must have done over the years.

'Stop making a tit of yourself,' Gene barked from the darkness. 'Just 'coz I can't see you don't mean you don't look like a right prat clawin' at that door. Pack it in, park your arse somewhere and pull yourself together.'

Sam threw a last, furious punch at the door, and then slumped down, his back against the hard surface. He had no choice but to trust in Annie, that somehow she had got herself to safety, that she could indeed take care of herself.

Sam gently placed his palms together. The skin was neither hot nor blistered.

Perhaps I had no chance to change the past. Perhaps all I witnessed was a replay of what happened, a glimpse of how Tony Cartwright died, and how Clive Gould got his hands on Annie. And, of all people, it was McClintock who tried to stop him!

He could hardly believe it. And yet, it made a curious sense. McClintock was uptight, a disciplinarian, a by-the-book sort of man. Ten years ago, as a serving police officer, before he switched and joined the prison service, he'd be just the sort who'd stand out from the others, refuse to take bribes, refuse to be corrupted.

Like me, Sam thought. *Maybe we're more alike than I could ever have imagined.*

McClintock stood up, he defied Clive Gould, he tried to save Tony Cartwright – but he failed, and in the process he was burned.

He died in that fire – and he ended up here, in 1973, just like me. But, unlike me, he brought something with him – something solid, an object from Life. He brought that watch. It's not just evidence to link Gould to murder – it's a direct link to Life itself!

He had sensed it, right from the start, at the very moment he clapped eyes on that fob watch nestling in McClintock's uniform pocket. He had sensed there was something about it, something vital – and yet also something repellent.

But of course. It's not just a physical link to Life – it's a physical link to Clive Gould. Gould handled that watch – it was in his possession during those final moments before Tony Cartwright died. That watch is graced by its connection to Life, just as it is contaminated by its contact with the Devil in the Dark.

Sam shook his head to clear it. This was no time for sitting about, fathoming out riddles in the dark. They had to get out of this damned punishment cell – right now!

'Get your cigarette lighter out, Guv,' Sam said. 'Let's at least have a look around, see if there's any way we can get out of here.'

'Bad news, Samuel,' Gene intoned sadly. 'I lost me lighter in the crush outside. *And* me packet of Players. It's a tragedy I don't deserve. I'm fagless, Tyler. Fagless in the dark. Now *that* is what I call punishment.'

'We could be stuck in here for days, Guv. Just you, and me, and the darkness.'

'And no snout.'

There was a pause, and then Gene said, 'Shit, let's get that bloody door open.'

They moved about clumsily in the darkness, running their hands over the door in search of the mechanism.

'How good are you with locks, Tyler?'

'So-so. But this one's going to be a real pig.'

'I think you're right. Let's force it.'

'Force it? Gene, this door is solid iron.'

'So am I.'

'It's built to withstand a bloody tank rolling into it!'

'So am I.'

'It's donkey's years old and covered in shit and graffiti.'

'Tough luck, Sammy boy, I ain't walking into *that* one!' He sighed and shuffled away from the door. 'There's nowt for it. We're not getting out, not for the foreseeable. It's just you, me, and the slow passing of time. Think of it like a camping holiday, Tyler, only worse.'

They settled down again in the pitch blackness.

'Remember what you said to me first time we came to this borstal, Tyler?' Gene said.

'I'm not in the mood to chat, Guv.'

'No, it weren't that. It were that these lads, locked up here, they could've been prime minister given half a chance. Summat like that. You remember?'

Sam sighed. 'Yes, I remember.'

'And what do you reckon now, mmm? Still a bunch of future Winston Churchills, are they? I mean, now you've seen what a scummy, nasty, shitty, treacherous shower of shite they really are?'

'I'd say, Guv, that given your description of them they've got the perfect character reference to go into politics.'

'Oh very good, Tyler. Right off the flamin' *Frost Report*, you are. *God*, I wish I had me fags!' There was a pause while Gene hunted through his pockets, just in case, then admitted defeat. 'I only mention that stuff, Tyler, 'coz I think you're wrong.'

'You *always* think I'm wrong, Guv.'

'That's because I've been around and I've seen what's what and I'm not afraid to call a spade a spade. And, no, I didn't mean that racialistically.'

'I'm sure you didn't, Guv.'

'The thing is, Tyler, there's a reason lads end up in places like this. It's not about hard luck. It's about *choice*.'

'Spoken like a true Tory,' said Sam.

'But I'm right. You choose which way to go. You see different roads, and you decide which one to follow. Some blokes choose crime. Some blokes choose the path of least resistance. Me, I chose the path of the angels.'

'*The path of the angels?*'

'I was speaking poetically, Tyler. I thought you'd appreciate that. Something about sitting trapped in the dark brings out the poet in a fella's soul.'

Sam thought about that for a moment, then said, 'Weirdly, Guv, I think you're right.'

'Life ain't a cakewalk for any of us – except perhaps them born with the silver spoon. You can't avoid trouble, and you can't avoid getting shafted. But what counts is how you choose to deal with it. *You're* in the saddle, *you* tell the horse where to go, not the other way round. We're all skippers of our own souls, come fair sea or foul.'

The Guv was hopelessly mixing his metaphors, but even so there was a ring of truth in what he was saying. His words were making Sam think of his father, Vic, and the choices he had made. He could have played it straight, earned an honest living, but instead he had looked for the shortcut – and that had taken him into criminality, into violence, even murder. And then, later, when everything had unravelled for him – when CID had been closing in and the game was up – he could have stood by his wife and his young son. It would have meant arrest, and prosecution, and prison – but it would also have meant retribution, atonement, and the chance to stay in the lives of those who loved him, even if he was behind bars.

But Vic Tyler had chosen otherwise.

Not me, though, Sam thought. *I've made my choice – and that is to stand by Annie until the bitter end.*

He could not bear to think of her, not while he was trapped hopelessly in the dark, unable to get to her. He shook his head to clear it, fearing that panic and terror would get the better of him, and decided to distract himself by keeping on talking.

'Tell me, Guv,' he said. 'What you were saying just now.'

'Aye?'

'Where'd you get the bit about 'come fair sea or foul'?'

'Don't be patronizing, you saucy get.'

'Straight up, Guv, I'm not knocking you. I think it's rather sweet.'

'All I'm saying, Tyler, is that you spend too much energy trying to understand what makes a villain. Nobody gives a stuff about that! We're not bloody sociologists, Tyler. We're coppers. The people out there, them walking the streets and trying to make ends meet, the ones we're set to protect – all they want is *certainty*. Certainty, Tyler. The certainty that there's a blue line standing between them and the bad 'uns. The certainty that, for all its faults, the law's on their side. If you understood *that*, Tyler, you'd be a better copper.'

'I believe in fairness for all, and that goes for criminals as well as everybody else,' said Sam. 'It's being fair that makes *us* the good guys. The law is an ass – it really is – but it's still better than all the alternatives.'

'When asses don't budge, you gotta whack 'em up, right up the Khyber, and pay no attention to a load of bleedin' hee-hawing!'

'You *are* getting poetic, Gene!'

'That's your problem, Tyler, you don't actually *listen*. You're a mouthy Peter Cook smart alec but you don't *listen*. You tried to stick up for the shits in this place, and what did you get for your troubles. Eh? You think they give a damn about you and your namby-pamby botty-wiper's care and compassion?'

'Shhh!' hissed Sam.

'I see, you can't stand hearing the truth, eh?'

'No, no, I heard something. Listen.'

'What, Tyler? What is it?'

'Hear that, Guv?'

'If I could hear it, I wouldn't be asking what it was, would I?'

Dimly, as if filtering through to them from another world, they heard the squeal and squeak of feedback over a megaphone. At once, they caught Chris's youthful voice, massively amplified.

'Aye up, Ray, it's workin' now!'

'It's Chris!' exclaimed Gene, excitedly. 'I knew it! Him and Ray got out! They grabbed the shooter and they fought their way out! You see, Tyler – you get further in life with a Magnum in your hands than a—'

'Shut up, Guv, I can't hear!'

'That dopey-tits bird probably got out with them. She'll be safe and sound out there, filing her nails.'

'Guv, please be quiet.'

'I'm dead chuffed! Chris and Ray got out! You see, Tyler? You reckon my boys are just knobheads but it just shows what *you* know!'

'Guv, for God's sake ...!'

'School of Gene Genie's taught 'em everything they know. A couple of Gene Geniuses, my boys.'

'*Just shut your stupid face!*' Sam roared.

Invisible in the darkness, Gene went silent.

Sam pressed his ear to what he assumed was the outside wall. He could make out the howl of the megaphone, coming from presumably the far side of the prison walls, and then Ray's voice echoing out of it:

'Right! This is the fuzz. The game's up, the place is surrounded. No point playin' silly buggers, you ain't got a hope.'

Gene joined Sam at the wall, listening.

'That's it, Ray,' he muttered. 'Good 'n' tough.'

'You're all nicked, you hear me?' Ray went on. 'I mean, you're all nicked anyway 'coz you're in borstal, but now you're all nicked again.'

Chris's voice suddenly piped up, 'Double nicked!'

'Get your hands off the megaphone, Chris!'

'I want a go on it!'

'*I'm* senior officer. *I'm* negotiating.'

'I don't care, I want a go!'

'I said get *off* it!'

'Gimme the—'

'Chris, what the hell are ya—'

'Come out with your hands up!'

There was a high-pitched electronic howl, and then the megaphone went dead.

After a pause, Gene said flatly, 'When we get out of here, I'll send 'em on a course.'

'Shhh!'

'I'm not happy you shushing me like this, Tyler. it inverts the whole master–servant dynamic.'

'What's that noise?' Sam hissed.

They listened. Metal tapped hesitantly against metal.

'Is that you chattering your fillings, Tyler?'

302

'Somebody's unlocking the door, Guv!'

A key was clattering in the lock. Sam and Gene both tensed.

'The second that door opens, rush 'em!' breathed Gene.

Sam grabbed at him in the dark and got hold of his camel-hair coat. 'No, Guv!'

'Off the lapels, Tyler, and get yourself ready to fight your way out of here!'

'For God's sake, Gene, that lad out there is showing us *trust*. And we're going to prove ourselves worthy of that trust!'

'Prove ourselves worthy?' Gene sneered. '*Prove* ourselves? To *them* shites? Didn't you listen to nothing I was saying just now?'

'Listening? Yes. Agreeing? Nah.'

A line of light appeared and gradually broadened as the door edged open. At once, Gene burst forward, flinging the door wide and rushing through it. The lad who had released them – a tall, red-haired boy with powerful shoulders – jumped back, raising a length of lead piping to defend himself.

Gene clenched his fists and swaggered forwards. 'Thanks for opening that door, Sonny. But don't think it's going to save you from beating you so hard your nose'll end up sticking out your arsehole.'

'Wait, Guv!' Sam cried. 'I know this lad!'

'Know him?' Gene rolled his eyes. 'Oh, typical.

Tyler's got chummy with the lags. He must bloody love 'em!'

'Priest, it's me,' said Sam holding up both hands. 'It's okay, nobody's going to touch you.'

Priest kept his distance. He backed up against a wall and held the strip of pipe in both hands, ready to take a swipe.

'Why'd you let us out of there?' Sam asked.

Priest shrugged. 'Owe you one.'

'You owe me one? Why? Was it because I stepped in that time you were getting a beating out in the punishment yard?'

'You didn't have to stand up for me,' muttered Priest. 'But you did.'

Sam turned to Gene. 'You see, Guv? Treat them like human beings and see what you get.'

'Curryin' favour, that's all,' growled Gene. 'That little shit knows what he can expect when our boys come crashing back in here to secure this place.' He glared across at Priest, then seemed to relent. 'Fair enough. I'll put a word in for you, lad, tell 'em what you did.'

'What's happening out there?' Sam asked. 'Are the boys trashing the place?'

'It's pretty mental,' said Priest. 'You're going to have to be careful trying to get out. There's lads here who'll have you.'

'You reckon?' put in Gene, lifting his chin and narrowing his eyes.

'And what about Annie?' Sam asked anxiously. 'You know, the female officer I was with. She got out, right? She's safe, yes?'

'She's still around,' said Priest vaguely.

'Still around? You mean she didn't get out with the others?'

'She didn't get out. She's with Donner.'

'Donner! Why the hell's she with *him*?'

'Her and Mr Fellowes and Mr McClintock, they're all with Donner,' said Priest. 'He had a big knife from the kitchens, so …' He trailed off with a shrug. 'P'raps he's holding them hostage or summat.'

'Where?' demanded Sam, grabbing Priest by the denim straps of his prison-issue dungarees. 'Where? *Where?*'

'I dunno, honest!' Priest insisted, his eyes wide. 'I let you out, remember? I played fair! I been good!'

But Sam had already let go of him and was racing away along the corridor. Gene dutifully lumbered after him.

'Hold up, Tyler! Me knees ain't what they were!'

Sam sprinted on. At every corner, he braced himself to find Annie lying sprawled on the floor. His imagination tormented him with every horror it could dredge up.

I brought McClintock's System crashing down – but I was wrong! McClintock's not the enemy!

In destroying the System, he had also destroyed the only glue holding Friar's Brook together. Now, all was anarchy. The boys were running riot – and Annie was lost somewhere amid it all.

If anything's happened to her, it's my fault! I let her come here, I smashed the System, I unleashed this chaos. Oh my God, is this what was decreed for her? By trying to change Fate, did I just play straight into its hands? What have I done? What have I done?

CHAPTER TWENTY-ONE

UNDER SIEGE

Running through the borstal, Sam and Gene found nothing but wreckage and ruin. Like a medieval army sacking a city, the boys had rampaged through the rooms and corridors, destroying everything. The once shiny corridors were strewn with trashed furniture and broken glass, the sharp stink of bleach now obscured by the choking smell of smoke. And everywhere – scattered on the floors, tied to the bars on window frames, ripped, burned, trampled – were ragged patches of brown cloth, the so-called 'Stain' ordered by McClintock to be worn by every boy as a mark of his criminality, his sinfulness, his fall from grace.

And yet there was no sign of the boys themselves – or, for that matter, the warders.

Turning a corridor, they stopped at one of the huge painted slogans on the wall: 'SILENCE – RESPECT – DUTY'. It had been defaced with a single word: 'BOLLOCKS'.

Gene strode over to a door that hung limply on wrecked hinges. Glancing inside, he said, 'It's even worse than *your* gaff in there, Tyler.'

Sam looked through the door into what had once been a dormitory. The beds had been violently attacked and smashed to pieces, the broken remains heaped up along with the shredded blankets and ruined mattresses to form a chaotic, smouldering mountain of wreckage.

Gene reached down and picked up a warder's peaked cap. It had a hole in it, and the lining was stained with what could well have been blood.

'And you think they're all innocents,' he growled.

'We don't have time for any of your bullshit, Guv,' Sam snapped. 'Our priority is to find Annie.'

'Well *I* ain't holding you back,' Gene barked at him. 'Where d'you want to start looking?'

Sam looked about him, desperate for some hint or clue as to which way to go. And then he caught the sound of boys' voices echoing along the corridor. He sprinted off in search of the source, Gene lumbering and wheezing behind him.

At a broken window, Sam skidded to a halt and carefully peered into the yard outside. It was filled with boys, all shouting and jeering. They were massed around the tall punishment frame where Priest and Capps had been abused and beaten, and where Sam had broken ranks and stepped in to defy McClintock's System. But, instead of inmates hanging from the crossbar, Sam saw two warders, upside down, dangling by their ankles, their battered, swollen faces streaming with blood.

The image of Annie's father flashed into Sam's mind.

'Lynching the screws, are they?' breathed Gene, stepping up close to Sam and glancing through the broken window. 'What you going to do, Sam? Go out there and appeal to their better natures? And what about the widows and orphaned kiddies of them warders? What you going to say to *them*?'

But the warders weren't dead, not yet at any rate. The boys were rampaging about them, armed with splintery chunks of furniture, lengths of metal, even pieces of broken guttering; they aimed blows at the warders, whacking them as if they were piñatas, but the warders were still alive and conscious, glaring back at their attackers through the blood that flowed over their faces.

At that moment, something appeared above the perimeter wall of the borstal, rising up slowly. The boys turned and started screaming abuse at it. They furiously threw lumps of wood and shattered bricks and even spit-balls. But the object of their derision was undeterred; it just kept on rising.

'What the hell is it?' whispered Sam, struggling to see.

'It ain't a 'what',' Gene replied. 'It's a 'who'.'

And that particular 'who' was Ray Carling, riding high atop a slowly rising cherry picker, peering down into the punishment yard from over the barbed wire that topped the wall. He had discarded his jacket and rolled up his shirtsleeves, heedless of the cold wind that whipped in from across the moors and plastered the pale-blue nylon of his shirt hard enough against his body to clearly reveal the outline of his string vest beneath. His low-slung tie danced and fretted on the wind.

As disdainful of the cold as he was of the missiles being lobbed at him, Ray lifted the megaphone to his mouth. A metallic howl cut through the air, making even the boys in the yard wince.

'Right you lot!' he boomed, his voice distorted and dehumanized by the loudhailer. 'This is the fuzz. You are all completely nicked!'

Gales of abuse, laughter, threats and farting noises blasted back at him.

But Ray was undeterred. 'There's five thousand armed officers out here, ready to come steaming in there and stamp your bollocks flat, every one of you!'

'Five *thousand*?' said Sam.

'Artistic licence,' muttered Gene. 'Mind games.'

Ray went on. 'Now then. You little shitters can either pack it in with this nonsense and open them front gates, in which case you can expect to get duffed up a *bit* but nuffing out of the ordinary – or, you can carry on playing silly buggers and *wwaaaarh*!'

The megaphone squawked deafeningly.

'Jesus, that cut right through me!' they heard Ray exclaim. Then he tried to regain his composure. 'You know the deal, you bastards. Open them gates, or else.'

'Or else what?' one of the boys yelled back at him.

'Or else we'll starve you out, you saucy sod!' Ray barked back at him. '*We* can sit out here till bloody Christmas. *We* got food, *we* got fags, *we* got access to telly. What have you got, eh? Once you've scoffed all your grub, you'll be knackered! And don't bother turning the taps on, we've had the water cut. *And* the lecky. So, all in all, you ain't got *nuffing*!'

The boys in the yard were shouting and howling, pointing at the warders hanging from the punishment frame. Evidently, they felt that what they did have was worth more to them than 'nuffing'.

'You let them warders go, right now!' Ray ordered. 'You hear me? No hostages, that ain't fair! This is between you lot in there and us lot out here! Let them men go or I'll— Oi! What you bloody doing?'

Without warning, Ray had suddenly begun trundling majestically sideways. The driver of the cherry picker seemed to have made up his mind he needed to be somewhere else.

'I ain't finished up here! Oi!'

But for reasons of his own the driver just kept going.

'I'll be back, you bastards!' Ray bellowed at the boys as he rolled away. 'I'll be back!'

He descended to a hail of abuse and missiles, and vanished below the wall.

'Well, that was impressive,' muttered a distinctly unimpressed Gene Hunt. 'Ray's handling this wrong. He's turning it into a siege, and I hate bloody sieges. It ain't the Middle Ages. He's going to get sucked in. This whole thing'll start dragging, with negotiations and demands and *quid pro* flamin' *quo* this way and that until we're rattling round this flamin' borstal with walking sticks and incontinence knickers. He needs to kick doors down, storm the gaff, and crack a few skulls.'

'Maybe that's what he wants to avoid,' said Sam. 'Maybe even *Ray's* squeamish about ordering riot police to attack children.'

'They *ain't* children – not any more!' Gene retorted, and he indicated the two screws dangling upside down and dripping blood, surrounded by jeering, knife-wielding boys. 'Right, Tyler, I'm taking charge. First thing we do is open the gates to this place and let the heavy mob in. And, before you start bleating on like old Mother Riley, the sooner we get this place under control the sooner we can find Annie.'

312

Sam glanced back out of the window. The boys were rampaging about in the yard like savages, jabbing at the warders, flicking cigarette lighters under their flushed faces, waving kitchen knives at them. Were McClintock and Fellowes faring any better? And what about Annie herself? Terrible images flashed into his mind of what might have become of her. He screwed up his eyes and shook his head, forcing himself to think clearly.

'No time for dicky-fits,' Gene barked at him, grabbing him by the collar and dragging him roughly along.

'You're right, Guv. This *is* no time for dicky-fits!'

'Good boy. Now, let's get them front doors open!'

They found the main corridor that led to the front entrance. The doors had been wedged shut with a heap of smashed chairs, broken bed frames, and shattered office furniture. Two boys in regulation denim dungarees – a barrel-chested, mean-eyed bastard and a smaller, more weaselly companion – were piling more debris onto the mound. They reacted with shock when they say Sam and Gene striding up the corridor towards them.

The barrel-chested boy grabbed a chunk of wood and rushed forward. Gene caught him square in the face with a ferocious blow, splitting the lad's nose and upper lip and sending him slithering half-conscious to the floor.

At once the smaller boy was on his knees, grovelling.

'None of it was my idea!' the lad howled. 'I didn't do anything! It was all the others!'

'Shut your gob and start shifting this lot!' Gene ordered, wrenching away handfuls of rubble. 'I want these doors open in one minute flat or you, sonny, are going to find yourself intimately acquainted with *this*!'

He thrust his fist in front of the boy's wide and terrified eyes. It was more than enough: the lad leapt up and frantically started hauling wreckage away from the doors.

Outside, there were voices, and the sound of movement.

'Get yourselves ready!' Gene bellowed. 'We're getting these doors open!'

'Is that you, Guv?' It was Chris, calling through from the other side.

'No, it's Raquel Welch in search of some rumpy. Of course it's me, you berk!'

Between them, Sam and Gene and the lad in dungarees cleared away the wreckage. When he could reach them, Gene grabbed the handles and dramatically flung the doors open, revealing Chris and Ray standing there, backed up by a host of coppers carrying riot shields and truncheons. While all the excitement had inspired Ray to pare down to his shirt and tie, Chris had chosen to bundle himself up beneath an enormous, grey parka. So cold was he that he had zipped up the snorkel hood. He peered out from a fur-lined tunnel.

'Stone me, it's Madam Cholet,' growled Gene. And then, looking past Chris at the massed riot police behind him, he added, 'And he's brought the dancing girls. There's plenty of work here for you, ladies, take my word.' With the toe of his loafer, he contemptuously nudged the prone body of the barrel-chested boy lying beside him. 'This one's busted, but there's more inside. Enough for everyone.'

Chris pushed forward, moving clumsily in his bulky parka, and spoke from the depths of his snorkel hood: 'Oh, Guv, it's great to see you! I was worried sick about you in there!'

'I'm touched,' grunted Gene. 'But tone it down, Chris, you'll start rumours.'

Ray stepped forward and, with a certain solemnity, held out the Magnum for Gene to take.

'She got us out of there,' Ray said. 'She did us proud. But her place is with you, Guv.'

Gene nodded gravely, like a knight regaining his sword, and took hold of the Magnum, curling his fingers almost sensuously around the handgrip and trigger.

The boy in dungarees was trying to sneak off, but Sam stepped in front of him.

'Not so fast, lad,' he said. 'I'm looking for someone. A woman. She was here when everything kicked off. Did you see her?'

The boy nodded. 'Aye, I saw her. Dishy lass, brown hair, tasty.'

'What happened to her? Eh? Don't just stand there gawping at me, *tell me what happened to her!*'

'She were with that lad, the weirdo one,' the boy said.

Gene rolled his eyes. 'Well that narrows it down.'

'Are you talking about Donner?' Sam demanded, looming over the boy.

'Donner, aye, the nutter.'

'Annie was with Donner? What was happening?'

The boy shrugged. 'Donner had a knife or summat. I only caught a glimpse.'

'Where is she?' Sam yelled, grabbing the boy by the straps of his denim dungarees. '*Where is she?*'

'Dunno!' the boy cried back.

'Was she hurt? Did anyone touch her? What happened to her? *Tell me where she is!*'

'Swear to you, sir, I dunno, I just don't know!'

Sam thrust the boy away and turned towards Gene. 'Right, that's it, Guv. If Annie's a hostage, we need to keep things as cool as possible round here.'

'No, Tyler, we don't need to 'keep things cool' – we need to storm the place and get her back.'

'It's too dangerous, Guv! The emotional temperature in here's high enough already. Let's start calming things down rather than whacking up the pressure.'

'What are you on about, you noncey twiglet?'

'Guv, if I hadn't stepped in that time when Priest was getting a beating, we'd still be locked in that bloody pitch-black cell! I showed him respect, and he returned it. The same will go for all these other lads.'

'So what you going to do, Sam? Stroll out there and offer 'em a fag? Tyler, *look* at 'em. Barbarians, the lot of 'em!' He renewed his grip on the Magnum. 'There's only one thing they respect, and it ain't good manners.'

'Put the gun away, Guv, that's not going to help.'

'Oh, you think not, eh? It didn't do Ray and Chris no harm when they had it – they got straight out of here, no problemos.'

Ray nodded his agreement.

'If Donner's holding Annie hostage, I can talk to him!' Sam said instead. 'I talked to him before, I won a tiny ounce of his trust, I can do it again – but not to the backdrop of the riot police and guns going off.'

'We don't have time to prick about, Tyler!' Gene snarled. 'One of our officers is in here somewhere, unaccounted for. If I have to plug a few borstal brats to get her out of here in one piece, it won't put *me* off me pie 'n' mash.' And then he bellowed, 'Saddle up, boys! *Wagons roll!*'

Fearlessly, Gene strode ahead, flanked by Ray in his shirtsleeves and Chris in his snorkel parka, the massed forces of the riot squad bundling along behind. Unable to stop this juggernaut of men and weapons, Sam hurried along with it, his mind in a whirl, his imagination tormenting him with images of Annie suffering at the hands of the psychopathic Donner.

Hunt led his army straight into the punishment yard where the two screws were dangling from the crossbeam. At once, the boys stopped, and every head turned. Every pair of eyes focused on him, on Chris and Ray, on the sudden phalanx of armed police officers drawing up around them – and on the huge gun the Guv'nor had pointed straight at them.

'Oh 'eck,' muttered Chris, and like a frightened animal he seemed to retreat further into his snorkel hood.

But the Guv was in his element. He planted himself squarely in front of the boys and glared at them, taking his time, letting them mull over just what that Magnum would do to their soft tissues if he unleashed its awesome power. He cocked the hammer.

'Okay, boys. Who wants candy?'

The yard fell totally silent. Nobody moved. The boys were motionless. Even the warders, hanging by their ankles, watched and waited.

Sam rushed out into the yard. He didn't know what the hell he was going to say, but he'd think of something. He'd get Gene to put that damned gun away, he'd start talking to the boys, he'd persuade them to let the warders go and realize the hopelessness of getting drawn into a siege. He'd reach out to them, treat them like human beings, appeal to that spark of decency he knew still burned somewhere deep in the heart of every one of them. And Donner – watching, perhaps, from some high

318

window somewhere – would see that Sam was a policeman he could trust, that he didn't need Annie or anyone else as a hostage, that if he cooperated and behaved it would all be in his own best interests.

Or will I fail, just like I failed to save Annie's father – just like I failed to kill Clive Gould when I had the chance?

But Sam didn't get a chance to say or do anything, as out of nowhere there came a scream. A female scream. Everybody – Chris and Ray, Sam and Gene, the riot squad and even the borstal boys in the yard – instinctively looked about them, glancing from one barred window to another.

'Over there!' suggested Gene, pointing.

'No, no, over *there*!' cried Sam, pointing in the opposite direction.

'I thought it came from up there somewhere,' put in Chris, indicating vaguely towards the sky.

The matter was decided for them. From a smashed window on the first floor Annie cried out again, 'Donner, please, stop, think what you're doing!'

Sam's blood froze in his veins. Without hesitation, he raced forward, making for a wrecked door that hung limply on the remains of its hinges.

His sudden movement galvanized the borstal boys. A high, childish, unbroken voice called out, 'Come on boys, let's get 'em!' and there was a disorganized rush of bodies and clubs as the lads pressed forward, jeering and shrieking. Instantly, the riot squad responded, clashing their truncheons against their shields as they surged forward. Sam found himself caught slap-bang in the middle.

A chunk of wood caught him square in the ribs and sent him sprawling hard against a wall. He struggled up, managing to deflect one blow with his arm, but taking another straight in the stomach, doubling him up. He fell to the ground, covering his head with both hands as he took hits to his flanks and his spine. Bolts of pain shot through his body, but all he could think of was Annie and whatever the hell that lunatic Donner might be doing to her.

A powerful explosion resounded across the yard. It was the roar of a cannon. It was the blast of an atom bomb. It was the very crack of doom.

Quite suddenly, like a tap being turned off, the blows ceased. So did the whooping. Sam peered up from under the shelter of his hands and saw the boys all surging away in panic. Then, amid the confusion of rushing legs and bodies, he caught sight of a pair of off-white leather loafers planted firmly a few yards away, then a pair of eggshell-blue slacks and the hem of a camel-hair coat, a pale green shirt with a chevron-patterned kipper tie loosely knotted, manly stubble over an even more manly chin, and, at the end of an outstretched arm, a hand gloved in black leather, grasping the handgrip and trigger of a duly glittering Magnum. But the barrel of that monstrous weapon was pointed *upwards*, into the sky.

That single, deafening warning shot was enough. The boys were madly scrambling away, their resolve broken, their nerves in tatters. In a split second, they had gone from young men on the rampage to frightened children fleeing in terror. The riot squad swarmed after them, truncheons flailing.

He's broken the siege, thought Sam, *but he's also broke what little trust I'd established with Donner. How the hell will that boy react? He could do anything. Anything!*

Gene strode over and hauled Sam to his feet. 'See that? You may knock 'em, Tyler, but my methods ain't half boss.'

But Sam was already sprinting away in search of Annie.

'A thank-you don't cost nothing, Samuel,' Gene called out, and then he loped off after Sam, spinning the Magnum showily on his finger, just like a *real* cowboy.

CHAPTER TWENTY-TWO

WATCH ON A CHAIN

'This way! This way!'

Sam bounded ahead, Gene lumbering along after him with his camel-hair coat billowing.

'You sure, Tyler? This ain't the time for a magical mystery tour.'

'Save your breath and keep up!'

'Hey, what's that?' panted Gene, peering ahead as they ran.

Sam looked. Something appeared to be lying in a pool of spilt liquid at the far end of the corridor.

No, no! Sam's suddenly numbed mind could think of no other word. *No – no no no!*

As they drew closer, they saw that it was Fellowes, the borstal governor. He was lying face up in a lake of his own blood, his throat torn wide open. Guiltily, Sam felt an overpowering sense of relief.

Gene peered down at the mangled corpse, wrinkling his nose. 'This is getting serious.'

'Damn right it is, Guv. This was Donner's doing. And he's got Annie with him.'

Gene's eyes narrowed. 'Not for long.'

They ran on, reaching the end of the corridor. The only way on was through an open doorway and up a flight of steps.

'Annie's up there,' panted Sam.

'You sure?' Gene wheezed back, hungry for oxygen.

'I'm sure. Nowhere else for them to have gone. He's a chess player, he knows what pieces really count in this game. We know he's got Annie – and ten-to-one says he's got McClintock too.'

'Unless Jock McTavish's come to the same sticky end as his guv'nor,' Gene intoned. He reached under his camel-hair coat and pulled out the Magnum. Light gleamed along its huge barrel. 'Time to introduce that slag Donner to Uncle Genie's favourite nephew.'

'No, Guv! Put that thing away!'

'Put it away? It's saved your girly arse once already today, Tyler!'

'But not this time! Guv, please, listen to me. Donner's up them stairs – he's not going to be intimidated by you waving a shooter about. Annie was right about him: he's a psychopath. If you start raising the temperature, there's no telling what he'll do. This is a game that has to be played *psychologically*, not with your precious Magnum!'

Hurt and offended, Gene gave his gun a wounded look and said defensively, 'I got a licence!'

'Yes, but no *sense*, Guv! Leave this to me.'

'To you, Tyler? What you gonna do, bore him to death playing your poncy feckin' prog-rock albums? You try that and I warn you, the first bullet goes straight through your stereo, Tyler, and the second goes straight through *you*!'

But Sam blocked his way, refusing to let him past.

Gene's face flushed with fury. 'You want WDC Knockers to get out of this alive? Then get out of the way!'

'You think you can solve everything with that bloody cannon of yours! Gene, stop and think, damn it, just stop and *think*. We need Donner alive; we need him in one piece. We need to speak to him, keep him as calm as possible, and arrest him.'

'And failing that we plug him!' Gene barked back, cocking the Magnum with his thumb.

'There's a little thing you're forgetting about here, Gene. It's called the law!'

'I *am* the law!' Gene declared.

'No, you are not! You are *not* Dirty Harry and you are *not* Judge bloody Dredd and you are staying right *here*!'

With all his strength, Sam shoved Gene back. Gene

stumbled, his face forming into a complex expression of surprise, confusion, incredulity and sheer bloody outrage.

'Tyler, how bloody dare you—'

But Sam slammed the door on him and threw the bolt, then went pounding up the stairs.

Panting and sweating, he burst into an unlocked office, and stopped dead in his tracks. The first thing he saw was Annie, standing nervously in the far corner. She shot a tense glance at him, but remained where she was.

Then Sam saw McClintock. He was sitting motionless in a chair, his head back and his mouth open as if he were at the dentist's, a few trickles of blood drying across his cheeks and along his chin. Donner was standing behind him, holding a huge knife from the kitchens; the blade had disappeared into McClintock's open mouth, the sharp tip pressed against the back of his tongue and making him gag. At the first hint of trouble, all Donner had to do was push down with that knife.

'Nobody move, nobody do anything,' Donner said flatly.

'I'm not moving,' said Sam, holding up his hands.

'Me neither,' added Annie.

'Everyone stays exactly where they are, or this man dies,' Donner announced, without emotion. He jerked the knife, and McClintock choked and flinched, and a fresh line of blood ran from the corner of his open mouth.

'Annie?' Sam called softly across the room.

'I'm fine,' she said back.

'Stop talking,' Donner ordered. 'I'm in charge here. Everybody has to do what I say.'

'And what is it you want, Donner?' Sam asked.

'My freedom.'

'You know that's not possible.'

'Make it possible.'

'I can't. No one can.'

'*I* can,' Donner said, and for the first time Sam caught an inhuman, insane glint in the boy's eye. 'I can do anything.'

'At chess, maybe, but this is real life.'

'No difference. I'm brilliant at both. Now – sort out transport and a safe house.'

Sam slowly shook his head. 'You're living in cloud cuckoo land if you think that's what you're going to get. The riot police are securing this place even as we speak. It's all over. Nobody's going to negotiate and nobody's going to do a deal with you. Come on, Donner, you're no fool, you know you're clutching at straws. Throw the knife away and let's be done with all this.'

'Like I said, *I'm* in charge. There's a telephone on that desk. Ring whoever you have to ring and make all the arrangements.'

'They've cut the phone lines.' Sam edged closer, very carefully. 'Get rid of the knife. Let Mr McClintock go. And I promise I'll see you're treated fairly.'

'Promise, promise, promise,' mocked Donner, and now a hint of real aggression was creeping into his voice. 'You've promised things to me before. You promised to transfer me if I cooperated with you. I cooperated! And what did I get?'

'Donner, I—'

'I said, *what did I get*?' The boy's eyes flashed at Sam. 'Empty words. All I've ever had, from anyone. The world is shit. You're all shit.'

From downstairs came a series of heavy thuds.

'What's going on?' snapped Donner.

'It's my guv'nor,' said Sam. 'He's trying to force the door.'

Donner frowned. 'You locked him out?'

Sam nodded.

'Why did you lock him out?'

'Because I didn't want him up here. I wanted to speak to you myself.'

Donner's eyes narrowed suspiciously.

'I trusted you,' said Sam. 'I believed what you told me. About this place. About Mr McClintock. I believed you, and I stood up for you, and I put my faith in you. But it was all lies.'

'I told you the truth,' Donner said.

'You murdered Mr Fellowes.'

'He went for me. *She* saw what happened.'

Donner jerked his head towards Annie.

327

Clearly lying, doing everything she could to keep things calm, Annie said, 'Yes. Mr Fellowes went for him, Sam. He did.'

'I defended myself,' Donner went on, 'just like I'm defending myself now. If I let this bastard go' – he jerked the knife, making McClintock cry out – '– then I've got no protection. As long as I've got him like this, you won't touch me.'

'But you lied to me, Donner,' Sam said. 'Craig Tulse's death in the kitchen – it was *you* who set him alight, wasn't it – just like it was *you* who killed Tunning in the cell that night.'

Donner didn't react at all. And his total lack of reaction – his blank, expressionless gaze – seemed to Sam the ultimate proof of the boy's guilt. These deaths meant nothing to him. All he was thinking about was how to play the here and now to his advantage.

'And Coren,' Sam went on. 'Mr McClintock *didn't* change the work detail, did he. He knew nothing about Coren's escape until he was reported missing. But *you*, Donner – you knew. You wrote that letter for Coren, but you deliberately put in the wrong information. It made you feel powerful, didn't it, knowing that you could control the situation, make Coren's brother steal the wrong lorry – and all the while, as he thought he was saving his brother, Andy was dying inside that crushing machine?'

'You people *owe* me,' Donner declared. He looked

sulkily across at Annie. 'You owe me most of all. If it wasn't for me, the other boys would have had you. They'd have had you, over and over, and then strangled you and left you lying out there in the courtyard. But they didn't touch you because *I* was there. They didn't dare! They saw how I dealt with Fellowes. They knew they couldn't take *me* on. You are alive because of *me*. Because of *me*!'

'Yes, Donner, you certainly frightened them off,' said Annie, shooting a glance at Sam. 'You and your knife, you were certainly – intimidating. But now you've got to put the knife down and trust us.'

Sam could see in her expression that she knew, even as she spoke, that her words were useless, that Donner was beyond reason and rationality.

Gene's still trying to get in, Sam thought, hearing another set of frustrated bangs and bashes from downstairs. *Perhaps he's already drafted in the riot boys to help him. I only hope that door's strong enough to hold. The last thing we need is him and the goon squad storming in here, throwing petrol on the fire. Me and Annie can handle this situation, I know we can – we can get all of us out of here alive – just so long as the Guv doesn't come steaming in like a caveman!*

As he inched closer, a reflection on the floor caught his eye. It was McClintock's fob watch. Its chain had broken in the struggle and it had fallen from his waistcoat pocket. Very carefully, Sam reached down and picked it up.

'What do you think you're doing?' Donner demanded. 'What have you got there?'

'Something with a history,' Sam said, almost to himself. 'Mr McClintock knows about it, deep down – not that you're giving him a chance to tell us. I know about it too, though I'd be pushed to explain how. We'll just say I – I saw things.'

Donner's face was impassive, but his voice betrayed a hint of unease. 'Stop talking. Give that gold thing to me.'

But Sam ignored him. 'History. I was never much cop at it at school. But recently I've become pretty good at it. You could even say history's my strong point.' He looked over at Annie and smiled. '*Your* history, *my* history – even Mr McClintock's. And all this history, it's been teaching me things. All sorts of things. Not always easy to put into words what I've been learning, but ...' He shrugged. 'It's made a better man of me, that's all I can say.'

He found his gaze had shifted from Annie's pale, wide-eyed face to McClintock's burned hands, which were flexing anxiously by his sides.

'How can I say that I was there?' Sam said, looking at that pink, smooth scar tissue. 'How can I say that I felt that pain – the flames, the burning? How can I say that I saw what you saw, Mr McClintock – that night – ten years ago? How can I say that I *lived* the past that's embodied in this little pocket watch?'

What would they all be making of his words? Annie

no doubt would be assuming that he was stalling for time, or trying to undermine Donner's confidence by talking so obliquely. If McClintock could hear him at all, would he be recalling Tony Cartwright's death, and the fire, and how he failed to defeat Clive Gould? Would he be wondering just how the hell the impertinent detective from CID knew about all this?

And what about Donner? What would *he* be thinking? Or was that an impossible question for Sam to answer? Was the broken mind of that poor, ruined psychopathic child too far beyond his understand and imagination?

And what about me? *What am* I *thinking?*

Sam was thinking about how he had misjudged everything, how he had looked for the Devil in the Dark and seen it manifested in the wrong guise. McClintock wasn't that murderous monster. Indeed, once he had been a fine copper – upstanding and brave. He may have lost his way since then, but maybe he was damaged, like the boys in his borstal.

I was wrong about McClintock – and I was wrong about Donner. The System that I need to break, it's not represented by this borstal at all – and it's not represented by Donner either. It's somehow here, in my hand.

The fob watch sat in his palm, innocently ticking.

Here is my link to Life itself. A physical object from the world of the living, carried through to this world of the dead. A living relic – and maybe something more.

This innocuous-looking timepiece had already granted him glimpses of the past – of Tony Cartwright's violent death, of McClintock's own demise amid the flames, of the monstrous Clive Gould at the height of his powers. This watch had witnessed so much horror – and, as an object from Life, it brought with it into this afterlife the taint and aura of all that death and betrayal. So powerful was that resonance that Sam had detected it at once, and been transported by it back into the past.

Here is my link to Clive Gould. Through this, somehow, I can get to him – and then, maybe, I can destroy him once and for all.

He looked up at Annie and felt an overpowering need to protect her from Clive Gould, no matter what the cost to himself. He had killed her father, then turned his attentions to her, drawing that poor, orphaned girl into his filthy life and into his bed and then, in time, murdering her with his bare hands. Yes, she had suffered enough at his hands already, although she could not remember it. He vowed to himself then and there that she would suffer no more.

But, before I can protect her, I've got a desperate, knife-wielding psychopath to deal with. First things first, Sam.

Sam slipped the watch into his inside jacket pocket and zipped it up.

'No,' said Donner. 'Give it to me.'

'Oh, I'm not listening to you any more,' said Sam dismissively.

'You *will* listen. I'm in charge.'

'I trusted you!' Sam snapped. He felt genuine indignation rising within him. 'I was the only one out of all of them to take your side, to give you the benefit of the doubt! I stood up for you, do you know that? I saw you as a human being, not just some borstal slag to be treated like filth. I *listened* to you. But all you were doing was stringing me along!'

'Give me that gold thing you picked up,' said Donner, his face blank.

'Oh yes, here we go, the dead-eyed-killer routine!' sneered Sam, and he wasn't play-acting. 'The great player of games! The puppet master! The pint-sized Hannibal bloody Lecter, messing with all our minds! But you're just a kid. A sad, broken little kid.'

Sam glimpsed Annie's face, drawn and bloodless, her eyes wide and staring. Her whole body was tensed in anticipation of a sudden move from Donner. What would it be? Would he plunge the knife wantonly into McClintock's windpipe? Would he attack Sam? Or would he blindside them all with something totally unforeseeable?

'Why aren't you doing what I say?' Donner said. 'I'll kill this man if you don't take me seriously. Give me that gold thing you've got.'

'Threats,' said Sam, unimpressed. 'Violence. Fear. That's what it all comes down to. That's what we're all supposed to be running from. 'Oh please, don't hurt, I'm too weak to defend myself, have mercy, I'm begging you ...!'' Who was he addressing his words to? Was it Donner? Or was he speaking *past* Donner, to that lurking, brooding, shadowy menace that had been faceless and nameless for so long, but that now he knew to be a stinking lowlife called Clive Gould? Maybe the two had become one, so that, when he confronted Donner, he also – if only symbolically – confronted Gould. Whatever the truth, it felt good to stand up and speak out, to refuse to be afraid, to make a stand. Sam puffed his chest out and planted himself squarely in front of Donner, fixing him with his stare. 'You're just a killer, and I've met plenty of killers before now, believe me. They're nothing special. I thought *you* were something special. I told the others, 'This lad could have been prime minister if he'd been born a few doors down the road. His only problem is bad luck. He was brought up wrong, that's all.' But now I see I was wrong. Sometimes, what's shit on the outside is also shit at the core. You do your best by someone, you look for the good, you give them every opportunity to prove themselves – and what do they do? Lie, kill, wave a knife around.' Sam shook his head contemptuously. 'But even now I'll bet you think you're the only victim in this room.'

'Stop saying things or McClintock dies right now,' Donner ordered. He held out his free hand. 'Give that thing you picked up to me.'

'You want it? said Sam. 'Swivel.'

Annie pressed herself back against the wall. McClintock's bulging eyes screwed up in anticipation of a terrible death. Even Donner's eyes seemed to cloud over for a moment.

'You've turned against me,' the boy said.

'No. You *made* me turn against you. You've given me no choice, you little bastard.'

'You're playing games.'

'I thought you liked games.'

Donner thought about this. He tilted his head to one side. The boy was staring at Sam, but he did not make eye contact. He glared at Sam's mouth, at his forehead, at his jacket, at the space to either side of him, but never into the eyes. He was utterly disconnected, regarding Sam not as a fellow human being but as an object – an object that, for reasons he could not understand, was not behaving as it was ordered. Whatever went on in that brilliant but broken mind of his, it was not reflected at all in his face. And that was why his next move was so completely unexpected.

Donner pulled the knife from McClintock's mouth, slicing deep into his upper lip as he did so, and lunged ferociously at Sam. As McClintock tumbled from his chair, clamping his scarred hands to his face to stem the gush of blood, Sam grabbed hold of Donner's wrist with both hands and wrenched the boy's arms with all his might. Donner refused to let go. They locked together, fighting for possession of the blade.

Without warning, Annie rushed in, aiming a sharp blow across the front of Donner's windpipe. The boy's blank face hardly changed expression; a flicker of the eye, a slight twist of the corner of his mouth, no more than that.

But, despite his impassive face, Donner was struggling wildly. He swung a calculated blow back at Annie, catching her hard across the side of her head and sending her crashing into a glass-fronted cabinet, smashing it.

Sam felt his gasp on Donner's wrist loosening as they both thrashed and writhed.

Don't let go! For God's sake, don't let go!

A knee shot upwards into Sam's groin. He let go.

The huge knife flashed before his eyes. He felt it slice through the leather of his jacket, just missing the vulnerable flesh beneath. Sam fell back, and at once Donner was on him, stabbing downwards with the knife. It hit his chest.

That's it, he thought, very clearly. *I'm dead.*

In the next moment, a concussive boom resounded across the office. A spark leapt from the knife blade as it jerked from Donner's hand and clattered across the floor. Donner had time to turn and glare upwards at the imposing figure who strode briskly towards him – and then a hand, clad in a black-leather string-back, struck him with the force of a speeding locomotive. The boy was lifted clear off the ground for a moment, carried helplessly by the sheer power of the blow. He landed hard, and at once tried to leap back up. But a second blow, this time from the butt of a smoking Magnum, knocked him out cold.

'Norman Bates – you're ruddy nicked,' Gene growled, planting a leather-loafered foot firmly on the boy's motionless body, like a big-game hunter posing for a photograph. With his black-gloved thumb he clicked the Mangum's safety catch back on, and glanced across at Sam. 'Still think my toys ain't no good, Tyler?'

'They have their uses,' admitted Sam, aching and battered.

Annie rushed over to him and threw her arms around him, holding him tight.

'I thought you'd had it!' she said, very close to his ear, her voice unsteady with emotion. 'I thought that knife had gone right into you!'

She released him from her hug and looked down at his jacket. It was ripped, right above the heart. Sam felt inside, his fingers reaching into the inside breast pocket, and pulled out the thing that had saved him. The gold casing of the fob watch was dented inwards where it had taken the force of the knife.

'Shaves don't get much closer than that,' said Sam.

Annie hugged him again, even tighter than before, and kissed him full on the mouth.

'Get a flamin' hotel room, you two,' Sam heard Gene growl. 'It's like one of them Swedish films down the Roxy, only crap.'

CHAPTER TWENTY-THREE

THE FACE OF THE DEVIL

Night had settled over the city, and it found CID A-Division quiet and almost deserted. The phones were silent, the typewriters unmanned. Chris and Ray had both repaired to the Railway Arms to get thoroughly bladdered. Only Sam and Annie remained behind – and the Guv, who emerged from his office after taking a late-night call.

'McClintock'll live, apparently,' announced Gene, looming out of his office. 'That was his quack on the blower just now. They've got him in the hozzie being fed porridge through a drip in his arm.'

'As soon as he's well enough, I'm going to go speak to him,' said Sam.

Gene frowned. 'Go speak to Tavish McTwat? What the hell for?'

'I just – have a few more questions for him.'

'Maybe I'll come with you, Tyler. Bring him some oats. And catch up with that nurse down there who's got the hots for me.'

'I'm not sure your company would be appreciated,' Sam said tactfully.

'I don't see why not. I'm a charmer. And I do a brilliant Tommy Cooper – that'll bring a smile to his face.'

'I think in this instance, Guv, discretion is the better part of valour.'

'Discretion is my middle name,' Gene said. 'And valour. And tripod.' He winked at Annie. 'Oh, maybe you're right, Tyler. What are me and that Jock going to say to each other, eh?'

The Guv shrugged on his coat, straightened his broad tie, adjusted his cuffs and checked his reflection in one of his office's nicotine-coated windows. He gnashed his teeth, smoothed back his hair and flicked out a bogey from his left nostril.

'Killer,' he told his reflection, and fired a finger-pistol at himself. And then, sauntering across to the door, he called over his shoulder, 'Don't forget the lights on your way out, kiddies. See you bright and breezy first thing.'

And, with that, he was gone.

'So,' said Sam, getting a little closer to Annie, 'it's now just the two of us. Alone.'

'In CID, of all places. How romantic.'

'We could always go back to my place. It's crap and it's cold and the bloke next door plays Thin Lizzy at all hours, but still ...'

Annie gave him a serious look. She thought hard for a moment, and then, with great deliberation, said, 'I really like you, Sam.'

'That sounds like one of them sentences that continues with a 'but'.'

'Well ...' She looked for the right words. 'I *do* like you. A lot. I really care about you.'

'There's still a 'but' on its way.'

'Some of the things you say ... The way you talk sometimes ...'

'You mean the things I said about your father?' Sam asked. 'Forget about it, Annie. I talk daft sometimes, you know that. But I'm still me. I'm not like Donner, I'm not a psycho.'

'I don't think you're a psycho,' Annie said, trying to find the right way to express her thoughts. 'Perhaps I thought you were a bit bonkers, you know, when you first said it, but then – something happened.'

'What, Annie? What happened?'

'That watch. The gold one that McClintock had. When I saw it, it sort of ... seemed like it was familiar.'

Sam watched her as she furrowed her brow and chewed her lip, trying to make sense of whatever was going on inside her mind.

'Not just familiar,' she went on. 'Important, somehow. And for a moment, Sam, it was like – like it was like when you're trying to think of a word and it's right on the tip of your tongue.'

'And *did* you remember, Annie?'

She sighed and shrugged. 'The next thing that happened was that Donner went for you with that knife, and then *everything* went out of my head.' She tried to banish that awful memory from her mind. 'What I'm trying to say, and making a total pig's ear out of, is that I really do like you, Sam – and that I don't think you're bonkers for saying all that stuff about my dad. I think you know something – about me – something really important that I've forgotten. I – I don't understand how you know, or what it is, or why I've forgotten it or what it means, but ...' Her troubled expression all at once cleared. She smiled at Sam, as much with her eyes as with her mouth. 'I like you, Sam. And I trust you. And I know that, even if here and now ain't the right time, that one day – very soon – you'll tell me what you know. Because you've got a secret, haven't you, Sam?'

Sam looked at her for a long time, and then, at last, he said, 'Yes.'

'A secret about yourself – and about me.'

'Yes, Annie.'

'And one day, when we're not as knackered as we are right now, and when it's the right place, and the right time, you'll tell me, won't you. And then—'

342

'Chuffin' Nora! You two still here?'

It was Gene, sweeping back in. Sam and Annie jumped, the fragile mood between them shattered.

'I hope you ain't thinking of using my office for hanky-panky,' the Guv declared, stomping over to his desk and rummaging through a drawer. 'Any fanny up for grabs between these hallowed walls is sole property of G. Hunt esquire. And no disrespect luv,' he added for Annie's benefit, 'but I prefer 'em fuller up top and less boysy in the leg department. With pins like yours you should be playing for Bolton Wanderers. Aha!' He suddenly flourished what he had been looking for: the keys to the Cortina. 'The reins to my trusty stallion. Every knight needs his horse, Tyler – and I can see you've got yours.'

Sam looked him straight in the eye as he spoke. 'Guv, this degree of personal abuse you feel the need to dish out, don't you think it suggests you might have some sort of behavioural problem?'

'Nah,' said Gene, jangling the keys to the Cortina as he strode back across towards the door. Then he paused, thought for a moment, and said, 'McClintock's shitty little watch. You still got it, Sam?'

'I have. Why do you ask?'

Gene shrugged. 'Dunno. Something about it set me thinking.' Sam and Annie shared a glance. Gene thought for a moment, then contemptuously waved his own thoughts away. 'Ach, forget it. Ain't got time to fanny about like this – the boys are expecting me to join them for a nightcap down the Arms.'

'Give my regards to Nelson, Guv,' Sam said.

'I ain't your flamin' messenger boy,' growled Gene as he strode out. 'Christ, Tyler, you're a saucy little get when you're showin' off to the crumpet. Birds in the department – it's gonna spell the ruin of this place, you mark my words.'

Puffing his chest out and squaring his jaw, Gene thrust his hand flagrantly down the front of his trousers to shift his balls into a more comfortable position, cleared his throat loudly, and went striding off along the corridor lustily whistling the theme from *Van der Valk*. A few moments later, from outside, came the revving of a Cortina's engine, and the squeal of tyres. Then there was silence. This time, he was definitely gone.

'Do you reckon he's got kids?' Sam asked.

'The Guv?' Annie balked. She thought about it. 'It's possible, I suppose. But I don't think he reproduces like us humans do.'

'Oh? And how do us humans do it, then? I'm only a young 'un. I'd love to learn.'

Annie drew closer. 'We'd better see about fitting in you in for some lessons, then.'

'Evening classes?'

'Night school.'

As Sam took Annie's face in his hands and moved in to kiss her, there came the sudden clattering of a mop and bucket, and the high-pitched howl of a dodgy hearing aid. It was Deaf Aid Doreen, the night cleaner.

'Oi, you two, you can't 'ump in 'ere, I need to do under the desks.'

Annie laughed and drew away from Sam.

'Come home with me,' Sam said.

'I need to sleep. So do you.'

'We can talk. I can – I can tell you about—'

She rested her finger against his lips: 'Another night.'

She got her coat and handbag, then looked slyly across at him. 'Looks like you'll just have to wait for the start of term for them lessons.'

'Any chance of some private tuition?'

'We'll see.' She smiled at him – a warm but teasing smile – and walked a seductive tightrope towards the door, wiggling her hips and glancing alluringly back over her shoulder like Betty Grable. 'See you in the morning – *Boss*.'

And, with that, she was gone.

Doreen nudged Sam in the ribs with the end of her mop. 'Bit of a goer, is she?'

'I haven't had the chance to find out yet,' sighed Sam.

'Eh? You what, luv?' She fiddled with her hearing aid, making it whistle.

'I've got to be going – early start in the morning,' Sam intoned back at her, and he left her to her mopping.

Back at his desk, Sam put a few things away, got his jacket – then paused. From his jacket pocket he pulled out the gold-plated fob watch and its slender chain.

Everything's coming to a head, he thought, letting the chain play across his fingers. *Soon – very soon – I will tell Annie everything: about me, about her, about where we are; about the violent past that she cannot remember; the father who was murdered; and that monster Clive Gould. And, together, we'll face that monster. Because he's close now. He's right around the corner. He's breathing down our necks – and this watch in my hands is the link between me and him. Somehow, it is the bridge that brings us together.*

He shoved the watch into his pocket and shrugged on his jacket.

That girl from the test card was wrong when she said the universe is too big for any one of us to matter more than a grain of sand. Me and Annie, we can be happy together, despite everything. I know we can – and that's all that matters. I will be with her, she will be with me, and the whole damned universe can go to hell.

As Deaf Aid Doreen lumbered about, working clumsily with the mop, her broad backside bumped against the Xerox machine, awakening it and setting it off making copies. Sam called to her, but Doreen heard not a word. She lugged her bucket away in search of fresh water.

Sam crossed over to the copier to stop it. It was churning out page after page of blank copier paper. He pressed various buttons, shook it, thwacked it, but the machine didn't respond, just kept sweeping its light and spewing out another blank sheet – or were they blank?

Frowning, Sam picked up one of the sheets. It stank of chemicals – and of something else, something like burnt charcoal. There, just visible on the surface of the paper, was the hazy suggestion of a face. He turned the sheet towards the light and peered closer, making out narrow eyes, a broad chin, a cruel mouth behind which sat a chaotic jumble of large, uneven teeth.

At once, he felt his skin tighten. The hairs tingled on the back of his neck.

The face, faint as it was, was unmistakable.

Sam grabbed the power cable of the copier and wrenched it from the wall. The machine fell silent. When he looked back down at the sheet of paper in his hands, it was blank. Totally blank. The face of the Devil in the Dark was gone.

'But not for long,' Sam said.

CHAPTER ONE

SHADOW OF THE PAST

It was Sunday morning. Manchester was still and silent.
And DI Sam Tyler was staring death in the face.

My God! It's him ...

His blood had frozen in his veins.

Don't run. Stand your ground.

His heart was hammering in his chest.

This is it. This is the showdown. Don't run –
be a man – it's time to finish this thing here
and now!

The silent confrontation between him and death had
been as sudden as it was unexpected. He had been
walking through the city on a typically dead Sunday
morning. Manchester was lying in, its curtains still
drawn, its head under the covers, refusing to budge.

Here in 1973, Sunday trading was still just a promise – or a threat – that lay in the future. Apart from a few corner shops and wayside cafés, all the shutters were down. Hardly a car moved in the streets. An elderly man walked his elderly dog. A solitary council worker gathered up discarded cans of Tennent's and stinking chip papers. And, through this, Sam had made his way, lost in his own thoughts.

As he hurried past the Roxy cinema, a sudden movement caught his eye. He glanced up – and at once he gasped and stumbled to a halt. Stepping out silently from the dark façade of the cinema came a shadowy figure, blank-faced and featureless. It positioned itself in Sam's way, standing motionless in front of a gaudy poster for Westworld, which remained visible through its hazy, insubstantial body. Grotesquely, Yul Brynner's face – falling away like a mask to reveal robot mechanics underneath – could be seen where the shadow's own face should have been.

Sam knew at once what – or rather who – that phantom was. He knew the aura of horror that hung about it, had experienced before the unreasoning terror that surrounded this dreadful apparition.

Running a dry tongue over dry lips, Sam said as calmly as he could, 'So. Looks like you've found me, Mr Gould.'

There was no sign of response. Yul Brynner glared

back at him through the blank mask of the Devil in the Dark.

Sam tried to pluck up the courage to take a challenging step towards this thing of darkness. But his feet would not obey him. He remained rooted to the spot. Acting tougher than he felt, he said, 'How are we going to do this? Do we fight? Or do you just zap me with a death ray? Whatever it is, let's do. Right now. Let's finish this.'

Brave words. But he felt anything but brave. A bead of sweat rolled down his face.

The shadow shifted its position, and now, through its hazy form, Sam could see the Westworld poster's tagline, perfectly readable through Gould's chest:

> **The playcentre for sensation seekers,**
> **where robot men and women**
> **do <u>anything</u> for you,**
> **and nothing can possibly go wo**rng...

'Don't just stand there,' Sam said, lifting his head and refusing to be cowed. 'You want Annie? Forget it. You're not getting her. She's with me now, you filthy, bullying, murdering bastard. You're never going to lay so much as finger on her ever again. You and her are history, done with. But you and me, Mr Gould, we have business to finish.' He raised his fists. They felt puny and weak, like the fists of a child. 'So let's get on with it.'

Clive Gould, the Devil in the Dark, remained still and silent, an insubstantial shadow, a dark, hazy stain upon the air. But Sam could still recall the broad-nosed, snaggle-toothed face of Clive Gould as he had seen it for himself that awful night he had witnessed the murder of Annie's father, PC Tony Cartwright. In dreams and waking visions, the Test Card Girl had shown him more of Gould's cruelty, the sickening treatment Annie had suffered in life from this brute, the beatings, the assaults, the psychological torture. And, although he had not seen it for himself (thank God), he knew that it was at Gould's hands that Annie had died. She had died, just as Sam had died, and Gene Hunt and all the rest of them, and wound up here in this strange simulacrum of 1973 that lay somewhere between Life and the Life Beyond.

And at some point Clive Gould died too, Sam thought. But, unlike Annie, he shouldn't have come here. His place was elsewhere. But that hasn't stopped him. He's forcing his way into 1973, strengthening his presence here, becoming more and more real. At first, he was a dream, a glimpse of something awful in the dark recesses of my mind. Then I saw him personified in the monstrous body tattoos of bare-knuckle boxer

Patsy O'Riordan. Then, in Friar's Brook borstal, I saw his face, and I saw how he murdered Annie's father.

And now – right now – I'm seeing him again. A shadow – a ghost.

Sam frowned, tilted his head, thought to himself.

'You're not saying very much, Mr Gould. What's the matter? Don't you want to kill me here and now? Or is it – is it that you want to, but you're not strong enough yet?'

The shadow stirred at last. It seemed to push back its shoulders as if about to attack. But Sam sensed it was all for show.

'I'm right,' said Sam, and he felt emboldened. 'You're not strong enough to beat me yet. You're just trying to psyche me out before the showdown. You sad, pathetic bully. Well you might not be ready for this fight, but me ...'

Sam lunged forward, hurling a blow at Gould, putting all the weight of his body behind it. He lost his balance and staggered forward, righting himself at once and throwing up his left arm to deflect a counterattack. But no attack came. The street outside the cinema was empty. Sam stared at Yul Brynner, and Yul Brynner stared back, but of Clive Gould there was no sign.

'Run if you want to!' Sam shouted into the empty street. 'I'm not running any more! I'm done with running. I'm coming for you, Gould! I'll find you, and I'll beat you, and I'll send you back to the hell you came from!'

His blood was up, he was ready for battle – but his enemy had quit the field. Sam brought his breathing under control and unclenched his fists. He wiped the sleeve of his leather jacket across his glistening forehead. His knees were shaking.

Despite the fear that Gould's ghostlike appearance had instilled in him, Sam felt a strange surge of hope and defiance rising up from deep within him. Gould was getting stronger, but he still didn't have what it took for the final duel. He would delay the final confrontation until he was more powerful – unless Sam could track him down before then and finish him once and for all.

And I can do it! If I can draw him into a fight before he's ready for it, if I can provoke him into attacking me too soon. I can do it! I can win!

The sense that things were drawing at last to an endgame between these two mortal enemies renewed Sam's energies, even revived his spirits. Victory – or at the very least, the possibility of victory – was at hand. The chance was coming for Sam to dispel Gould for ever. He had no choice – he had to win this fight. The price of failure was too high. And, when he at last defeated Gould, his and Annie's future together would be wide open, like a shining plain beneath a golden sun, just as Nelson had shown him in the Railway Arms.

'I'm not here to carry your burden for you,' Nelson had told him. 'That's for you and you alone ... Be strong! It's the future that matters, Sam. Your future. Yours and Annie's. Because you two have a future, if you can reach it. You can be happy together. It's possible. It's all very possible.'

Possible – but not guaranteed.

'"Possible" is the best odds I'm going to get,' Sam told himself. 'Perhaps I can improve those odds with a little help. But who can I turn to?'

At that moment, he stopped, glancing across at a grimy, gone-to-seed, urban church out of which slow, wheezing music could just be heard. The organist was limbering up before the service. It took a few moments for Sam to place the tune. He hunted through his memory like a man rifling through a cluttered attic – and then, quite suddenly, he found what he was after.

'"Rock of Ages",' he muttered to himself. And from somewhere at the back of his brain, words emerged to join with the tune:

While I draw this fleeting breath,
when mine eyes shall close in death,
when I soar to worlds unknown ...

'Something something dum-dee-dum, rock of ages, cleft for me.'

Like photographs in an album, old hymns had a potency that no amount of rationalism and scepticism could entirely stifle. Deep emotions were stirred – part nostalgia, partly unease, part regret, part hope. Sam thought of his life, and of his death, and of Clive Gould emerging from the darkness, and of Nelson, breaking cover to reveal that he was far more than just a grinning barman in a fag-stained pub – and he though of Annie, whose memory, as always, stirred his heart and gave his strange, precarious existence all the focus and meaning he could ask for.

Despite everything – the threats, the danger, the approaching horror of the Devil in the Dark – Sam felt happy. He knew it wouldn't last, but, as long as it did, he let the feeling warm him, like a man in the wilderness holding his palms over a campfire.

Sam turned away from the church, strolled across an empty street devoid of traffic, and ducked into Joe's Caff, a greasy spoon which served coffee like sump oil and bacon butties cooked in what seemed to be Brylcreem. There were red-and-white chequered plastic covers on all the tables, bottles of vinegar with hairs gummed to the tops and ketchup served in squeezy plastic tomatoes. Joe himself was a miserable, bolshy bugger who covered his fat belly in a splattered apron and never cleaned his fingernails. He let ash from his roll-up fall into his cooking, and checked to see if food was ready by sticking his thumb into it.

Sam loved the place. It was everything he could ask for from a greasy-spoon caff, and he wouldn't have changed a thing about it.

'Morning, Joe,' he said as he strolled in, enjoying his brief inner glow of happiness. 'Any news on that Michelin star yet?'

THE END
Gene Hunt will return in
GET CARTWRIGHT

Printed in Great Britain
by Amazon

79691210R00212